THE VACATION BUBBLE

To Barcelona with Love Trilogy
Book 1

Marcella Steele

This book is dedicated to all the amazing women I've met on my journey; those in their fabulous forties and fifties, and even sexy sixties or seventies. The power of the female spirit to burn even brighter with each passing decade is a beautiful thing to witness, and I thank all of you for the inspiration.

A Note From the
Author

Content warning

Although my stories are romantic comedies, I touch on themes that reflect a more serious tone. Readers who prefer to have prior knowledge of content themes, please keep reading. Those of you who would rather not have advance notice can skip ahead.

One chapter in this book contains descriptions of domestic violence, including emotional abuse and a detailed account of a violent assault. While the reader does not witness the action happening in the scene and no central characters are harmed, it could be triggering for some. These elements are presented to illustrate warning signs and patterns of abusive behavior—and the importance of having a support system in place to break the cycle.

Contents

Prologue

I t had all seemed so perfect with Ron. Despite his thinly veiled narcissistic characteristics, I think I fell for him the instant he picked me out of a crowd of lonely divorcées, much like a lion pounced on a vulnerable wildebeest. It takes skill, stamina, and a keen mind to hunt in the Serengeti of an over-forty singles social event. Ron, as I would later learn, was widely considered the king of this jungle, wielding his charm like a fine-tuned weapon. Back then, I had been terrifyingly easy prey. Back then, I'd believed in love.

You might consider me a cynic, and you wouldn't be wrong. But I wasn't always this way. Like most little girls of a certain era, I grew up believing in fairy tales—the promise of a happily-ever-after if only the right prince came along, dedicated to winning my heart. Seduced by those tales, I became a hopeless romantic. Fast-forward a couple of decades: Romance has ghosted, gaslit, and gone full Shakespearean tragedy on me—I'm basically a one-woman rom-com with no third act.

All the current self-help strategies tell us to love ourselves, forget about that outdated idea of finding a prince, and get on with our happy lives. But here's the thing: there's no escaping the reminders of how we're missing out on romance. Singers croon about it (remember the Beatles proclaiming, All You Need Is Love?), poets have been writing sonnets about love for centuries, and the Hallmark Channel might be the worst offender of all in perpetuating fairy tales. And don't get me started on that stupid diamond ring commercial. Forever? Really? I want to hurl my pint of post-breakup Ben and Jerry's ice cream at the television screen every time it airs.

My story isn't unique by any means, so as I unspool the details, you might find yourself asking the question, "Is love worth the risk?" I'll let you be the judge.

Chapter One

"Hold that pace. Ready? Now, butts off seats and sprint!"

The instructor's voice cut through the pounding music and the whir of twenty spinning bikes. I stared at his impossibly white teeth behind a smile so wide it looked Photoshopped in real life. His relentless enthusiasm made me wonder if he was high on something or running on endorphins, protein powder, and pure delusion. How could anyone be this happy while endlessly spinning yet going nowhere?

My thighs screamed in protest. Fifteen minutes. Fifteen. I had forty-five more minutes of this torture masquerading as exercise, and I was already planning my obituary: Sofia Drake, forty-nine, died in San Francisco doing something incredibly stupid in the name of fitness. She is survived by her dignity, which she left at the front desk.

"That's it, ladies, you're doing great. Let's pick it up, go a little faster."

I would have laughed if I wasn't busy trying to keep my lungs from exploding. This twenty-something endorphin junkie was going to be responsible for my heart attack. Did the gym have a defibrillator?

He gripped the handlebars, biceps bulging, beaming that toothpaste-commercial smile at the class as if to say, "Isn't this the most fun you've had all week?" In defiance, I shot him back a look that said, "I seriously hate you."

Madison caught my eye from the bike next to mine; her face twisted in beautiful agony. She had suggested we attend the yoga stretch class down the hall with all the other mature women who'd made peace with their limitations. I'd been the genius who'd scoffed and suggested we prove we could keep up with the twenty-somethings.

She'd glared at me but accepted the challenge. I had known she would. My best friend lived by the motto I'll try anything once. However, this time, I suspected she was already plotting revenge.

Pride. It really was going to be the death of me.

My lungs burned, my vision blurred, and somewhere in the back of my mind, a little voice whispered that this was what happened when you tried to outrun time itself. Because that's what this was really about, wasn't it? Not fitness. Not health. It was about the number that was creeping closer every day—fifty—like some kind of deadline I couldn't negotiate with.

I'd been preparing for fifty the way some people prepare for natural disasters. Badly, and with a lot of denial.

The stages had become as predictable as seasons: First, came the refusal to acknowledge it was happening. If I didn't celebrate, didn't acknowledge the date, maybe time would just... pause. Then the fury at the cosmic injustice of it all—how was it that childhood summers had lasted forever, but now entire years disappeared like they'd been sucked into a black hole when I wasn't looking? Next came the bargaining phase, where I'd seriously considered what fifteen thousand dollars paid to a plastic surgeon might buy me. Groupon offered me bargain deals on Botox and filler. On my budget, I could only beat back time a year or two, but I'd take it.

Finally, despair always hit like a freight train. I knew it was coming, heard it roaring down the tracks, but couldn't manage to jump out of the way.

But acceptance? Though I'd spent my life counseling clients through psychological crises, I had never found the peace of acceptance within myself. Truthfully, the number didn't matter as much as the way it categorized me—fitted me with an invisibility cloak, imprisoned me in an inescapable box of age-related expectations.

Someone always had an unsolicited opinion to share. "At your age, you have to expect arthritis, heartburn, and...." the list went on. "You can't make your body do what it used to" (clearly, I proved that true). "Isn't that outfit a little too young for you?" "Of course you have more cushion around your middle. That's to be expected at your age." "Aren't you too old to be running around with that man (five years younger)?" "You need to adjust your expectations and settle for a nice, older man." "At your age, sex and passion aren't so important anymore; you need companionship and security in your golden years."

I vowed to flash my middle finger to anything that began with "You're too old for..." or "At your age..." Thus, I was on this godforsaken death machine, proving my youth—even if it killed me.

My legs had gone on autopilot, spinning mindlessly while my brain checked out entirely. It wasn't until Madison's hand landed on my arm that I realized the class had ended and I was the only one still pedaling furiously to nowhere.

"Sofia? You okay?"

I tried to speak, but only a wheeze came out. My legs, when I finally stopped them, felt like overcooked noodles. I swung them over the side of the bike and immediately crumpled to the floor, where the cool tile felt like heaven against my overheated skin.

"I'm going to die here," I announced to the ceiling. "Tell my son I love him. Tell my ex-husband... actually, don't tell him anything."

Madison bent over, hands on her knees, still catching her breath. "Well, that was horrific. I'm never listening to you again."

"That's fair." I managed a thumbs up from my position on the floor. "I deserve that."

"Don't you have dinner with Ron tonight?"

The mention of his name sent a little flutter through my chest—part excitement, part anxiety. "God, yes. This was such a bad idea. Help me up."

Madison, a good four inches taller and twenty pounds heavier, grabbed my forearm and yanked. Together, we limped toward the locker room like two survivors of some kind of athletic apocalypse.

"So how long has it been with Ron now? Six months?"

I caught my reflection in the mirror above the sinks and winced. My face was the color of marinara sauce, and my hair looked like I'd been electrocuted. "Something like that. There's not enough concealer in the world to fix this."

"The price we pay to get in shape." She ran the towel over her smooth, dark complexion, taming the stray hairs that had broken free from her tightly-woven black braids. "You know, I would've laid odds on Ron bailing by six weeks. No offense, but he has the attention span of a hamster."

"Thanks for the vote of confidence. But you're not wrong about his attention span. I think he could be diagnosed with ADHD." I opened my locker, and a Victoria's Secret bag tumbled out, spilling its contents across the bench. Black lace. Lots of it.

Madison's eyebrows shot up. "Well, well. What do we have here?"

I quickly stuffed the lingerie back into the bag, glancing around to make sure the prenatal yoga crowd wasn't watching. "It's nothing. Just... you know. Trying to keep things interesting."

"Uh-huh." Madison's expression was the one she wore when she was about to say something I didn't want to hear. "How are things really going with him?"

Madison applied her signature burgundy lipstick with the precision of a surgeon. This was her superpower—the ability to look put-together in any circumstance. Once, we had been splashing around in the clear, Caribbean waters of Punta Cana, and she'd trekked back to our lounge chairs to re-apply her lipstick, then skipped across scorching sand to reach the sea again.

"Fine. Great. Why?"

"Because Ron strikes me as the kind of guy who's allergic to anything resembling commitment. And you..." she paused, choosing her words carefully. "You get attached."

"What's wrong with wanting love—a real relationship?" Anger bubbled up, but down deep, I knew it wasn't about Madison. "Just because every damn time I try it blows up in my face, doesn't mean it doesn't exist." My poor gym bag bore the brunt as I kicked it, sending the contents all over the floor.

"Oh, honey, I know." Her voice softened. "We've all been there. Anyone who's single at our age has stepped on at least a few landmines. It's tough out there. Finding a man to go the distance is like panning for gold in a puddle."

"Look," I said, rummaging around the floor for something to tame my hair, "I know you think I'm being naive, but this feels different. Ron and I have something real."

"I'm only giving you my opinion because I love you. Just... be careful, okay? I've seen you go through this before."

The thing was, she was right. I *had* been through this before. Multiple times, including my divorce. Each relationship had started with the same breathless hope, the same certainty that this time would be different. And each one had ended with me sitting on my bathroom floor at two in the morning, wondering what was wrong with me.

"I know. And I'll admit he's been a little distant lately. But he's turning forty-five today. Men get weird about birthdays too, right?" Not for the first time, I felt a prick of doubt. It was like a sesame seed stuck in my sock—too small to worry about, but I hadn't been able to shake it loose.

Madison's reflection met mine in the mirror. "Oh, sweetie. When a man starts pulling away, it's usually not about his birthday. Take some advice from a woman who's dating a married guy. When you're last on his schedule, there's something up."

"Wait. Wasn't Kevin getting a divorce?"

Her shoulders shrugged. "Still pending, or so I'm told. And nice try, but we're not changing topics."

"I'm sure everything is fine," I said, as if mimicking a line from a positive thinking handbook. "People often get strange around their birthday, that's all it is."

Madison groaned. "Oh God, don't even mention birthdays. Mine's coming up soon. You want to see 'strange'? I guarantee it won't be pretty."

"Fifty is going to be an unbirthday year for me. I'm skipping that one and dealing with it later... maybe."

"How do you manage that?" She shot me an incredulous look. "Facebook knows. It announces it to all your friends every damn year."

I shoved the bag in the locker when a twenty-something body appeared, parading out of the shower in a mini towel, which could have easily been mistaken for a napkin. She was probably size zero, her muscles toned, with skin that didn't hint at the collagen loss to come in a decade or two.

Madison followed my gaze and spotted her too as she shuffled past us in flip-flops, heading for the lockers. I caught

Madison holding her hands outstretched as if measuring in the air. "I think if you put three of those skinny twenty-some-things side by side, it would be equal to one of me."

"And that's why I wait to shower at home. Let's get out of here before I start feeling even worse about myself."

As we walked past the mirrors, I caught sight of my reflection again and stopped short. Madison bumped into me.

"Don't," she warned.

"Don't what?"

"Don't do that thing where you catalog everything you think is wrong with yourself."

"I'm fifty."

"You're forty-nine. And so what if you were fifty? You're beautiful and still have a figure most women would kill for."

"Thanks, but things that used to be up here…" I cupped my boobs, then my ass. "They're now falling to the floor. Gravity's a bitch."

Madison spun around and grabbed me by the shoulders. "Would you stop? Ron is lucky to have you. If he doesn't see that, then he's an idiot."

"Would you write a note to that effect and pin it to my shirt so he can be reminded?"

The laugh that burst out of her broke the tension. "C'mon. Let's go."

I looked over my shoulder to see Madison striking a pose in her reflection, then nod in satisfaction. God, I envied her confidence, the way she was comfortable in her own skin.

I felt lucky to have her—she was my person—grounding me like no one else could. "Alright, Miss America, let's head out."

But as we rode the elevator down to the parking garage, I couldn't shake the feeling that Madison's words were more hope than truth.

"How was Ben's graduation, by the way? Did your ex behave himself?" she asked as we stepped into the cool space that smelled of exhaust and dank concrete.

"Trent didn't hurl insults, and I refrained from asking his date if she had a driver's license."

"He brought that chick? It's a good thing I wasn't there."

"You definitely could've taken her. Probably him too. But someone has to be the mature parent."

"Maturity is overrated."

"I do it for Ben. And, oh, he was beaming! It's hard to comprehend he's old enough to have finished college already."

"Have you started looking through his baby pictures and dragging out the videotapes? I did that last week during another phase of, 'where has the time gone?'"

"Been there, done that, several times. My eyes were puffy for days."

"So, what's the plan for tonight?" Madison asked, settling into her driver's seat. I was still trying to remember where I'd parked my car, as usual—always hopelessly lost. With a few clicks on the remote, I found the beeping vehicle.

"Dinner, wine, and then..." I held up the Victoria's Secret bag. "Operation Keep Your Man Happy."

"Good luck with that. Text me later."

As I drove home through the familiar streets, I let myself imagine the evening ahead: a candlelit dinner in San Francisco, his favorite bottle of wine, and me—decked out in that new, expensive lingerie the salesclerk had promised would drive any heterosexual man wild. Naively, I thought the evening would be wonderful.

I was so busy planning the perfect night that I didn't see the disaster coming.

If I had, maybe I would have driven straight home, thrown the lingerie in the trash, and saved myself the humiliation of hearing those four words every woman dreaded: "It's not you, it's me."

The look in Ron's eyes when his glance raked over my half-naked body clad in the skimpy lingerie told me it had been worth the investment. I'd made sure the lighting was soft, because let's face it, bright lights were just cruel.

His eyelids lowered when I feathered kisses along his neck, and his breath quickened as I straddled him, my breasts sliding gently over his chest. I knew what he liked, and after all, it was his birthday. At least my experience in the bedroom counted for something. That beat having a twenty-year-old body, right?

His voice was raspy, but there was no mistaking his words. "Stop, please. I can't do this."

"What's wrong?" I shot up and balanced on my knees as Ron flipped on the bedside table light. I glanced behind me. He wasn't kidding. Man down.

"This... you and me... it's not going to work." His words rammed me like a punch to the gut, my breath stalling somewhere in my diaphragm.

"You're... breaking up with me? Now?"

"I'm sorry. I should've told you sooner, but—"

"But what? You thought you'd let me humiliate myself first?" I scrambled off the bed, hunting for my clothes with hands that shook with more than cold.

"It's not like that."

"Then what is it like, Ron? Because from where I'm standing—half-naked in your bedroom—it looks pretty much like the worst possible timing in the history of breakups."

Frantically searching the floor, I yelled, "Where are my damn clothes?"

"They're on the chair in the corner. Please, Sofia, don't be so upset."

Ron propped himself up on several pillows and pulled the sheet up to his abdomen, but it didn't stop me from being distracted by the sight of his broad chest. The scent of his cologne—of him—still lingered on my skin.

"Upset? Why would I be upset?" My trembling fingers fumbled with the dexterity of cocktail sausages as I attempted to pull on my skirt. Trying and failing to hook my bra, I stuffed it in my bag and wriggled the lace blouse over my head. I didn't care if the neighbors witnessed the show when I slunk out of his apartment.

"Just because you said we were a couple…" A lump knotted in my throat. I paused before the words tumbled out of my mouth. "And now you're dumping me? What girl would have the audacity to be upset?" I was vaguely aware my voice was approaching the decibel of a dog whistle.

"Sofia, honey, calm down. These things happen. People change."

"What the fuck does that even mean?" I jammed my feet into my second-hand pair of Louboutins and sank onto the bed. The sting of tears pooling at my bottom lids threatened my composure. "Why? Give me that much."

He slung his forearm over his brow and blew out a heavy breath. "I want to have a family, kids of my own. Turning forty-five this week made me realize I have little time. I need to get serious if I'm going to take a shot at making this happen. If we stay together, I won't have that chance. Isn't it better we end things now before it goes any further?"

"I was under the mistaken impression we were important—I was important. But apparently, I'm disposable, simply because I'm too old to have kids?"

"It's not about your age—"

I reeled on him. "Oh, it absolutely is."

It wasn't fair, I thought, as I pried myself from the edge of the bed. The prime of my life was just a glance away in the rear-view mirror, but to Ron, I was useless. I glanced surreptitiously at my abdomen and wondered if my ovaries now looked like shriveled prunes. While I'd dreaded those monthly visits—the ones that made me curl into a ball, clutching a heating pad to my belly and cursing the day I'd been born a female—when they'd stopped coming around without so much as a "goodbye, it's been fun," it had left me shattered. Ron's answer felt like a punch landing on a still tender bruise.

"Look, you're a fantastic woman. You're beautiful, smart, and fun to be with. It's not you. It's me. You'll find the right guy."

The look I gave him was like a lightning bolt straight at his eyes. "Don't you dare patronize me." Anger boiled up once again, anesthetizing the pain momentarily. Fury was a useful shield when one was preparing to make a grand exit, though like a shot of lidocaine at the dentist's office, I knew it would be temporary.

After snatching my purse from the chair, I rummaged under the covers until my fingers located the black silk lingerie, then stuffed the delicate fabric inside my bag. It was tainted now, but I'd be damned if I was going to leave it behind. I scanned the room to make sure I hadn't forgotten anything, because after I walked out the door, there was no coming back.

Panic joined anger and spread through my insides like wildfire. I couldn't think. Did I have my phone and car keys? It wasn't fear driving me as much as an urgent call to action—to run. I needed to get the hell out of his apartment.

"Good luck out there. In case you haven't noticed, the dating scene at our age is about as fertile as a stagnant cesspool. And don't worry about me. I'll be fine." I squared my shoulders and hurled a defiant stare in his direction. With that, I flung open the bedroom door.

Ron didn't respond. Not that he could've said anything to make this moment less humiliating. He never moved from the bed and didn't offer to walk me to my car. To my credit, I didn't slam the door behind me as I left. Even filled with anger and hurt, I resisted the temptation to key his Mercedes-Benz GT as I passed it on my way to the parking lot, although it crossed my mind to slander him on Facebook before he knew what hit him. But no.

Sometimes I wished I was that kind of woman, one who could erect protective barriers fueled by anger. But it wasn't in me to strike out in retaliation. I'd handle this failure as I had the others that had come before—with a modicum of grace and a dollop of self-recrimination.

Unleashed tears clouded my vision as the lights of on-coming traffic sent blinding prisms through my windshield; a kaleidoscope of streetlights and regret. I thought about Madison's warnings, about the signs I'd chosen to ignore, about the way hope could make you stupid. I blamed myself for being naïve, for rushing toward that irresistible state of euphoria with zero regard for the risks.

When I finally reached the solitude of my house, my back pressed against the front door, I allowed the tears to spill, sobs erupting as old wounds bled into the fresh cut. It might have been minutes, but it seemed like hours before my heart rate slowed.

"Okay, enough," I told myself. Swiping my palms against my damp cheeks, I kicked off my pumps and padded into the kitchen, grabbing an entire bottle of wine from the fridge. This had to change. I had to be different.

I curled up on the sofa, flicking on the TV for company. Maybe that's the only company I'd ever have—me, the TV, and cats in this lonely house—if I had a cat. Could my life get more pathetic? Swigging wine from the bottle, flipping through stations while fat tears fell on my blouse?

Cats, big cats, caught my attention on the screen. On an African desert, antelopes gathered around a watering hole, their noses to the wind, ears perked to sense danger. When the big cat took a step and a twig cracked beneath its paw, the antelopes ran like their lives depended on it (which, of course, it did). Hoofbeats thundered across the plains—the lion left to go hungry.

Suddenly, I knew what I had to do. I had to be the antelope, ready to run at the first sign of danger. My ex-husband used to say my spirit animal was the golden retriever. Yes, he was a little strange, but he had a point. He claimed my attributes included loyalty to home and family, just like our precious dog. She had become fast friends with any human who walked past our house, trusting everyone—no questions asked.

But in my life, having the attributes of a golden retriever wasn't serving me.

Collecting the pile of tissues on the couch, I padded into the bathroom, tossed them in the trash, faced my tired, tear-streaked face in the mirror, and vowed to break this pattern. I would have to morph from a golden retriever into an antelope. There was no other rational choice.

As I pulled on my comfy nightshirt and climbed under the covers, I swore a whispered oath into the darkness. "Never, ever, will I let this happen again." No longer would my heart's careless antics go unchecked. Love might be blind, but, by God, I would keep my eyes wide open, my senses alert, and my feet prepared to sprint.

Chapter Two

There should be a law banning Monday mornings, especially when one has spent the previous day in bed drowning in despair, complete with episodic sobbing. It had been an epic pity party of one. Classic, really. Curtains drawn, the television burbling incessantly, tissues and junk food littering my favorite blue duvet sprinkled with white flowers.

Why in the world had I thought the Hallmark Channel was a good idea? In hindsight, I suppose a case could be made for the cathartic value of viewing one sappy romance movie after another—a desensitization exercise. I gave myself the day to mourn. According to psychological theories, by now my tear ducts should be dehydrated, my memory flushed free from the remnants of humiliation, and my professional persona intact to start the work week. But no, I was still a mess—a jumble of emotions taunting my mind even as I hid behind dark sunglasses and strode into the office.

"Good morning, Ms. Drake." Patty, the perky young receptionist, called the greeting from her desk perched on the massive metallic podium, the luminescent sign above her glowing green today: Bay Area Tech Innovations. For the life of me, I couldn't understand the genius behind changing the color of the sign each day, but it did command attention.

Some days, I questioned my decision to hang out my shingle in the corporate world. I'd set out to become a psychologist to help the disadvantaged. I had loved my work with children and families, especially adolescents, but as the years went by, several things changed. The teens no longer trusted that I could possibly understand their world. Anyone over thirty was considered ancient in their minds, and they lumped me in with their parents, teachers, and all uncool authority figures. Despite my efforts to keep up with the ever-changing trends in social media and fashion, I wondered if I had aged out of this calling.

Then my divorce was a wake-up call. I needed to fend for myself. No longer a two-earner family, I had to up my game with a higher salary, stock options, and a damn good 401K plan. So, when a colleague suggested I apply for the position as an in-house psychologist and management consultant for a major tech firm, I chose security over noble ambitions. After all, I had managed an entire non-profit clinic. How different could this be? Later, I would learn that I'd boxed myself into a well-paid corner. Was I happy working in the corporate world? Happiness was relative, I rationalized. Was it survivable and a decent trade-off for security? Most definitely.

So, I pasted a smile on my face and gave a nod to Patty. "Oh, Ms. Drake—"

I paused my trajectory past her desk. "Patty, please, it's just Sofia. We aren't formal here."

Her pale cheeks flushed. "Right. I'm sorry. Mister—I mean Andrew—wants to schedule a meeting with you today."

I skimmed through my mental calendar. "Tell him I'll check in with him after I see a client."

As I made my way down the hallway, my heels clacking on the polished marble floors, I couldn't help noticing an odd vibration floating in the air. My spidey senses detected a storm brewing. Passing cubicle after cubicle, I caught glimpses of co-workers huddled together, speaking in hushed tones, their words indecipherable. It was the anxious looks, the furrowed brows, and eyes that darted furtively from side to side that confirmed my suspicions.

I thought of heading straight to Andrew's office and reporting my concerns to my boss, but when I saw Ajay standing by my door for his session, rocking from one foot to the other, I didn't have the heart to ask him to wait. Unlike his co-workers, there was nothing unusual about seeing a look of panic flash in his eyes, since he suffered from a chronic anxiety disorder.

"Sorry to keep you waiting this morning. Come in and have a seat," I said. While I retrieved a notebook and pen, then settled into my chair, he positioned himself in his usual spot—the chair closest to the door.

"Now then, how have you been feeling since we met last week?" It was a routine question I had to ask, but the answer was clear before he spoke. His right eye blinked rapidly, the skin below jerking upwards due to the facial tic.

Ajay blurted out, "What do you think? Do I look like I'm doing alright?" He placed his palm against the side of his spasming face.

"Have you been able to eat and sleep regularly?"

He laughed at my absurd question. "My stomach is in knots, and I wake up every night with the sweats. I'm so tired by the time I arrive at work, I can't think straight."

I jotted down a few notes, then looked up. "Has anything happened this week to exacerbate your symptoms?"

"I heard a rumor that I'm going to be fired."

"Ajay, your employee reviews have been excellent. Why would you believe the rumor?"

His hands were tapping on the arms of the chair now. The tat-tat-tat sound growing more frenetic. "Isn't it obvious? I'm almost forty, the oldest one left among the entire programming team since Peter was let go last month. They're hiring kids straight out of college to replace us at half the salary. I can't work those long hours anymore, it's not fair to my wife. She needs help with our boys at night." He jumped out of his seat, pacing the small patch of carpet in front of my desk. "And then what am I going to do? I have a house with a huge fucking mortgage."

While I hadn't heard any rumors, I knew the culture of the organization and the pressure it placed on the workers with families. But at the moment, the priority was to help Ajay cope.

"Ajay, please sit down. These thoughts are leading you down a destructive path. We can plan to speak with your supervisor, but right now, we must work on reducing your response to the anxiety."

He complied, and for the next ten minutes, I guided him through breathing exercises and visualizations. At least his tics had slowed considerably by the time we finished.

"Are you willing to reconsider medication treatment as an adjunct to therapy?" I asked.

After a moment, he nodded, and I reached for the stack of cards on my desk, handing him Dr. Qadir's card while saying with reassurance in my voice, "This psychiatrist is one of the best. He won't steer you wrong. Make an appointment by the time we meet next week."

The minute Ajay stepped out of my office, I looked up to see Sarika's tall frame barreling through the door, her eyes flashing with... anger? She turned and closed it carefully behind her.

"Did you know this was coming?"

"What? You'll have to be more specific." As the office manager, Sarika was privy to everything that went on in this company, so it wasn't unusual for her to fill me in, but she was always composed. The look on her face set off alarm bells.

She stood over me, pressing her palms against my desk. "Don't tell me management didn't inform you of the layoffs."

"Who's getting laid off?"

"Oh, this is priceless. They put you in charge of company morale and—"

"Sarika, what's going on?"

"This place is about to be gutted. Some bullshit about restructuring and containing rising costs."

Outside my office, the sound of angry voices drifted from somewhere in the hallway. Instantly, my anxiety level spiked to a ten. *So, Ajay was right about the rumors,* I thought. I had to get to Andrew immediately. I flew out of my chair and lunged for the door, then turned back and faced Sarika. She'd been here longer than most of us, but did seniority matter at all?

"Did you receive a notice?" I asked.

Her face crumpled. "On my desk this morning. Sanjay and Tomika too."

"Fuck." I yanked open my door and stormed down the hall to Andrew's office. Ignoring the secretary's protests, "Sofia, Andrew is busy just now. You can't go in there. Sofia—" I burst in to find him with a cell phone pressed to his ear.

"Uh-huh, yes, I know that. Legal is on it." He motioned me to have a seat, but I opted to remain standing. "I'll call you back in twenty. Yeah, I have someone in my office."

"What the hell is going on here?" It came out as an accusation rather than a question, but I was fuming. It was only then that I noticed the beads of sweat on his forehead, his brows knitted together. Andrew was an executive in his mid-thirties, a little young for an ulcer, but he popped two antacids in his mouth and chased them down with a glass of water before answering.

"We lost a government contract. We had no choice but to eliminate positions," he said flatly.

"Andrew, people are freaking out. You could have at least allowed me to prepare them."

"The board wanted to roll this out without advance notice. It wasn't my call."

"And let me guess. They're sacking personnel with higher salaries? You are aware that it targets the older workforce, right?"

Andrew's eyes slid away from mine. He knew the truth, and that made him equally culpable.

"Jesus Christ, you know exactly how this looks. They can't legally do this." Despite my assumption, I knew they must have figured out a way to frame the layoffs to avoid lawsuits.

"It's just a numbers game, Sofia."

"Have you considered how this will affect morale?"

Before he could answer, his secretary popped her head inside the door. "Andrew, Mr. Grayson at corporate is on the phone. You'd better take his call."

"Give me a minute." Her disembodied head retreated abruptly, and he turned back to me, his skin becoming redder by the second. I wondered briefly if an early heart attack was in his future. "I would appreciate it if you would stay on to handle the... um, morale issues, but I understand if—"

"Wait! So, I'm on the chopping block too?"

He cleared his throat, a dry, rasping sound. "It is simply more cost-effective to contract out for psychological and consulting services, rather than employ a psychologist on staff full-time. But, um, we do value your work and could really use your help in the interim."

My hands became clammy, my heart pounding so hard I could feel my temples vibrating, but the injustice of it all fueled my anger and kept my legs from crumpling beneath me. "Let me get this straight. I've put ten years of my life into this company, helped it through a myriad of growing pains, and navigated management's negotiations with staff to maintain a positive culture. And now, you want me to clean up your mess before I lose my job?"

Andrew didn't answer. His mouth opened, but he let his jaw close without uttering a word. Outside the window of his office, the secretary held up a phone, gesturing to it with urgency.

"There's not a chance in hell I'll do that." Andrew's eyes swung from the secretary back to me. "I want the severance package on my desk today, commensurate with my long tenure of service here."

I straightened my spine and stormed out the door. I would not break down. I would not let them see me defeated. Holding my head high, I stomped down the hall, now viewing the wrecking ball in full swing. Despondent staff carried boxes to the elevator, escorted by security personnel. Those left in their cubicles were either clutching tissue packets or held their jaws so tight I could almost hear teeth grinding. I had to wonder how the corporate head honchos could be so heartless. How could they justify ruining lives in the name of a profit margin?

By the time I reached my office, I realized with new clarity that I didn't belong here. That, in the end, nothing I had accomplished had mattered. It was almost a relief, if it weren't for the fact I was losing my security.

I kept it together long enough to pack boxes and shred documents. No one interfered or attempted to escort me out of the building. Maybe Andrew held out hope that I might change my mind. After taking my license down off the wall and packing the pictures of my son that had held a place on my desk for so long, I strode out of the building. No fanfare, no goodbyes. I'd ask them to send a courier to my home with the severance paperwork.

It wasn't until I was tucked inside my house that I allowed myself to fall apart, once again.

"Hey, girl, I'm on my way to the salsa club. Want me to stop by and pick you up?" Christy's voice emerged through the phone's speaker, the sound of traffic noise crackling in the background. I groaned a response and plucked another tissue from the box. My pity party tonight was in full swing on the couch in my living room, and my drink of choice was a nice, buttery chardonnay.

"I can barely get off my sofa. Sorry, but you'll have to go it alone."

"What's wrong? You sound all stuffed up. Did you catch a cold?"

"Not exactly. It's a long story, but in a nutshell, as of today, I no longer have a boyfriend or a job."

At the sound of her voice screaming into the microphone, I almost dropped my cell. "Hey! How dare you cut in front of me?! What an asshole driver. Sorry, Sofia. So, what the fuck happened?"

"With my boyfriend or work? Strike that. The boyfriend thing was Saturday. Ancient history. I found out today that the firm is trimming the fat, and coincidentally, those of us past forty are considered over the weight limit." Just saying it out loud made it more real. I needed more wine. To the kitchen I went, my fluffy slippers shuffling along the hardwood floor.

"That must be illegal. You need a kick-ass attorney."

I refilled my glass, then took several gulps. "Nope, it's no use. They have a team of lawyers. I'll take the severance package and look for another job."

"Perfect. You can come with me tomorrow night to a job networking event. I need a wing woman anyway."

"Are you looking for a man or a job?"

Her laugh rang through the speaker. "It's a kill-two-birds kind of event, which apparently suits your needs at the moment. Great hunting grounds."

"Oh no, don't even go there," I warned. "I've sworn off men for the foreseeable future." I grabbed the bottle and a bag of chips, then shuffled back to the couch.

"Tell yourself whatever you want, girl. The last time I went, I met a gorgeous guy who was building his own start-up company. He took me out a few times."

"Yes, but you're thirty, and the inventory of men around your age is about a hundred times greater than the ones around mine."

"So what? You'll just have to date younger."

"Um... been there, done that. A lot." After my divorce, I had been shocked at how many thirty-something men wanted to date me, until I learned that "date" was merely code for hook-up. Granted, it had been fun for a while, except that, ultimately, I grew tired of the games and found that what I really craved was another chance for a real relationship—a chance to start over and get it right this time. But after Ron, that hope had died.

"What are you eating?" she asked. My hand dipped into the bag again.

"I'm in savory mode, so the appetizer is chips tonight. I'm planning to skip the main course and go straight to a pint of ice cream."

"Oh my God, you have to get out of the house. I'll order the tickets. There'll be a spread of free food, and the drinks there are to die for. I've gotta run. My call waiting just beeped. Ciao."

"But..." The line went dead before I could protest. I pressed the cool glass to my forehead, water droplets dripping down my nose. Looking back, it seemed like an insignificant decision to make. Much like, should I go to Trader Joe's or hit Safeway today?

But I never could have anticipated that one decision—that one night—would make me question the entire course of my life.

Chapter Three

At seven o'clock, I stood on my front porch wearing a figure-flattering, classic black dress and a wool coat. I would have preferred to encase myself in a suit of armor, since it would more accurately reflect my current state of mind, but I hadn't yet found an affordable one on eBay. Still, I had chosen well. Professional, attractive—somewhere between too conservative and overly provocative.

In the distance, a blanket of fog began to roll across the sky, threatening to pour over the Sunset district, already carrying with it a blast of cold air. I pulled my collar up against my neck. Christy had texted to say the event was at a fancy venue, so I had reluctantly slipped my feet into stiletto heels. I'd pay for it later.

In an effort to sound prepared, I practiced my lines in a whisper. "Hello, I'm Sofia Drake. Do you know of any jobs for a middle-aged woman who's burned out but has mad psychotherapy skills? I'm great at helping others, but I suck at getting out of my own way, especially when it relates to dating." *Not a good sell,* I thought. *Strike and revise.*

Mr. Peterson lifted his head from under the hood of his beat-up truck next door and caught me mid-speech. I closed my mouth, managing a tight-lipped smile. He shot me a nod, then picked up a wrench and disappeared behind the hood. For the last twenty years, he'd promised to get rid of the jalopies piling up in his driveway. While all the homes in this neighborhood were painted in civilized colors, a putrid shade of green buckled and peeled from the siding on his house. I'd long since given up hope that he'd haul away the junk and spare car parts littering the front yard. On the upside, he made my 1940s Victorian-style house look good, even with overgrown trees nearly obscuring the porch.

At five minutes after seven, Christy pulled up in her red sports car and whistled at me. "Get in, sexy lady."

I rolled my eyes but complied. "Thanks, but I'm not going for sexy tonight. It's a professional event."

"Whatever. You're sexy. Get over it." She shifted gears and peeled out, the tires screeching around the corner. With the window down, her long blond hair fanned across her glowing, fresh face as the wind whipped it in all directions.

We were a contrast in every way, yet we complemented each other. She dressed in pastel yellow, the color reflecting on her creamy skin and making her look like she could be cast in a commercial for the quintessential California girl. As for me, the black ensemble worked best with my Mediterranean tones. One has to play to one's strengths. Mine, I'd learned, was a dark, sultry effect. Blessed with my mother's olive complexion and chestnut curls, I'd accentuated my lids with the blackest liner and a smudge of opaque shadow in the crease. Together, we looked like the symbol of yin and yang.

Christy caught me batting strands of hair away from my eyes. "You good with the windows down?"

"Actually, all the work I did with the curling wand is literally being blown out the window. Mind rolling them up?" Her pin-straight hairstyle appeared unruffled.

She turned her radiant, white smile at me and pressed the button. "Sure, no problem."

"By the way, what are you looking to find this evening?" I asked.

Holding her view on the road ahead, she said, "Tall, dark, and handsome."

I rolled my eyes. "Besides that. Jesus, you have a one-track mind. It's a networking event, remember?"

"I'm keeping all my options open tonight." There was a pause while she checked her lipstick in the mirror. "I can go in a variety of directions with my business degree, but I'm thinking of finance. It must be more lucrative than marketing for these broke start-ups. What about you?"

"Tall, dark, and handsome, always." With a sideways glance, she caught me smirking. "My field of expertise is narrow, but I'm hoping to find work opportunities in the government sector. I've had it with corporations."

The engine whirred as Christy pressed her foot to the floor and wove through the traffic toward downtown.

"You could get another job as a psychologist, right?"

"It's about security," I began. "At my age, I have to consider things like retirement or 401K plans."

"I get it," she said. "My mom is dealing with the same thing."

Oh, that's perfect. I'm her mother's age? I deflated like a popped balloon, my confidence evaporating in the air.

"She's a registered nurse in a hospital, but the work is brutal. I think she wants to be a midwife, but you know, she needs retirement benefits."

"See what you have to look forward to?" I quipped.

"That's depressing," she said, her eyes slicing to mine for a second.

"Yeah, well, my mood is a tad somber right now. I probably shouldn't have come tonight."

"Look, things will get better." Adding with a cheery lilt, she said, "Who knows? You might find an exciting opportunity tonight!"

I settled back in the seat, closed my eyes, and tried to reconstruct my confidence, hoping she'd turn out to be right.

Christy cranked up the radio, salsa music blaring from the speakers. Dancing was our common interest. The salsa club was the one place my age didn't matter. I'd proven my skills with the best of them and invariably had partners waiting to hit the dance floor. We were both rocking in our seats to the Latin rhythm when my attention wandered to the view of the white-capped waves and the East Bay Bridge in the distance as we drove along the marina, the sun's ribbons skating across the water. Here, the sky was clear, and the brilliant rays made the city glow, the light reflecting off the windows of tall buildings that stood clustered in the dense cityscape.

Christy pressed a button on the steering wheel and lowered the volume. "Are you going to tell me what happened with the boyfriend? Ron, right?"

I let out an exaggerated sigh. "Not much to tell. I thought things were fine, but he blindsided me. Turning forty-five clicked his biological clock into gear, and he realized his priority was to knock up some young thing and have kids."

"That sucks."

"Tell me about it."

"It's so unfair. At thirty, I feel the pressure to decide if I want to have kids or not, because as a woman, we only have a small window of time. Men get to play around all they want and choose their window. Nature is cruel to women."

"In so many ways," I added. "Enough talk about guys or I'll be too depressed to do anything tonight except drown my sorrows in multiple cocktails."

Entering the city center, we wound our way through the busy streets teeming with pedestrians and cyclists. Men in suits hailed cabs alongside shivering tourists in shorts and their newly purchased San Francisco sweatshirts. Traffic snarled in the shadows of the endless skyscrapers, but soon we were in the tourist district where the cable cars made their routes. Due to sheer luck and the tiny size of her car, we found a rare parking space only several blocks from the event on Geary Street.

"Ready?" Christy asked, her fingers gripping the door handle and a tone of conviction in her voice like we were heading out on a mission.

I tried to sound enthusiastic. "Yep. Let's hit it."

It was a relief to take shelter from the brisk San Francisco wind when we ducked in the entrance of the Hawthorne. A cute twenty-something girl smiled up at me from her seat at the long table, crossed my name off the list, and handed me a color-coded name tag. She noticed my puzzled expression. "Green is for mental health. That's the field you entered when you signed up for the event." I glanced at Christy and gave her a thumbs up. At least she'd registered me in the right category. The receptionist pointed to a chart. "Each job market has their own color, so when you meet people, you'll automatically recognize if it's a match for you."

I sidled up next to Christy after she received her tag. "You know, I think men should have to wear a color-coded tag so when you meet them at a bar, their status is crystal clear. Like, if the guy is married and looking for a hook-up, his color would be red."

"That's genius! Bartenders could hand out the name tags with the drinks."

"Divorced, bitter, with a load of baggage and three kids would claim a yellow tag." I snorted out a laugh. "Plaster that sucker right to his forehead."

Christy got into it. "Single, searching for a one-night stand might be orange. Because, hey, it could be fun if you know the score ahead of time."

I added, "Single, middle-aged, and looking for the mother of his future children but doesn't want to disclose that detail…"

"Forget the label. Just put a target on his ass that says kick me!"

"Nothing would make me happier."

As we moved up in line and entered the event, she commented, "Pretty impressive place, right?"

I nodded, taking in the surroundings. The brightly lit, cavernous room stretched long and narrow, the perimeter lined with bench seating. Its red brick walls and industrial ceiling contrasted with the elegant chandeliers and draped purple fabric, giving it a late-night club vibe. I imagined the scene with the lights turned low, the gleam of the disco ball hanging over the dance floor. Then I zeroed in on the food tables opposite the enormous black marble-top bar where people clustered holding small plates of appetizers.

"I'm heading towards the bar," I shouted, the din of conversations swallowing the sound of my voice.

"Let's mingle a little, check out the crowd. Don't limit yourself to name tag colors. You never can tell who you might find. If we get separated, we'll meet back here, okay?"

I nodded, and we launched ourselves into the room, squeezing past elbows while trying not to tip cocktail glasses. Ahead by a few steps, I saw Christy veer to the left, headed toward a group of men whose colored tags indicated finance. I inched my way over to the bar, filed in behind ten other people, and glanced in both directions, catching snippets of conversation while keeping my eyes peeled for the green labels in the crowd. It was his voice I heard first—deep, with a sexy tone that rumbled through me.

"I'm in the mergers and acquisitions department. Possibly you're acquainted with the bank?" he asked the balding man next to him. "It's a global company whose headquarters are located here in San Francisco and in London. We're looking for fresh talent, someone with experience in finance. The organization has an excellent training program."

The line moved up, but I hung back, waving at people to take the place in front of me. Obvious? A few sideways glances confirmed that my chivalry wasn't going unnoticed.

His voice came from my right, only a few feet away. I shifted in my high heels and casually pretended to brush a piece of lint off my shoulder, then caught sight of him. It may have been only four or five seconds, but as my eyes raked across his features, time seemed to slow, as if watching a movie at half speed. To say he was gorgeous wouldn't do him justice. That face belonged on the cover of GQ magazine. Tall, dark, and handsome with refined, perfectly symmetrical features, luscious full lips, and, God help me, a chiseled jawline resembling Adonis. That was the moment I knew I was in trouble.

He continued his pitch to the short man in a suit. The man wasn't over thirty-five, but the back of his head was already thinning. Sexy guy stood over six feet tall, his bronzed olive skin and tousled dark curls effortlessly stylish without seeming overdone. Even his clothes were sexy, although it was more about the way they fit his frame. My eyes scanned him from bottom to top, taking in his leather shoes, indigo-blue designer jeans, a white-collared shirt, and a black sport coat cut close to his body, revealing broad shoulders that led to a slender waist in a V shape. When he raised his arm to retrieve a business card, his bicep bulged against the sleeve of his jacket. Holy shit.

A buzzing sound rang in my ears, muting the conversation, but I watched as his face broke into a wide smile, dimples forming like perfect punctuation marks on his cheeks.

Without warning, his head swiveled a fraction to the right and his eyes caught sight of mine—sparkling, deep blue eyes that held me transfixed for a split second. Then, in one swift (not obvious at all) move, I brought my hand to my hair and, as I flicked it over my shoulder, my gaze shifted to the blond woman directly in front of me. Thank God I was next in line.

A flush bloomed on my face, not solely due to the hot flash racing up my neck. *Stop right there, missy,* I told myself. *He's too young, probably in his thirties.* I'd never needed a drink so desperately. Forcing my view straight ahead, I ordered a gin and tonic when I reached the edge of the bar.

"Make it two, please," his voice rang in my ear.

Oh, dear God.

"I hope you don't mind if I join you." He stretched out his arm and offered a handshake. As our hands folded together, a rush of heat surged through my body. "I'm Ryan. Ryan Hunter."

I shook my head, waiting for the words to untangle from my tongue. "No. Not at all, thanks for the drink." Silence.

"And you are?" He glanced at my name tag. "Sofia Drake?"

"Oh. Yes." My finger tapped against the green badge. "That's me." I couldn't have felt more unbalanced and idiotic. Here I was, an intelligent, confident woman reduced to monosyllabic communication. I lifted myself a little taller and straightened my shoulders. "Sorry, this is my first time at one of these events."

"They can be overwhelming, but maybe I can help if I know what you're looking for."

Several things converged in an instant. Just as I took a hefty gulp, I flashed on Christy's question in the car. What are you looking for? Well, tall, dark, and handsome was right in front of me—drinking me in with those deep-blue eyes, a seductive smile lifting a corner of his mouth. Unfortunately, the distraction caused me to inhale the liquid, which was now barreling down my windpipe. I broke into a coughing fit and, to my horror, the lovely gin and tonic spewed out of my mouth, droplets landing on his jacket. With one measly cocktail napkin, I swiped his lapel, my apologies stuttering out between coughs. But he didn't move his body out of my trajectory, and there was no sign of irritation. His eyes only held a look of concern.

He patted my back, brows pinching together. "Easy there. Are you okay?" While the gentle blows didn't clear my windpipe, they did send me wobbling on my high heels. He didn't miss a beat, catching me by the shoulders until I was steady again. I already knew this was one of those embarrassing moments I would reflect upon later. Over and over again. Much like when, on a first date, gas had escaped me after eating Mexican food at dinner. I blamed the beans. It had happened several years ago, but I still cringed every time I pictured the look on my date's face. There hadn't been a second date.

I cleared my throat, blinked at the sting in my watering eyes, and tried to speak again. "I'm fine. Um, your tag is purple. Does that mean you're in finance? What exactly does your work entail?" I dabbed my cheeks with the useless napkin to mop up the tears.

"I'm in banking. Specifically, mergers and acquisitions."

"Oh." I shook my head. "Forgive my ignorance, but does that involve buying and selling corporations?"

"It's close. I'm a professional advisor with a worldwide bank. The job involves brokering deals with large firms, advising chief executives on structural changes and strategies. And yes, buying, selling, or taking over other companies."

He paused, the corner of his mouth ticking up. "Your eyes just glazed over. I know, boring stuff."

"No, not at all," I lied. "Where do you work?"

"My office has its base here, but I also travel to the London branch to meet up with my team there."

"Where do you call home?"

"Right here in San Francisco. I have an apartment on Nob Hill."

I resisted the urge to drop my jaw again. That was one of the most exclusive areas in the city. Much like when a painting comes alive, all the colors and shading blending to form recognizable shapes, I was forming a picture of him. But something didn't quite fit. Was he older than he looked? I crossed my fingers, then took a chance.

"Pardon me if this sounds rude, but you seem to be pretty young to have built such a successful career."

In the way he cocked his head, a one-sided grin breaking on his lips, it was clear he caught me fishing for his age. "Not so young to realize what I want in life. I just turned thirty-five."

Damn. I felt something in me sag with disappointment.

The mass of bodies pressing in seemed to double, swallowing us in the crowd. A man in a suit pushed his way to the bar, his elbow stabbing my ribs. In an instant, Ryan's hand was on the small of my back, pulling me out of the fray. "I want to learn about you now, but let's get away from this noise. Would you like to get some fresh air?"

For a moment, I stood rooted in place, my nerve endings reverberating at the feel of his hand, the warmth penetrating through the fabric of my dress. The strength of his touch, the way he held me—that wasn't surprising, but it was the tenderness that undid me. As if a curtain opened, my defensive shield parted, and I dared to imagine the sensation of his hands roaming my bare skin.

"Follow me." He motioned with his other hand when I didn't move.

I blinked. "Oh. Right."

As he shepherded me through the crowd and we crossed the lobby, I threw a cursory glance around my surroundings, but there was no sign of Christy. And then I was exiting the hotel with tall, dark, and handsome—questioning my sanity.

Chapter Four

A gust of icy wind bit my fiery cheeks the moment we stepped onto Geary Street. A series of hot flashes had been rolling up my chest and making their way to the top of my head. Now, I tipped my face to catch relief in the breeze. I needed to ground myself again and stop fantasizing about this man.

"So, your green tag," Ryan began as we walked side by side, "what's the corresponding profession?" His feet halted on the pavement. Facing me, he added, "Wait. Let me guess." He studied me. "You're in the corporate world. Upper-level management. Possibly human resources?"

"That's not far off. I've been working in the corporate sector but as a psychologist."

"Seriously? You don't look like most of the shrinks I've known."

A laugh honked out of me. "So, you've had some experience with shrinks?"

"A few, yes." He stared past me into the distance, lost in his thoughts. "I guess you might say I had a troubled youth, a pretty chaotic family life. I believe the term is 'dysfunctional?'"

I slipped easily into character with a grin on my face. "Go on, this is getting interesting."

"That right there…" His face lit up. "You sounded just like my second therapist."

"Hah. How many therapists have you gone through?"

He shrugged. "A few. But in my defense, some were horrendous. No offense."

"None taken."

Ryan slowed as we approached a homeless man sitting on the sidewalk, his back leaning on the front of a building. A small dog of indistinguishable breeding lay sleeping against his leg. Normally, I wouldn't make eye contact in these situations. Not alone, anyway. But I noticed the man's gaze swing up to meet Ryan's. His eyes conveyed the weariness, the desperation of his circumstances.

When I was on actual dates, I always gauged a guy's character by how he treated others. I watched to see if he was kind or rude to the waitstaff; if he had an air of entitlement. When I saw Ryan pull a ten from his pocket and drop it in the man's cup, my estimation of this man skyrocketed.

"Well, all that therapy seems to have helped. You turned out okay in the end," I said.

"Thanks to a good therapist. If it wasn't for her, I'm sure I wouldn't have gotten this far in life." When he captured my gaze and smiled, a river of warmth trickled through me. "I have a lot of respect for what you do, helping people."

As his eyes bored into mine, I saw more than flirtation—a window opened, and I witnessed a depth in him that surprised me. For a moment, I glimpsed his heart through kind eyes. That, I was certain, would push me over the edge, so I fixed my gaze on the street ahead. "You just made my day. It's nice to receive validation for my work."

"Can I ask why you came to the event tonight?"

I stumbled slightly over a crack on the sidewalk, recovering on my own. I didn't want to delve into my current situation and ruin the moment, so I simply said, "I'm looking for new opportunities, maybe to make a change." He waited, his expression urging me to divulge more. "Currently, I'm working with an IT company, but they're restructuring. It's messy."

Ryan nodded, and we were both temporarily distracted. Drunk twenty-somethings were pouring out of bars, shouting and celebrating a night out in the big city. Per the usual, a guy was relieving himself against the side of a building.

Ryan shook his head. "Damn tourists." Turning to me, he asked, "Do you live here in San Francisco?"

"I have a house in the Sunset. Been there about twenty years. The city is changing, or maybe it's just me, but I'm getting tired of being here. To be honest, I'm in serious need of a vacation and a change of scenery." *Especially now*, I thought to myself.

"So... are you flying solo or with a partner on this getaway?"

I had to smile at the way he slipped in the question. "I'm divorced and single."

He shot me a sideways glance, and I glimpsed those dimples. "Surprising, again, Sofia. Any specific destination in mind?"

"Oh, I don't have any plans in the works."

"But if you were to make an escape...?"

Without thinking, an answer immediately pinged into place. "It's been ages since I've been to Europe. I'd love to go back." Memories of the trips I had taken after college flooded my mind like it was yesterday. The red-tiled rooftops of Italy, French pastry shops lining the streets of Paris, the haunting history within the walls of the Tower of London. I still recollected the offending odor of unwashed socks while sharing a sleeper car on a night train with my two girlfriends and several male backpackers. No hardship, including hitchhiking on a freeway to catch our flight in Nice, had diminished the thrill of experiencing a world so different from the one I grew up in.

With a sudden stab of regret, I was painfully aware too many years had slipped by without ever leaving home. Marriage and family had changed my priorities. The furthest I'd traveled was to the east coast for our yearly trip to visit my in-laws. You learned a lot about your husband when thrown into the middle of his family dynamics, and believe me, it was no vacation. How did my life veer so off-track?

Just then, Ryan whistled, flagging a taxi. The driver pulled to the curb.

"Let's go. I know where I want to take you."

My feet stayed planted on the sidewalk while he opened the door of the taxi. "I can't just run off with you. My friend is still inside."

With a wink, he dared me. "Where's your sense of adventure, Sofia? I promise I'm not an axe murderer. You're safe with me."

My feet betrayed me. I stepped into the backseat, saying, "I'm pretty sure that's exactly what an axe murderer would say."

I heard Ryan tell the taxi driver, "Beldon Lane, please." I thought to myself, *This is the stupidest thing I've ever done*, or... maybe it was the universe opening new doors for me. What I needed was inspiration about now—not a new man. On that issue, I was clear.

The taxi deposited us at the destination within minutes, and when I looked at the alleyway filled with restaurants and their covered terraces lining the lane, I realized he'd just delivered me inspiration. The old-world European vibe condensed in this little street was like a shot back in time, a mixture of several countries to choose from lying ahead. I felt myself beaming.

When Ryan held the door open and ushered me into a restaurant, his smile conveyed his pleasure at my delight.

"What is this place?" I asked.

Ryan caught the attention of a server who was rushing by with a steaming pot of mussels. The scent of garlic and wine almost made me swoon. The server said something to him in Spanish and pointed to the terrace. Ryan took hold of my hand—let me repeat: he held my hand—while leading me to our table on the covered patio. Sometimes it was the little, sweet gestures that zinged straight to the heart. But no. I couldn't allow it to affect me.

"This, Sofia, is a Catalan restaurant."

I stared blankly at him across the table with a candle burning in the center. The server appeared and greeted Ryan with familiarity, speaking in Spanish again. He ordered vino and some other things I didn't recognize. Then, when the man disappeared into the restaurant, he explained, "Barcelona is one of my favorite places in Europe to visit, so, last year, I found this restaurant that serves Catalan cuisine. It comes from the particular region in Spain where Barcelona is situated." He paused, checking for my reaction. "I take it you haven't been there?"

"No, I haven't been out of the country for a long time," I admitted.

"Then you're past due for a trip. Barcelona is an amazing city. You should make it a priority to visit there."

The young server appeared again, bringing the wine and something he called tapas. Delicious scents wafted off these little plates, demanding my full attention. Ryan invited me to dig in, and he didn't need to tell me twice. I savored each mouthful, his eyes sparkling while he watched me.

"By the way, are you Spanish?" he said.

"That's random. Why do you ask?"

"You have those Spanish eyes... they're dark, quite beautiful, and wildly expressive."

I felt a blush rising on my cheeks. Okay, maybe it was another hot flash. I took a sip of wine. "Um... Thank you. I'm half Spanish, on my mother's side."

"Do you speak the language?"

"Does cursing count?" His eyebrow lifted. "She rarely spoke Spanish unless she was mad or yelling at my dad. I don't think that's going to help me communicate in a foreign country."

Ryan leaned in, a grin lighting up his features. I couldn't take my eyes off those dimples. "I have an idea," he said. "You want a getaway in Europe, and it so happens I'm headed to Barcelona for a vacation in a couple of weeks. I already have an apartment reserved. Come with me."

I placed my wine down on the table without taking a sip, afraid to take any more chances swallowing while stunned. "Wow... Um... That's..."

Ryan jumped in. "Impulsive? Maybe. But why not?"

"Because this is not what grown women do. You're thirty-five. Impulsive trips are perfectly acceptable at your age," I said, immediately regretting sounding old.

"Oh, so there's an age limit on taking a vacation?"

"No, but I have responsibilities."

"So do I." He batted the ball to my court, and I sent it right back.

"It's not practical to just... just run off."

He volleyed. "Because life always has to be practical? Everything neatly planned out?" That ball landed squarely at the heart of the matter, so naturally I got defensive.

"I can be spontaneous and impractical sometimes, when I want to." This time, I downed the rest of my glass.

My phone vibrated on the table, a text appearing from Christy. Damn. She was looking for me. Without thinking, I opened the Uber app and booked a ride, then met Ryan's questioning gaze. "It's my friend back at the event. I've got to go." I popped out of my seat and grabbed my bag, prepared to sprint.

"Wait. I'll come with you."

"No, it's fine. You stay and finish the food. The Uber driver will be here in two minutes." I reached inside my purse for my wallet. "I can leave you some cash for—"

He held up his hand. "It's my treat. But can I get your number? I'd really like to see you again." Now he was standing inches from me, his eyes pleading with me to concede.

I shifted my gaze to the alleyway. Those beautiful eyes were tempting me, but I held steadfast. "I don't think that would be a good idea. But thank you for everything." It took all my strength to turn away from him. Even as I did, I questioned my decision. Then I reminded myself of the promise I'd made. *I won't ever let this happen again.*

"Wait." He reached for my hand and pressed a business card against my palm. "In case you change your mind."

My phone pinged with an alert. The Uber driver was at the end of the alley. "Goodnight, Ryan."

It wasn't easy to sprint on cobblestones with stiletto heels, but I propelled myself down the alleyway like it was midnight and I had to reach the car before it changed into a pumpkin. But princes didn't exist, and those shoes were too expensive to leave one behind. As I opened the door to the coach—or rather, the car—I ventured a last look back. Ryan was standing by our table, still watching me. I tucked his business card in my purse and slipped into the back seat.

The fluttering in my chest, just in the center of my heart, only slowed when I arrived at the venue.

There didn't seem to be any point in sharing the evening's events with Christy, as I could predict the lecture I'd have to endure. When she dropped me at home, I walked through the door and set my purse on the table, questioning why I felt an overwhelming sense of disappointment. It had been the right decision. Still, I retrieved his card from my purse and stared at it for a few seconds, then suspended it over the trash can. My fingers refused to release it. For reasons I couldn't comprehend, I slipped the card back inside the pocket of my purse.

With a heavy sigh, I pried off my high heels and limped into my bedroom. I may have walked away, but my mind—the sadistic thing that it was—kept conjuring up images of Ryan, and I wondered if I'd dodged a bullet or if I was missing out on the opportunity of a lifetime.

Chapter Five

"Girl, I can't believe you lost a boyfriend and a job in the span of a few days. Have you checked your horoscope?" Madison picked up her phone, searching for the app. Yep, she had an astrological app on her home screen. "There must be some serious conflict in the alignment of your planets."

"It must be Mercury's fault. Isn't it always in retrograde?"

Madison and I had parked ourselves at the bar, and for the last thirty minutes, she'd listened intently while I filled in the details. At least this place was peaceful, with its dim lighting and soft jazz playing in the background. Far from the newer and flashier bars, it was more of a lounge, appealing to an older, classier clientele, with its overstuffed chairs and a view high above the city.

Her face contorted as she presumably read my astrological predictions, uttered an, "Uh- oh," then placed the phone back on the bar. "Well, that was depressing, but on the upside, you look better than you sounded last night. I half expected bags the size of my Gucci clutch purses under your eyes." She chortled a laugh.

My fingers patted at the lingering puffiness above my cheekbones. "Thanks to my miracle serum that cost almost

as much as your treasured Gucci, the bags have been reduced to the size of coin purses."

"I hate to say I-told-you-so about Ron, but it doesn't
surprise me he changed course so suddenly. And was he
really the one?"

"I don't know. Maybe I was so tired of dating that I
wanted to believe he was the one. But he did some damage.
Madison, I'm done with men. There's no way I'm getting back
on that dating roller coaster."

She opened her mouth, no doubt prepared with a pep
talk, but a male voice broke into our conversation.

"Seriously?" My gaze lifted to find a new bartender swiping a cloth over the wood surface, sopping up the remnants
of spilled beer several seats down. His lips curved up in a
bemused grin. "You're writing off half the population on the
planet?" He looked barely old enough to order a drink, let
alone mix cocktails.

"You wouldn't understand," I said, then added, "And excuse you for eavesdropping."

He slapped two paper mats in front of us and, decidedly
not excusing himself, barreled into the conversation. "It's not
any easier for men. Do you know how many times I've sprung
for dinner with a girl whose photos didn't remotely resemble
how they appeared in person?"

Madison leaned in over the bar, nearly tipping over her
stool. "Oh, don't even get me started on the online dating
thing. What's your name?"

"Rick." He retrieved a tumbler from a tray.

"Well, Rick, there are a million women out there competing for that one right guy who is actually single, has a job, and wants a serious relationship," Madison said.

"A million?" I interjected.

She flung a hand in the air. "Whatever. You know what I mean. Most of the time, you spend weeks texting back and forth and then suddenly he drops off or clicks the unmatch button and you don't have a clue what you could've done wrong. All before you've even met."

"Rick, you probably can't imagine what it was like before the dating apps," I said, joining the rant. His face swung toward me, a grin twitching the corners of his mouth, which I took to mean, okay, lady, I'll humor you. "Twenty years ago, dating was straightforward—you met a guy at a bar or a party, and if you liked each other, he'd call. Or he'd leave a message on your home answering machine, which of course you could monitor while he was speaking, leaving about fifteen seconds to decide if he was worth the chance before that beep cut him off. And if your decision was 'No,' he wouldn't be certain you received the message or interpret it as rejection because everyone knows those tapes jam up, and he couldn't stalk you on social media because... well, you get my point."

"Wow." Madison shook her head. "He has no idea what you're talking about. That was like being jettisoned back in a time machine to the dinosaur age."

I glanced at Rick, whose eyes had glazed over.

"Oh, dear God." I buried my face in my hands, then recovering, I barked at Rick. "Will you just bring us a couple of margaritas?"

"I can't solve your dating problems, or even begin to understand what you said, but that... I can do."

When he left, Madison nudged my shoulder with hers. "What got you on a roll tonight?"

My forehead hit the sticky bar with a thump. "General frustration, I guess." I hesitated, considering whether I should confess the one secret I hadn't divulged, then huffed out a breath and lifted my head. "There's something else, but you can't get all excited when I tell you."

She raised one eyebrow, bracing herself. "Okaaay."

"Remember that night I went to a job networking event with Christy?"

She nodded; her fingers swiping across her lips as if zipping them closed.

"I met a guy. A guy I can't stop thinking about."

Madison, the poor thing, was trying very hard to keep her cool. She pressed her lips together and her hands remained tightly clasped on the top of the bar. I might as well have tied her wrists and taped her mouth. "Fine, you can ask me questions."

Unleashed, the words tumbled out. "Spill it. Who is he? What's he like? Is he hot? What's his name? Details, woman."

There were never any secrets we didn't share; no topic was off limits. Since the day we'd met at a salsa event, it felt as though I'd found the sister I'd never had. Still, I hesitated. Although Ryan had never left my thoughts, speaking about him would alter the fuzzy, dreamlike quality of the image I held. I wasn't sure I wanted to bring him to life.

Rick returned with our cocktails, but instead of moving on to the other patrons, he lingered. I narrowed my eyes. "Thank you...?" Nothing. "Okay, off you go." After he skulked away, I lowered my voice and leaned into Madison.

"You know, there are very few guys who... stimulate me. At least not at first sight." I looked down at my lap, avoiding her probing stare. "Ryan. Mr. Ryan Hunter got to me. He's not like all the rest, he's intriguing—exciting." A grin crept across my face as I pictured him. "And he's so fine. I mean really fine."

She blew out a faint whistle. "Deadly combination."

"I know. He could charm the pants off any woman, but I didn't get the sense he was a player." I raised the glass to my lips, slugging down half my drink.

"You sure about that? Guys can be sly." Given her experience, she had good reason to be suspicious.

"Maybe I'm a fool, but there's something about his cycs. They're kind... sincere." My body instantly recalled the feeling I had when he'd placed his hand on the small of my back, his gaze sending fiery shards of heat up my spine. "We had a few moments... like there was this magnetic force pulling us together. Dear God, I thought I was going to combust!"

"Girl, I'm so happy for you," she exclaimed, clapping her hands like a giddy child. "When do you see him again?"

My smile fell away. "I'm not. I can't," I stuttered.

"Why not? What happened?"

As only a sister could, one who knows you so well she can read your thoughts, she blurted out the answer. "He's young, isn't he?"

My eyelids squeezed shut as I winced. "Thirty-five. But it wouldn't matter if he was fifty. I'm not risking my heart again."

"So don't. Just have fun with him. You can't be hurt if you give up having expectations."

I stared at her, my mouth hanging open. "Have you met me?"

"Ladies, can I get you another round?" Rick's timing wasn't accidental. "You know, Madison makes a good point. Why limit yourself? Have some fun."

I repeated for both their benefit. "He's thirty-five! The last thing I need is to look like a desperate cougar."

"Yeah, but you're a hot cougar and you don't seem desperate. I'd take you out."

In perfect unison, we both barked, "Shut up, Rick."

"Okay, I'm going."

Madison swiveled on the bar stool and scanned the seating area. It was far from packed, with only a handful of tables occupied. Suddenly, she blurted, "Let's play a game of I Spy."

"What the hell are you talking about?"

She proceeded, ignoring my question. "I spy with my little eye... something gray with something red."

"Are you kidding me?" When she rolled her eyes at me, I gave in and scanned the room. I spotted a gray-haired man in a dark gray suit. He was speaking directly to the woman's cleavage, fringed by a red dress. "Do you mean that couple over there?"

"Ding. You earned a point. How much younger is that hussy in red?"

"I'd say a ratio of thirty-five to sixty." Now I realized what she was up to. I picked out another couple. "I spy with my little eye, something bald with something blond."

Madison barked a laugh. "They're making this way too easy," she said, her voice too loud. The bald man noticed her stare, given that their table was only a few feet away. He shot her a look, his gray eyebrows lifting against the lines on his forehead. It could have meant anything, but I laid odds he was thinking, "WTF?"

As soon as Madison opened her mouth to speak, I preemptively cringed. "Sorry, my friend thought you looked familiar. Our mistake. You and your daughter have a nice evening."

The man glowered at us at the same time Rick broke into a hysterical fit of laughter from behind the bar. Not even the noise of ice rattling inside the shaker could disguise his utter amusement. Simultaneously, we pivoted, our backs to the bald guy. I covered my face in my hands, nearly imploding trying to stifle the giggles. After my shoulders stopped vibrating, I said, "How do the men get away with it?"

Madison answered, "They just can. It's socially acceptable. And if they have money, there are no limits. Women fall for money, status, and power."

"So much for gender equality. It's the same old status quo. If I did that, I'd be labeled a predatory cougar. Women are judged for dating even five years younger."

Madison took a long pull of her drink, then slammed her glass down on the bar. "So, fight back. There must be a way to find this Ryan dude."

After a moment, I peeled his card out of my purse. "There's one thing I neglected to mention." Cringing, I plunged ahead. "He invited me to go to Barcelona with him."

She glanced at the card—then at my face—her mouth a perfect O. "Woman, what the hell are you waiting for? You want to travel, you've lost your job but gained a hefty severance package that will sustain you for months, and this guy comes along with an invitation? I'd trade places with you in an instant."

I opened my mouth to protest, to cite the reasons it wasn't possible, but she cut me off with a swish of her hand. "Don't overthink it. Carpe diem the fuck out of this opportunity. At the very least, go on this trip and check him out."

"My idea of carpe diem takes months of planning, not two weeks' notice. Besides, I should be looking for a job."

Madison gave me the fisheye. Her mom look. Loosely translated: You're being ridiculous.

"Okay, I know, but how am I supposed to go all carpe diem when I don't know what the future holds? I need a secure direction."

"Honey, that's exactly my point. Take a break, and a direction will come to you. Time in Barcelona would do you a world of good."

I sipped on my drink and caught Rick giving me a thumbs up. "Ben and his girlfriend are touring Europe this summer. I think they're stopping in Barcelona." As I considered it, excitement rose in my belly, tickling my insides like tiny bubbles. "It seems like a lifetime ago when I was his age and doing the same thing. I always dreamed of going back, maybe living abroad for a while."

"Why didn't you?"

"Life happened. I became an adult with responsibilities—which I still have, by the way."

Madison placed her hand on my arm, her voice pleading with me. "Sofia, you have to go."

My head lolled onto her shoulder. "Then come with me. It would be good for you to get away from Kevin."

She exhaled a long, exasperated sigh. "Kevin has returned to his wife again."

"Let's see... how many times does that make this?"

"I've lost count." She leaned her elbows on the bar, perching her chin against her hand. "He comes in and out when it suits him. But what am I supposed to do? I can't find anyone else."

"I can give you advice and tell you to take care of yourself, but I'm not sure it's going to do any good. Seriously, Madison, I'm worried. Don't let him take advantage of you."

Simultaneously, we both lifted our glasses, swigging down the liquid as if tequila would anesthetize all our pain.

"At the risk of sounding like a psychotherapist, what are you getting out of this relationship?" She shrugged, the corner of her mouth lifting in a lopsided grin. "Besides the obvious," I interjected.

"Besides the mind-blowing sex? Not much, I suppose. All I get are vague promises, such as, 'One day, we'll take an exotic vacation together.' Or this one is his favorite: 'When the kids grow up, I'll have more time for you.'"

"Then why?"

She shrugged her shoulders, and I already knew what she would say. "I love him."

"Okay, I get that. But someday, I hope you realize your worth. You are an extraordinary lady. Besides being incredibly giving, you are an annoying combination of brains and beauty and have enormous reserves of strength. My God, woman, you've raised five children while working."

Her hand wrapped around mine with a squeeze. "Back at 'ya. You have a door opening in your life. Go inspire me."

"I'll think about it. I promise."

From down the bar, Rick curled his fingers in the shape of a heart and held his hands in front of his chest. Madison and I gave him an eye roll, then she shouted, "Check, please!"

Chapter Six

Whenever I needed to make a major life decision, I taped poster paper on the wall and divided it into two columns: Pros and Cons. I would begin by listing every factor, big or small. This gave me a clear visual representation of which list was longer. Everybody knew this method, but that was child's play. Being an overachiever, I had advanced it to include weighted point systems, probability calculations, and—yes—a separate chart for my feelings about each pro and con.

Pro tip: I put colored stars on the most important elements, ranking them in three colors, which then were assigned point values. Red was ten points, green earned five, and yellow had a value of two. When all the points were tallied, I'd have a concise, quantitative answer to my quandary. Or so it would seem. The probability calculations and feelings chart would require a book in itself to explain.

I had used this method to analyze everything, including my choice of boyfriends, which car to buy, and the direction of my career. The scary part was, I'd started this well before high school. Admittedly, it freaked out my parents first. They loved how I was responsible and reliable, but in an age where children were supposed to do what they were told just because their elders said so, I drove them crazy with my arguments. I could run circles around them with my perfectly articulated reasoning until they became so frustrated they resorted to the only weapon in their toolbox: Go to your room!

In college, I ran the risk of being slapped with a diagnostic label, but my professors couldn't quite pin me down to one category. Sure, I was a bit anal. Did that mean my potty training had been too strict and I was obsessed with control? Possibly. But I always had a plan, which meant I met my goals.

But now, as I stared at the poster paper, I didn't have a clue where to start. Losing my job was a huge part of feeling adrift in a sea of uncertainty, because charting a new course at nearly fifty was a much different task than it was at twenty. The world of possibilities had shrunk down to the narrow end of the funnel and, realistically, I was far less likely to be hired at my age.

I tossed the markers aside and opted to pick up a wine glass instead, then plopped down on my couch; the poster paper taunting me. The clock on the wall ticked by the minutes while I stared at the blank slate. Tick, tick, tick. God, it was like listening to a dripping faucet. With my eyelids shut, I tried to block out the sound and focus on the rhythm of my breathing. In for three, out for four. I don't know how long I sat there like that, but something shifted. Memories began swirling in my mind, attached to images and scents and emotions.

Suddenly, my eyes shot open, and I was on my feet, headed for the bedroom closet. There, on the shelves, I retrieved my old photo albums hiding behind a stack of shoe boxes containing the elegant high heels I could no longer wear but couldn't bear to part with. Thanks to my anal tendencies, I found the exact one I was looking for, since its label listed the date and subject.

Clutching the album, I sprawled out on my bed and began carefully turning the pages. Sure, the plastic covering had yellowed and the photos had faded, but the memories they held were still vivid. I saw myself as a gleeful twenty-five-year-old, experiencing Europe for the first time on an epic girl's trip. Scanning the pictures of me posing at iconic sights—the Tower of Pisa in Italy, the Royal Palace in London, the Arc de Triomphe in Paris—I remembered the excitement I felt at exploring foreign lands. But it was the candid shots that captured my attention.

In one picture, my friend had surprised me by snapping the shutter while I was singing lines from The Sound of Music during a hike in the Alps. My arms opened wide against the backdrop of green fields dotted with wildflowers, as if I was embracing the entire blue sky. In Paris, I wore a pink beret, my forefinger and thumb tipping the fuzzy material at an angle near my eye, my long neck stretched upward in a pose reminiscent of Audrey Hepburn.

My cheeks ached from smiling as I continued my journey through the memories. In so many shots, I appeared wide-eyed, my eyes sparkling with an energy I hadn't felt in so long. I recalled the sensation of freedom—of discovering new experiences, of pure indulgence in delights. Very little had been planned in advance. We hopped on a train just to check out a cool place a fellow traveler had mentioned. Instead of booking ahead, we rolled into stations with no clue where we'd stay. We would pull out our guidebook and wander the streets until we found a room to spend the night. I could never imagine traveling that way now—or sharing a communal bathroom.

Once, in the Amsterdam train station, we met an old woman with a room for rent, and the next moment we were following her through the alleyways. It didn't matter that the shower cost a few coins and only lasted five minutes, because she took us on a tour of the red-light district and drove us to the poppy fields for a picnic. Now, when I looked at her picture, I was stunned to see she probably wasn't much older than fifty. That stung.

During a train ride between Italy and France, I'd fallen in lust with a charming boy. He didn't speak English, and I didn't understand a word of French, but somehow, our love language sufficed to generate an explosion of chemistry. My friend took a photo when she caught us kissing, preserving the memory forever.

Though I couldn't remember his name, I instantly re-called the feeling of abandoning my inhibitions and going for it. That, I thought, was my carpe diem—proof there had been a time in my life when the poster paper list was abandoned, when I took risks, when I was an adventure seeker. I'd all but forgotten this version of me.

After turning the last page, I removed my favorite photo from the album, hopped off the bed, and headed for the kitchen, where I grabbed a magnet and fixed it on the refrigerator, just like I used to do with my son's childhood drawings. Then, I stood back and memorized the image. In the picture, I was waist-deep in the blue sea of the Côte d'Azur, my string bikini top dangling from my fingers, the nipples on my perky breasts pointing toward the sky. The camera caught me mid-laugh; my neck arched, face tipped toward the sun. I wanted—NO—I needed to feel that way again.

Since it wasn't the 1990s anymore, technology could bring me to Spain in an instant. I pulled out my laptop, my hands shaking as I searched for images of Barcelona. In no time, I was convinced Ryan was right. I had to go. However, I wouldn't be going as Ryan's guest. Experience had taught me impulsivity had to be tempered with a good amount of reason. I wasn't about to throw caution to the wind, but I was ready to dip my toes into a new adventure, though the thought of traveling alone was enough to set off a firestorm of panic. I didn't even go out to dinner by myself.

But if there was one thing I'd learned from my first trip abroad, it was that setting off to a foreign place provided the chance to step outside of yourself and experiment with a new persona—to be a different kind of person. Just maybe, I could venture beyond my comfort zone and transform into a new character who would play the role of Sofia. Because right now, I was tired of being the person who needed the poster paper to plan out her life.

And so, I took the leap, excitement driving me forward and, at least temporarily, numbing my trepidation. My fingers flew over the keyboard, searching... Those B&B days were over—I wanted basic comforts and pre-arranged lodging. Since it was last minute and summer availability was scarce, I had to book two apartments, affording me thirty days in Barcelona. I had never taken such a long vacation in my life, but this was long overdue.

When I finished booking my flight, I let out a long breath and reviewed my itinerary. Was I really doing this? Inside, my heart was doing a happy dance. But I was certain of only one thing—I would have to be prepared for unexpected events, glitches along the way, and probably a few surprises. Away from home, I wouldn't have much control over my world.

Little did I know how my life was about to be turned upside down and inside out.

Chapter Seven

T he screech of an alarm blared into the darkness of my bedroom. My arm swung, striking the lamp, which tumbled to the carpet, followed by the clock. I saw the blinking red light pronouncing the time was four a.m. and bolted upright, heart pounding, just as the backup alarm on my phone went off.

A rush of adrenaline propelled me out of bed and into the shower. Despite the insane hour, I rushed through the make-up and hair routine and dressed in the outfit I'd set out last night. Everything was going according to plan. After running through a quick checklist in my head, I grabbed my purse, confirming I had my passport, then wheeled my suitcases to the doorway and... stopped. My breathing was too fast, too shallow. I dashed into the kitchen to grab a paper bag from a drawer. A text alert sounded from my purse. My Uber.

With the paper bag flapping at my side, I skittered back and called out to the driver. "I'm coming." The keys shook in my hand, and it took several tries to lock the door. I grappled with the fear, telling myself everything would be okay. That lots of women traveled alone to foreign countries. I failed to convince myself.

"You alright back there?" the driver asked while I furiously breathed into the paper bag. I nodded and shot him a thumbs up. *This has to be a bad sign*, I thought. Who has panic attacks on their way to their dream vacation?

We'd just pulled onto the freeway on-ramp when dawn broke on the horizon, illuminating San Francisco's jagged skyline in a pink glow. My breathing had barely returned to normal when the seat belt jerked and tightened against my torso, the car screeching to a stop. Not ten seconds later, the sound of police sirens blared from behind. Cars veered into the adjacent lanes, making room for a police vehicle to pass, followed by two more, then a fire truck. The car's engine idled, then chugged as he turned off the ignition. It was clear we weren't going anywhere. A sea of cars and minivans littered the roadway, forming a barrier between me and my dream escape.

I assessed the odds. It was two and a half hours before departure, which left thirty minutes to be at the check-in desk. Looking ahead at the traffic jam, it wasn't likely. If we arrived in an hour, I could still make it in time—maybe. There was nothing I could do but cross my fingers. I had predicted glitches and unexpected surprises but not before I even arrived at my destination. I wondered again if this was a terrible omen. If I should ask the driver to turn around and take me back home.

"Can you get a traffic report? What's going on up there?"

"Ma'am, there is an accident up ahead. My GPS estimates a thirty-minute delay, but you never know how long it will take to clear the road," he said in a slow drawl. In contrast, it made my voice sound like a high-speed version of Alvin the chipmunk. "I'll do what I can after the road clears, but right now we're stuck." He offered me a bottle of water, like that was going to sedate my nerves.

"Got a Bloody Mary up there?"

He burst out laughing. "I wish."

During the thirty minutes trapped in claustrophobic uncertainty, my stomach clenched into a knot. I checked and rechecked my carry-on with obsessive anxiety. With each examination, I was relieved that I hadn't forgotten any crucial item, but still, we remained stuck.

At minute thirty-five—and yes, I was counting—I heard engines firing up and traffic began funneling to the right. An officer blew a whistle and waved the vehicles past the accident. Even more frustrating was the sight of two SUVs with scratched bumpers.

As the car pulled up to the drop-off zone, I opened the door before the wheels stopped rolling. Ignoring the driver as he shouted, "Ma'am, please slow down," I leapt from the car at curbside, waited for him to unload my suitcase, then bolted through the revolving entrance. Panic tightened a knot in my chest as I searched for the blue insignia of United Airlines. *Why are so many people jamming the airport at this hour?* I set off in a sprint, cursing a family of five carting ten pieces of luggage, creating a blockade in my path.

When I finally reached the line, my chest heaving for air, I counted twenty people ahead of me. Desperate times called for desperate measures, I reasoned, as I found an agent and pled my case. Relief washed over me as she escorted me to the check-in desk, past the disapproving stares of waiting passengers.

But by this time, I was hot, sweaty, and nerves had replaced excitement. Not at all the image I had in mind as I set off on my adventure. After hoisting my large bag onto the conveyor belt, I cringed when the woman behind the counter gave me what my mother would call the evil eye.

"You're cutting it close. Next time, try to get here earlier."

I glared at her. Before she could change her mind, I snatched the boarding pass out of her hand and ran. By the time I exited the security screening and raced to the gate, the announcement sounded over the loudspeaker: Last call for Barcelona.

With one more dash down the gangway, I entered the plane, my knees nearly buckling with relief. Shoving my carry-on suitcase and shoulder bag into the overhead compartment, I slumped into my aisle seat, thankful I'd paid the added charge for the bulkhead location. Even though I was only five feet four inches, the extra legroom would make the cross-country flight bearable before I changed planes.

Around me, passengers were firing up their tablets and stowing small bags under the seats, preparing for takeoff. Amidst the bustling aircraft, flight attendants scurrying up and down the aisles, I allowed the excitement to bubble to the surface again and exhaled a long breath, slowing from the frenetic pace of the morning. Then I remembered I needed my phone, earbuds, and a sleep mask. Damn.

Bone weary, I heaved myself into the aisle between oncoming traffic, saying, "Excuse me. I just have to get my suitcase." A large man wearing a flowered Hawaiian shirt huffed out an irritated sigh, nearly knocking me over with whiskey fumes. His sandaled foot tapped on the carpet as he waited.

"Can you take your seat, please? We need to keep the aisle open." A flight attendant with a curtain of chestnut-brown hair stared insistently at me.

I obeyed, pulling the bag onto my lap. Hawaiian shirt guy muttered, "Finally," as he passed, and when the aisle cleared, I saw a man ahead, standing in business class. His back was to me, but for a second, an image of Ryan flashed in my mind, with his tall frame and curly, dark hair. It was incredibly irritating. I hadn't been able to get the man out of my head, and now I was seeing visions of him in a crowd.

I leaned back, momentarily closing my eyes, then gathered myself, remembering my task. At the end of my row, an older woman with a striking silver coif sat at the window, engrossed in her book. I placed my bag on the empty seat between us, and as I was rummaging for the items, I couldn't help wondering when Ryan was heading to Barcelona.

In my mind, the running dialogue sounded like two talking heads: It doesn't matter when he will be there because you're going solo on this trip. But... it wouldn't hurt just to get some tips from him, for sightseeing purposes, right? Oh, Sofia, who are you kidding? You totally want to see him again, and then you'll wind up on a slippery slope. Kind of like when you tried snow skiing, and you barreled down the hill out of control, dodging trees, with your poles uselessly waving in the air, until you fell and slid halfway down on your back. I had to admit, the last voice made a good point.

Still, my fingers landed on his business card tucked in the side pocket of my purse. I stared at it for a moment, then put it away. Briefly leaning my body over the armrest, I peered up the corridor. No sign of Ryan, of course. My obsession had reached new heights. But then, images of him hadn't left my mind since the night we'd met.

"Excuse me," I said, bumping butts with a woman across the aisle as we simultaneously stood to stow our bags. She was too preoccupied corralling her two toddlers to notice me. My eyes darted to the nearest bathroom just ahead, next to the galley. It had been a rushed morning, to say the least, and the two cups of coffee I'd had before leaving reminded me it would be a good time to take advantage of the lavatory.

A quick glance confirmed the flight attendant wasn't nearby, so I determined it was safe to move. I slid in front of the door, eyes fixed on the red occupied sign illuminated above, and waited, praying she wouldn't send me back to my seat, because my bladder was about to burst.

It had been a while since I'd been on an airplane; that's how I rationalized what happened next. But really, how was I supposed to know sometimes the loo's door swung out instead of in? I heard the click of the lock sliding, and suddenly it flew open, smacking me straight in the face.

"Oh my God! A panicked voice cried out, "I'm so sorry." I barely registered the apology, because I was covering my face with both hands, searing pain shooting up my nose. "Come in here, let me see."

I separated my fingers, and through watery eyes, I could just make out the man whose voice was prodding me into the bathroom. Ryan. Oh, my frigging God.

Of course, at that moment, my favorite flight attendant pushed her way past me as I hovered at the edge of the doorway. Half blind, I couldn't see what was happening, but suddenly I was hurling toward him, our bodies pressed together inside the miniscule space. Absently, I wondered how anyone managed to have sex in airplane bathrooms, because the two of us barely fit.

Over the roar of the idling engine, I heard the clunk of something hitting metal behind him. He growled out, "Fuck."

"You both must return to your seats." There was no mistaking that sound, her tone more insistent and far less polite now.

"Give us a minute. The lady is hurt."

I heard her exasperated huff as she closed the door, trapping us inside.

"Can you move your hand away? I need to check the damage."

Slowly, I complied, and when our gaze met, there was no denying it was him.

"Sofia?!"

I wanted to cry, overwhelmed with pain, embarrassment, and weariness. I blinked back tears.

"Oh, no. How badly does it hurt?" His beautiful blue eyes filled with concern.

And me? I could only imagine how I must have looked. My fingers stained red; I felt the blood trickling from my nostrils. "Not bad," I lied, then winced.

With the tips of his fingers, he gently examined my nose and cheeks. "I don't think it's broken, just bruised."

He reached behind, grabbed a paper towel, and held it under the water. Dabbing the cleft of my lip, he instructed me to pinch the bridge and tip my head forward. I complied, though the metallic tasting liquid continued to drip down my throat. But as he held me steady, I became aware of other things besides the throbbing. I felt the pulsing of his heartbeat against my chest, the hard muscles under my hand where I gripped his arm, the tender touch of his palm on my back.

Abruptly, I pulled away from him. "I think the bleeding has stopped." Glancing in the mirror, I determined it was no longer dripping, but dark circles formed under my eyes.

"Here, take some towels with you, just in case." He pressed them into my hand.

"Um. Could you...?" I gestured toward the door. "I need to use the bathroom."

His head drooped, mournfully gazing at the toilet. I followed his sightline, and then I saw it. "Sorry, it must have fallen out of my pocket when..."

"When I fell on you? Jesus. That's not good."

We both stared at his phone resting against the metal bowl, a slight film of iridescent blue coating the cover.

Something in me released. Amid the stress of the morning, the shock of seeing Ryan, the blood everywhere, and the sheer absurdity of it all—I collapsed into the kind of uncontrollable laughter that made your sides hurt. His face broke into a grin, then he joined me, laughing in breathless bursts—our chests heaving in gulps of air, pressed together in that tiny loo. For now, I was glad to have lost my sense of smell. I crossed my legs, trying not to pee myself.

Wiping my eyes, I attempted to speak between gasps. "How... are... you...?" Tears trickled down my cheeks. "Oh my God, what's the plan for getting the phone out of the toilet?"

"You don't have any tongs on you by any chance?" he asked, still chuckling.

I handed him a few paper towels. "Wrap it in these. I have a packet of disinfectant wipes in my bag."

He gingerly rescued his phone, the blue dye streaking through the flimsy paper. "Got it. So gross."

Jostling to change places, the only option was full body contact as he gingerly held the cell in one hand, his other gripping my shoulder. "Okay, here we go. Just turn..."

I turned. "Like this?"

"No, the other way."

But it was too late. As I rotated, I knocked his hand off my shoulder and it slid straight to my chest—his palm splayed over one boob.

"Shit. Sorry," he muttered, but I saw his lips press tight, suppressing a grin.

Frozen, I sucked in a breath through my teeth. With the heat of his body pressing against mine, I had no desire to move, because the tingling sensation igniting my core felt so damn good—except for the fact I still had to pee. "I... um... if I just keep turning, I think we've got it."

When our bodies untangled, I wasn't sure if I felt relieved or disappointed. Finally, he burst out the door.

"It's all yours," he said, heaving in a breath as if he'd just run a marathon. "Oh, where are you sitting?"

"Bulkhead," I mumbled, my nose swollen and clogged.

"I'll come find you."

Sometime later, securely buckled in my seat, I caught the flight attendant narrowing her eyes at me as she passed through the cabin before takeoff. As the plane roared down the runway and ascended into the air, I closed my eyes and replayed the debacle. Despite everything, a giggle escaped me. Lost in my thoughts, I heard the telltale ding of the seatbelt light turning off, signaling we had reached flying altitude.

"How are you feeling?" His velvety deep voice rang in my ear.

My eyelids flew open. "Oh! I'm fine now."

His gaze traveled to the unoccupied seat beside me. "Can I join you?"

The voices in my head battled, but I stepped onto the top of that ski slope. "Sure, but will you grab my bag from the bin?"

As I scooted into the middle chair, he opened the compartment and presented me with the black travel case. "This one?" I nodded, and he squeezed himself into the seat, his long legs extending out to the divider wall. He had to be six feet tall, maybe three inches more.

Unzipping it, I located the wipes. "Here, these should help."

"Thanks. Luckily, I have a waterproof case." As he gingerly wiped down his phone, he eyed me sideways. "Sofia, do you believe in fate?"

The answer flew out of my mouth before I could think. "That's absurd." Heat rose from my chest, radiating to the top of my head. Fate? Really?

"I'm not sure I buy into the fate thing, either. But this is weird, right?"

A laugh huffed out of me. "It's fifty shades of weird."

His eyes narrowed for a split second, our gaze locked while an undercurrent of thoughts went unsaid, and I scrambled for a way to stuff those words back into my mouth. "Well, anyway, I'm glad we bumped into each other again." He shook his head. "Although not so literally, I suppose."

I ran my fingers over the bridge of my nose. "Do you think I'll have a black eye?"

His hand cupped my chin, inspecting my face. "I doubt it. Even with the bruising, you're still beautiful, Sofia."

I felt a blush rising, and in my peripheral vision, I caught a glimpse of my seatmate glancing our way. Now I felt even more self-conscious, wondering if she was about to offer a piece of unsolicited advice that began with, "At your age..."

"How long are you staying in Barcelona?" he asked.

"A whole month, thirty days, to be exact."

His lips broke into a mischievous grin. Those full, perfectly shaped lips were exactly as I remembered them. "Huh. Interesting."

"Why is it so interesting?"

"Because I'm here for the month, too. I'd love to give you a tour. The city will amaze you." When I hesitated, he persisted. "Do you think I could get your number? Lunch is on me. After all, it's the least I can do after smashing your nose."

I grimaced. Fate or not, he'd cornered me. With a dizzying mixture of excitement and blinding fear, I held out my hand. "Fine. Give me your phone." Before typing in my information, I used a wipe to clean off the remaining purple slime, then passed it back to him.

"Thank you. Now, was that so hard?"

"Something tells me you're accustomed to getting what you want."

"You say that like it's a bad thing. Tell me, Sofia, what is it you want?"

"I'm not sure what you mean."

"Imagine you had a wish list, not exactly a bucket list, but things you most want out of life. Name the top three on your list."

I stared at the pixelated screen on the seat in front of me, watching the tiny winking plane as it traveled over the ocean, stalling for time. My old list had included career, marriage, and a baby. I'd been on a steady course for so long, I hadn't thought of making a new one. "Umm..." I took a breath and prepared to launch into a plausible explanation, when my favorite attendant leaned over Ryan.

"Mr. Hunter," she began, her voice so sweet I could sense my blood sugar spiking, "lunch is being served, if you'd like to return to your seat."

His gaze swung to me, then back to her. "Sure, in a minute." When his eyes returned to mine, he hesitated. "I'll drop by later, if it's okay. Unless you're sleeping."

I flashed on an embarrassing image of me with my mouth ajar, possibly snoring. "I'm not going anywhere."

An amused look crossed his features. "I suppose not, unless you're planning to parachute off this plane." His palm brushed the length of my arm, then squeezed my hand, the warmth of his touch lingering on my skin.

"I'm looking forward to showing you Barcelona," he said, climbing into the aisle. "We'll come back around to my question. To be continued." He beamed a smile at me before turning to leave.

"He's hot. Don't let that one go." Startled, I pivoted toward the woman next to me, a grin crinkling the lines on her cheekbones. She wore a chic, black ensemble, more elegant than anything I had in my closet.

I laughed. "Yeah, well. If only."

"Do not argue with fate. The universe sometimes gives us gifts. It gave me Javier."

I stared at her. "Your... boyfriend?"

Her smile widened, revealing perfectly white teeth. "I met him on my last trip to Barcelona, and this time, we'll be traveling to the south of Spain."

"How nice." I smiled politely, picturing an older, distinguished gentleman at her side. "Are you going on a group tour?"

She scoffed. "Dear, I'm not about to travel with those old people. I may be turning seventy-five, but don't underestimate me. We're taking Javier's Porsche and driving along the coast." Then she shot me a wink. "He's pretty hot for sixty."

I barked out a laugh. "You go, girl!"

"But your man..." Her lips puckered in a whistle. "You could have some serious fun with him. And let me tell you, as the years roll by, you realize opportunities for romance don't come around too often. Grab all the fun you can."

I could have argued with her, pointed out the risks and pitfalls, but what was the point? Obviously, she seemed happy with her life. I wondered if I could ever be as free-spirited.

"You are an inspiration," I said. "I hope you have a great trip."

As soon as I moved back to my seat and buckled the belt, the unbelievable coincidence with Ryan had my mind reeling. The concept of unexpected surprises on this adventure had just taken on a whole new meaning, and I hadn't even landed in Barcelona. Palpating my sore nose, I wasn't sure if I should have stayed at home.

Chapter Eight

"Permiso?" a voice rang out from behind me. "Permiso." I heard it again, louder now. I pivoted and found a man with a loaded luggage cart staring at me.

"Oh. Sorry," I mumbled, realizing me and my two roller bags had stalled outside of the terminal exit doors, creating a blockade. With some maneuvering, I pulled the suitcases a few feet to the side and tried to get my bearings. I'd slept little on the flights, and even then, it had been in fits and starts. How in the world did people sleep sitting up? My neck had so many kinks, I had to turn my whole torso to scan the surroundings. An image of C-3PO sprang to mind as I rotated.

A thick layer of fog had settled over my brain, and I struggled to bring thoughts into focus. The heat wasn't helping. Unlike a sauna, where dry heat baked the sweat out of you, the air here felt more akin to a steam bath. When I had searched for the weather conditions in June, the temperatures weren't much past the eighty-degree mark, but I'd neglected to check the humidity index.

I peeled off my sweater, but it gave little relief since I was already sweating through my blouse.

When the brain fog subsided, anxiety filled the space. For a moment, I wished Ryan was there waiting for me. When we'd landed in New York, he'd headed off to a different connecting flight, calling out, "See you in Barcelona," as he sprinted to the gate. I told myself everything would be fine. I could handle this. Yet the unfamiliarity of my surroundings and the language barrier left me feeling unbalanced.

Okay, Sofia, you've got this. There must be a taxi stand somewhere. I peeked over the rim of my sunglasses and squinted as the glare hit me. Cigarette smoke plumed in the air, and I rotated to see a woman standing near the garbage bin. Based on her uniform, she had to be one of the staff at the airport. Gathering my courage, I took a stab at speaking Spanish.

"Excuse me. Donde esta el Taxi?"

With her free hand, she pointed to a line slightly over a hundred yards away. "Alli."

When I focused my eyes in that direction, I saw the sign 'Taxi' clearly marked. Maybe this wouldn't be so bad after all. "Gracias."

It was a relief to see the familiar yellow cabs, a little oasis of security in knowing some things remained the same no matter how far I'd traveled. After the driver piled my luggage in the trunk, I handed him a piece of paper with an address, then settled into the back seat and stared out the window with anticipation as the landscape flew by.

The view changed from freeway and undistinguishable suburbia to the architecturally rich facades of the city, which differed from any country I'd visited before. The delicate patterns carved in stone and the lacy wrought iron stirred images that reminded me of France. But the color palette reflected earthy tones, in contrast to the clean, white, intricate structures I had seen in Paris and Nice. And it didn't resemble Italy, where red tile roofs and a Renaissance quality dominated the landscape in Florence.

Closer to the city center, elegant buildings with grand balconies and stained-glass windows flanked the wide boulevard. Interspersed amidst the nineteenth century structures, stood the sleek, glass encased hotels and office complexes. I already sensed the character of this city was unique, a blend of charming antiquity and modern sophistication.

After about thirty minutes, the taxi veered into a cramped avenue and came to a stop at a corner where tourists swarmed like ants. They darted in and out of shops and streamed in an endless flow down a central promenade, which, I would later learn, was the famous Las Ramblas—the primary artery that stretched from the sea to city center, ending at the fountains of Plaza Catalunya.

The driver spoke to me in rapid-fire Spanish, hanging his arm out the window and pointing to a small side street.

"I'm sorry, I don't understand," I said, my anxiety spiking. Again, I held out the hand-written note which bore the address of my Airbnb. He responded by wagging his finger more insistently toward the slim alley jammed with shoppers, and suddenly I understood. Only pedestrians were allowed there. I imagined it would be a tight fit even if the street was completely deserted.

Horns blared from behind and the driver had already hoisted my bags out of the trunk when I peeled myself from the back seat. I thrust a credit card at him and waited for the receipt. Watching him drive away, I summoned what remained of my depleted courage and faced the alleyway.

Okay. I can do this. I straightened my spine and dragged the suitcases through the logjam of meandering tourists like a fish swimming upstream. The roller wheels clunked over the cobblestones, catching on the edges and almost toppling over my luggage more than once. I passed by storefronts and cafes, struggling to read the street numbers, barely visible against the gray stone. The panic wasn't subsiding. My mind whirled with the what-ifs. What if I can't find my apartment? What if my phone doesn't work here? What if I reach someone but they only speak Spanish?

I paused in a doorway, taking five deep breaths to quiet my racing thoughts. Why had I thought I could manage traveling alone?

Relief wasn't instantaneous; it took its time, coming in increments. First, when I found number '37' inscribed on the building. Second, when my phone successfully shifted to roaming mode and I fired off a text to the manager. Luckily, he responded within seconds. When his wiry frame appeared at my side and turned the lock on an enormous wooden door, the twist in my gut finally relaxed.

"Sofia?"

I nodded, then stepped inside. The door shut behind me with a heavy clunk.

"Welcome. I can help you with your bag." He grabbed the handle of my fifty-pound suitcase and started toward the stairs.

"There's no elevator?"

His eyes narrowed, giving me a look that probably meant, *stupid tourist.*

I trailed behind him with my carry-on, glancing at the crumbling plaster on the walls as we climbed the winding staircase. With each step, the poor man groaned, mumbling complaints in Spanish. Even in a foreign language, it wasn't hard to guess what he was saying, since some of the curse words rang out with familiarity. I couldn't blame him. Note to self: only book apartments with elevators or pack lighter. The latter was never going to happen.

The heavy door creaked open, revealing a worn and simple, furnished apartment. Dingy white paint peeled on the high ceilings, from which hung antique chandeliers.

"Um… are you sure we have the right one?" I rummaged in my bag to find the booking printout. "This doesn't quite match the photos on the website."

"Si. Portaferrissa cuatro." He dropped the keys on the table and headed for the door without a backward glance.

"But—" And he was gone. I was going to point out that the bed appeared to be nothing more than a mattress lying on the floor. Upon further inspection, I found a basic wood frame hiding below, but the three inches separation it provided was barely an improvement. It would only be for a week, I told myself, praying the second rental would be an upgrade. At least this place was in the center of the city. It was spacious and bright, with light pouring through several large balcony doors.

As I explored my new home, some unexpected surprises emerged. Of course. When I opened the kitchen drawers, small cockroaches skittered out of sight, causing me to scream like a little girl and hop onto a chair. It made no sense; I was way bigger than the bugs, but I couldn't help myself.

I thought it might still be tolerable except for the musty scent hanging in the air. I detected smells the way a sommelier used their nose to name the essences in a glass of wine. By my estimation, this apartment smelled like old plumbing, cigarettes, and dampness that had seeped into the walls. Black mold?

I pulled open all the windows, letting the cross breeze flush out the odors, then stepped out onto the small balcony which overlooked the bustling Las Ramblas. The layered sounds below—laughter and music and engines whining—drifted up in a continuous din of noise.

Despite the crushing fatigue, my stomach tingled with excitement—I was in the pulsing center of the city! I inhaled a deep breath, letting the unfamiliar scents wash over me, and my nose went to work again; this time finding another set of competing fragrances. The fresh baked smell of waffle cones coming from the gelaterias sparked a craving for ice cream. However, the updraft from the archaic sewer system created a noxious combination with the sweetness.

I closed the door and sprawled out on the mattress, giving in to exhaustion. By the time I woke up, the light in the room had dimmed, the floor lamp creating an elongated, thin shadow. Even before checking the clock, I guessed it was nearing sunset. I refused to spend my first day in Barcelona in bed, despite the new pain in my back that had me rolling to the floor on my hands and knees before pushing upright.

I rummaged through my suitcase and found a wrinkled long skirt and top, but there wasn't time to search for an iron. After running a brush through my hair and giving my armpits a spritz of deodorant, I tore down the stairs.

The air was cooler now, yet still balmy when I stepped outside. Retracing my steps to the corner, I turned left onto Las Ramblas, then joined the throngs of tourists strolling along the center promenade. All around me, the atmosphere vibrated with the sounds of life in a big city. Horns blared at taxis clogging the road as they stopped to unload passengers, and music joined the chorus of sounds. One guy was blasting rap on a boombox. A guitarist sat strumming Spanish songs. Teenage girls giggled with their friends, and from every direction, I caught dangling pieces of conversation as people passed.

Surrounded by tourists, an uneasy twinge sent a prickle up my spine. I was entirely alone in a strange country for the first time in my life. And yet it was as if this beating pulse had absorbed me into something greater than myself—a community of fellow travelers with a common mission. There was a difference between being alone and lonely. Yes, I was traveling alone, but oddly, I felt far less lonely than in the familiar surroundings of my home.

High above me, a canopy of lacy leaves glowed against the angled light as I continued strolling, passing by outdoor terraces, souvenir shops, and gelato stands. Something in me was shifting, almost imperceptibly at first. My mood brightened with each step. My shoulders relaxed and the muscles in my back lengthened. A little voice squealed in my head, *I am in Barcelona!* Halfway down the promenade, my face broke into a giddy grin for no particular reason at all.

When I finally reached the bottom of Las Ramblas, the sun had almost disappeared, sinking behind the hills next to the port; the horizon flooded with color. Clouds trimmed in pink and gold streaked across the darkening blue sky. The towers and spires of the Gothic style rooftops took on a magical appearance, as if silhouetted against a watercolor painting. It was the most stunning spectacle I'd ever seen.

I found an empty bench in front of the harbor and sat down, mesmerized by the fading sunlight shimmering on the water. Luxurious yachts rocked with the tide, tugging gently on the ropes, the angle of the light setting them aglow in golden hues. Seagulls swooped low as if preparing to make one last dash for a snack before calling it a night, their caws mingling with the sound of gentle waves lapping against the dock.

It was all so surreal, as if I'd landed in the middle of a dreamscape. I could hardly believe in just one day, I had crossed the ocean to arrive in Spain. And now, sitting on a bench in front of the Mediterranean Sea, my problems slipped into a haze, like a lens out of focus. *The magic of travel,* I thought, *presents itself in the contrasts.* Overnight, I had been teleported into a completely new world. It was exactly the balm I needed for my frayed nerves.

My nose appreciated the improved air at the port. With dozens of restaurants nearby, the fragrance of seafood and garlic floated on the soft breeze, reminding me I hadn't eaten since breakfast on the plane. I moved from the waterside with some reluctance and entered the labyrinth of tiny alleyways within the Gothic Quarter. I weaved around the lines extending from the cafes tucked away beyond stone facades, and even practiced my new word (permiso) when I found myself stuck in a logjam of tourists perusing the menu boards.

Restaurant windows displayed small plates containing what appeared to be fish, or a concoction of unrecognizable ingredients, atop slices of baguette. My stomach growled, urging me to woman-up and brave dining alone. As much as I hated the thought, hunger was a powerful motivator. When I found one with empty tables, I approached a server and held up a lone finger.

"Buenas noches. You'd like a table?" Of course he spoke English. This was the center of the tourist district.

"Yes, please."

While the young man showed me to a corner booth, I noted that all the other tables were occupied by families with children restlessly bouncing in their seats, or couples huddled together sharing their plates, engrossed in private conversations.

The menu he dropped on my table was in English, but it didn't matter as the food was still foreign. When the server arrived, I took my chances and let my finger point to random photos. By some stroke of luck, the food was delicious. My glass of wine was priced at three euros—a fraction of the price in California—a rich blend with notes of cherry. After draining a second glass, I paid the bill, leaving with a sense of accomplishment. I'd survived exploring on my own and had managed not to starve. *Not bad for the first day*, I thought.

My mind was still humming as I climbed into the lumpy bed, listening to the raucous sounds of the crowds on the street below. Barcelona, or at least this part of the city, didn't settle down at midnight. On my way home, the energy had grown electric with the promise of dancing and music and all-night parties. A wave of nostalgia swept through me, remembering how it felt to be twenty-five and full of anticipation of an evening out on the town.

A text alert pinged on my phone, and I nearly rolled onto the floor to grab it. Ryan. At the sight of his name on the screen, an unexpected tinge of excitement jolted me fully awake. I reminded myself I wasn't a teenager and there was no reason to get excited. Still, my heart raced when I read his message.

> *Meet me at Plaza Catalunya tomorrow at 2:00? I'll take you to lunch.*

I simply typed back, **Sounds good**, then added a thumbs up emoji, praying for no more surprises.

Chapter Nine

I woke to find the light streaming through the thin curtains in my bedroom, and my hand hit the tile floor, searching for my phone. Message alerts popped on the screen, one from Madison and another from my son. My mother had made me promise to let her know I arrived safely, but since she didn't use text or email, I set a reminder on my phone to call her landline later. She'd been surprised when I'd told her about my trip, and more than a little worried, launching into the safety lecture I'd heard a million times. There was no use arguing that I was a grown adult.

I reached for my laptop, propped myself up on pillows, and opened the email from Ben first. We'd spoken soon after I decided to come to Barcelona, and luckily, our timing would work out perfectly. He and his girlfriend were coming to visit Spain as part of their post-graduation European trek.

To: SofiaDrake01@gmail.com
From: BenandCallie@yahoo.com
Hey, Mom, did you arrive okay? How's the jet lag? Callie and I are in Brussels and it's hella beautiful here. You would love it! Is your apartment okay? I know it was tough to find

something at the last minute. We're excited to meet up with you next week! You can give us some tips on places to visit.

Later,

Ben

My heart let out a little sigh. God, I missed him. Since he'd left for college in New York, we had hardly seen each other except on holidays. In the blink of an eye, I had gone from being a devoted (and possibly hovering) mom to a single empty nester, barely enduring those dark, lonely days and tearful nights. Thinking back, should I have done things differently? Probably. The transition wouldn't have been so painful if I'd developed friendships with other single women or hadn't postponed dating until after he had left home. But being Ben's mom was a blessing, and it filled me with pride to know he'd turned out to be a well-adjusted, sweet young man who was confident enough to strike out on his own.

I wrote him a quick reply and clicked on the email from Madison, still wishing she could have joined me. Her check-in was similar, asking me if I'd arrived and to fill her in on every detail. I typed a response, knowing it would make her day to hear the big news.

To: Madison555@gmail.com
From: SofiaDrake01@gmail.com
Hey, girl. Yes, I arrived in Barcelona, and the city is spectacular. I'm feeling so invigorated already. I wish you were here to see it with me. You will never guess who I literally ran into on the plane. Yes, him. Mr. Temptation himself. He

now has my number and says he'll give me a tour. I'm still skeptical, but I'll keep you posted. I know you're rolling your eyes at me. Whatever.

Gotta run. I'm meeting him today for lunch, and you know how long I take to get ready. TTYL xo

By the time I stepped into Plaza Catalunya dressed in a cobalt blue sundress (decided on in my fifth wardrobe change) and reasonably comfortable sandals, I had successfully erected a cement barrier around my emotions by repeating the mantra: I am an antelope. That is, until I spotted him across the square, his piercing eyes drawn to mine like laser beams.

Mere moments before I sensed his arrival, I had been admiring the large fountain, one of two circular focal points at the far corner, water arcing high into the air. Benches lined the irregular angles of the plaza filled with tourists (and possibly a smattering of locals), many with a picnic lunch resting on their laps. A cacophony of cooing pigeons swooped down from the sky as gleeful children tossed handfuls of seed, the tiled surface becoming a solid mass of pecking creatures. Inching my sandaled feet backward, away from the beaks, I cringed. Images of Hitchcock's movie *The Birds* flashing through my mind. As I scanned the crowd for Ryan's familiar face, my head swiveled in all directions, and I fought the urge to panic, then told myself to stop freaking out. Even if he stood me up, it was no big deal, right? I hardly knew the guy. This was my vacation, and I'd be fine on my own.

I pulled my cell phone from my purse and checked the time: 2:07. A pigeon batted its wings, and I ducked out of its flight path. Then, I knew. Ryan was here somewhere amongst the skateboarding teenagers narrowly missing my toes, the vendors selling bird food, and the terrifying swarm of gray.

Beyond a group of young girls dressed in jean shorts cut so high they could pass for Brazilian swimsuits, I caught sight of him sauntering across the mosaics in my direction. Our eyes locked. Something hot shot through me, and I became a teenager again; unbalanced, palms sweating, heart racing.

"Finally, Sofia, I found you." He leaned in and planted a soft kiss on each cheek, then inspected my face. "Your nose looks perfect. Glad you're okay."

"Damn. I guess I can't sue for the injury," I teased. I took in the sight of him, dressed in blue Bermuda shorts and a white polo shirt, which clung to his broad shoulders. This guy made casual look good.

He laughed. "Were you waiting long?"

I shook my head, the warmth of his lips still lingering on my cheeks. "No worries, there is plenty of action here to keep me entertained." I glanced warily at an approaching pigeon. We had a brief stare down while I warned it with a glare, not today, buddy.

"Ready? We're going for lunch." Then he leaned in, his breath a warm gust against my cheek. "Later, I have a surprise planned for us."

I wasn't sure if it was the way his breath tickled my ear, the seductive tone in his voice, or the implications in the word surprise... but the ground seemed to sway under my feet. I held onto his arm and steadied myself. "I'm ready. Just lead the way."

Weaving through the snarl of tourists zigzagging in every direction, we emerged onto the sidewalk and traversed a wide, traffic-filled thoroughfare until we reached a tree-lined street. It was distinctly different from the ancient stone alleyways of the Gothic section. It was as if we'd crossed an invisible line and entered a more modern era, where the shops bore upscale brands and the restaurants glowed in opulent hues of golden light. Here, the sun's rays had plenty of space to filter through the trees.

"This is Rambla Catalunya," Ryan explained. "It leads up towards the hills and is part of the Eixample district, constructed in the 19th century. The area is still rather touristy, but it has a classier vibe."

My gaze swept across the lacy iron balconies, the delicate carvings of the facades. "It's beautiful. I'm sensing a French influence in the architecture. Wait, maybe Roman?"

From the corner of my eye, I saw his smile. "You're observant. Barcelona has a rich combination of styles influenced by various periods in Europe." He clasped my hand in his. "Hurry, I think we can grab that free table."

We darted in front of a taxi inching down a one-way street in bumper-to-bumper traffic and headed for the center island, where terrace restaurants stacked one on top of the other, stretching for ten, possibly twelve blocks. When I spotted another couple headed for the one free table remaining, I realized why we were sprinting. Ryan spun me into one chair, while he claimed the other, narrowly winning the race.

I was still catching my breath while Ryan caught the server's eye. He acknowledged us with a nod, and seconds later, the young man was at our table bearing menus. The guy's eyes swung from Ryan to me, then back to Ryan with a look, seemingly a question mark. Maybe I was being too sensitive, but was he wondering about this couple at his table? Were 'cougars' a thing here? Did he think I was Ryan's aunt? And lastly, why did I care?

"Would you like a drink to start?" Ryan asked.

"God, yes," I blurted out, a little too enthusiastically. Despite the warmth of the sun beating down on my skin, my hands trembled. *Get a grip.*

He ordered a liter of cava sangria, explaining, "It's similar to regular sangria except it's made with a type of Spanish champagne." It wasn't long before I realized that while it tasted like fruit juice, it turned out to be deceptively potent. After I'd guzzled down the entire glass, the trembling finally stopped and I slowly began to relax, my body sinking into the cushions.

I listened while he rattled off a list of the top ten sights of the city, then he asked me if I preferred museums or architecture, beaches or mountains, clubs or chill bars. Maybe it was the way Ryan made everything flow so effortlessly, the way he leaned forward while he waited for my answers, but I grew oddly comfortable, as if we'd known each other far longer than our brief moments together.

The server circled our table for the fourth time and finally asked, "Do you want to order food?"

Ryan nodded. "I'm starving. Do you know what you want to eat?"

"Actually, I don't have a clue what to pick. Everything looks delicious," I said, scanning the four-page menu. To be honest, his presence was a distraction, and though I'd only had coffee and a croissant for breakfast, my focus wasn't on food. "If you wouldn't mind, I'll let you choose a few things to share."

"Then I suggest we start with tuna tartare and the arugula salad with goat cheese and figs, followed by steamed mussels in white wine and garlic..." he paused, then added, "let's throw in a traditional dish from this region, patatas bravas."

"Potatoes what?"

"Imagine large steak fries in the U.S. covered in a special sauce, which varies between restaurants," he explained.

"You had me at fries, but I'm game for the rest, too. I'll try most anything... once."

A sly, crooked smile tilted his lips, a glint flashing in his eyes. "Does that apply to activities unrelated to food?"

An uninvited wave of heat fanned upward from somewhere in my core, but I tried to ignore the sensation. I rolled my eyes, and without answering, raised my glass.

By the time our meal arrived, I was beginning to understand his love for Barcelona. I learned his Spanish was decent, largely because he'd spent a few weeks in language school and later took online courses.

"So, is that where you made friends here?"

He lifted the pitcher of sangria and stirred the fruit with a long spoon, then refilled our glasses. "Barcelona is exceptionally international, so it's easy to make new connections. Aside from school, I met people at events or joined volleyball games at the beach. Friends multiply here. You make a few friends, and soon you find yourself swept into their social circle."

My gaze drifted to the view of the promenade, its vibrant energy palpable. Groups of weary tourists dashed for seats at the tables lining the avenue; their faces lit with excitement. Besides English, I heard voices speaking in French, Italian, and maybe Russian? Inspecting the tiers of balconies and facades, what looked like Roman columns stood alongside floral filigree inlays in stone, each structure different from the next. Compared to the plain, predictable lines of strip malls and office buildings in California, this was a feast for the eyes.

Apart from the servers scurrying from the restaurants to the terraces balancing trays of food and bottles of wine, the pace here was leisurely. Even the businesspeople in suits lingered over their meals, sipping wine or cocktails, apparently in no hurry to rush back to the office. I thought about how I'd usually eat lunch at my desk while I worked at the computer.

"What a dream it would be to live here."

"I'll admit, this city has its charms." Ryan eyed me from across the table. "Have you considered living abroad?"

"Once, I did." I paused to swallow a bite of tuna. "Did you taste this? It's amazing."

"Are you aware that you make this cute moaning sound when you're enjoying the food?"

I put down my fork. "No. I do not."

Chuckling at me, he said, "Yes, you do. But go on, finish your thought."

"Oh, right. That was a long time ago. It's something young people do when they finish college, when they've yet to amass responsibilities and debt. I'm way past that stage of life." Even as the words left my mouth, a tiny voice inside me rose in protest.

"Sofia, though I don't know you well—yet—I have a hard time believing you lack an adventurous spirit." A dimpled smile crept across his face, and it seemed as if he recognized the nagging inner doubts I was working diligently to silence. I shifted my focus, staring intently at my plate. He continued. "I'm just saying, you boarded a plane and came to Barcelona alone. A lot of women wouldn't have done that."

I considered that for a moment. While surfing the internet, I'd come upon blogs written by solo female travelers, but most were hardly out of their twenties. There seemed to be a whole new generation who bravely adopted, if not a nomad lifestyle, at least one that included exploring the world beyond the boundaries of the vast United States.

"You're right," I finally answered, "but you're a man traveling alone. Traditionally, men have been traveling for business and pleasure for ages, so why in the twenty-first century does it still seem like an anomaly when women set out for far-away places on their own?" Then I realized that while I was fighting for equality, my own fears about traveling alone had been pricking me like a thorn stuck in my shoe. "It's a rhetorical question. Don't mind me, I'm on a soapbox rant."

Ryan placed his fork neatly on his plate. "You make a good point, though in my experience, I've come across a broad community of people here, which includes women from many countries. Some are passing through or staying here briefly, and some have made this their permanent home. It's not as unusual as you might think."

I saw the second his thoughts shifted; the glint in his eyes gave it away. "By the way, I still can't believe we were on the same flight, let alone bumping into each other. Again, I'm so sorry."

As the images came rushing back, I shook my head. "I know, me too. I can't even fathom the odds of that happening." His words echoed in my mind... *Do you believe in fate?* "I've learned my lesson. No standing in front of bathroom doors."

He leaned forward, but for a few moments, his gaze shifted to the endless stream of tourists passing a few feet from our table, some stopping to study the menu posted on a stand, which conveniently listed the fare in several languages. Their eyes narrowed and glazed over, probably just as confused as I was. When he spoke, his tone was more serious.

"Why did you leave so abruptly the night we met? You specifically asked me about my age. Does it make you uncomfortable?"

My stomach sank to somewhere around my toes. Two tables over, a toddler resting on his mother's lap sent a glass toppling to the ground, and the shatter made me jolt in my seat. Reliving the awkward moments, the uncomfortable feelings of that night, I avoided his gaze. He'd laid the cards on the table face up, but I wasn't prepared for this discussion. Between the heat, the sangria, and his questions, I sensed my skin reddening.

"Um… if we're being honest, your age is only part of my reservation." I hesitated a few more seconds while he patiently waited. "Look, I've just had a bad break-up, and I'm not interested in getting involved with anyone. I've been disappointed too many times." I lowered my eyes to my lap, my fingers twisting a defenseless scrunchie band.

"I get it, but have you considered there's a good chance I might be different from those other guys?"

A laugh escaped me, along with an embarrassing snort. "And how are you any different, Ryan?"

With dramatic flair, he mimed plucking an arrow from his chest. "Oh, Sofia, you wound me. I'm not a player, if that's what you're worried about. I prefer dating women with some maturity because they have more life experience, which leads to more interesting conversation and… in my opinion, much better sex."

Something in me tightened. If he was aiming to seduce me, it was working. With one glance at the glimmer in his eyes, his full lips slightly parted, tiny fireworks exploded across my skin, but I couldn't let him know. "Are you inferring that we're going to have sex?" I cocked an eyebrow.

"Let's take this slow. I'm not about to risk scaring you away again. But think about it, every time we meet someone, we take a risk. I'll be the first to admit I don't mind living dangerously, but when it comes to dating, I'm not down with free-falling off a cliff. Then again, if we don't take chances, we might miss out on something great." His gentle smile almost convinced me, but there were a dozen rebuttals forming in my mind. My body, however, still reverberated with explosions—I ignored them. It was time to set boundaries.

"Let's take the word 'dating' off the table," I said.

"Okay, how do you want to define this?"

"You offered to show me around, so let's say you're my tour guide. Sound fair?"

He considered this for a moment. "I can live with that."

"So long as we understand the agreement—no free falling. We'll have some vacation fun for thirty days, and then, well... we'll go on with our lives. No expectations," I said, imagining Madison cheering me on.

"Agreed. A month of vacation fun and done. Should we notarize a contract?" His smile was so broad, those irresistible dimples popped on his cheeks. God, he was adorable.

"A handshake will do." I extended my arm, and he took my hand in his for a little longer than strictly necessary. Damn that electricity. Withdrawing my fingers from his warmth, I tilted my head. "How are you going to fulfill your guide duties? Are you on vacation for the whole month?"

"Mostly, yes, but I'll have to do some meetings over Zoom. I can make myself available to you, don't worry." He gave me a wry smile that made me wonder what kind of life he led. *Lucky*, I thought.

"So, what brought you here, anyway?" Ryan propped his chin against the broad palm of his hand, his eyes studying me with curiosity.

I reached for my glass and took a long pull on my drink, buying a moment to choose my words. "If you remember, you did say Barcelona was the place to visit." Thinking back to his invitation, I couldn't help but grin at him. It had seemed like a ludicrous idea, and yet, here we were. "As I mentioned, my company was restructuring, and I was shuffled out of a job."

"Damn. I'm sorry to hear that."

"Maybe it's not so bad. I got a decent severance package. It has given me the time to travel, to take a step back and reconsider my direction."

Ryan reached for his sangria, brushing his hand against mine, and I swear sparks flew. We raised our glasses in the air and toasted to new beginnings.

I let my gaze wander to a balcony overhead, where a couple was making out, and my cheeks flushed. Every time I was around Ryan, I was blushing or hot flashing. It was annoying.

"So, how do you manage to travel so much? Can you work remotely?"

"Sometimes. I have clients around Europe and the US and often commute to London, but when I'm in Barcelona, I tend to chill. Don't get me wrong, I work hard, but I allow myself time to play. I love my life, but there's one thing missing." He tilted his glass and plucked a slice of orange from the ice, then plopped it in his mouth.

His statement seemed illogical. Didn't he have it all? But I stepped off a cliff and asked, "What's that?" even though I instinctively knew the answer.

"Someone to share experiences with. The Eiffel Tower is stunning and the view from Machu Picchu leaves you awestruck, but it's not as much fun if there's no one special to relive those memories with."

I fumbled for words, afraid of revealing too much—afraid I might admit I was looking for the same thing. Instead, I shrugged and said, "I get that." Then a thought struck me. "Why don't you have a special someone in your life? Look at you... it wouldn't be hard to find a girlfriend."

"I could ask you the same question." He leaned back in his chair and our eyes locked. We played a game of chicken, raising our brows at each other. He backed down first. "Most women don't appreciate my travel schedule. My last girlfriend wanted me to settle down in London, but it wasn't possible at the time. Besides, we weren't a good fit. It's not easy to find the right person, but then, maybe I expect too much."

I leaned my elbow on the table and rested my chin on my palm. "Tell me, Ryan Hunter, what is it you expect?"

He laughed. "You're enjoying putting me on the spot, aren't you?"

"A little." I raised a mischievous smile.

"It feels odd to put it into words." He paused, shifting in his chair, his fingertips thrumming on the table while he considered this. "I wonder sometimes if it's even possible to find the right person or the ideal relationship, given I've yet to see a real-life example, but for me, it all comes down to a combination of chemistry, trust, respect, and compatibility. Like having a best friend to hang with, who you sort of want to have sex with every day."

Without my permission, my heart leaped against my chest, doing a happy dance—whirling in circles, screaming "Yes, yes, yes!" I ignored the commotion and kept my expression neutral. "It sounds like you've given it some thought. Your description sounds... perfect. A relationship with those qualities would have a good chance of going the distance."

Ryan leaned forward now, mirroring my position, his face only inches from mine. "And you?"

"You're distracting me." I waved my hand in the universal gesture to back up.

He complied, still grinning.

I could have launched into my two-page list titled, "Things I want in a man/relationship," which was definitely saved on Google Drive. Or I could have simply said... you, because he encompassed everything I'd been hoping for in a man, except for the age difference. Right then, I would have given anything to be fifteen years younger and far less jaded. But that wasn't going to happen, so instead, I answered, "Ditto. You nailed it. And I agree, it's not easy to find such a relationship."

Something quietly passed between us. A smile. A shared gaze that spoke volumes. We probably could have heard a pin drop if it wasn't for the cars honking. Our trance seemed to last several minutes, until the server showed up.

"Would you like anything else?"

"Just the bill, please," Ryan said.

It took another five minutes before he returned. The servers weren't rushing us out, making way for the customers waiting in line. As I sipped the last drops from my glass, a wave of calm washed over me, filling me with contentment for the first time in God knows how long. Admittedly, the sangria may have contributed, but somehow, he had put me at ease.

When Ryan paid the check, he thrummed his hands on the tabletop as if it was a drum roll. "Ready to go exploring?"

Chapter Ten

My feet bore the brunt of sightseeing all afternoon, blisters swelling where the straps rubbed at the sides, but Ryan fulfilled any expectations I might have had about his expertise as a tour guide. Since he had a Barcelona virgin on his hands, eager to be enthralled by the sites, I willingly gave him free rein.

"Show me your favorite places, Mr. Tour Guide."

"I'm afraid that's going to take more than a few hours, so consider this an introduction to the city. I'll have lots more to show you another day, but today we don't have too much time before the surprise."

I raised an eyebrow at him. "I'm not sure I can handle any more 'surprises' on this trip."

"I think you'll like this one."

"Hmm," I murmured, dubious.

His tour included some of the iconic sights. After purchasing a ticket at the metro station, we rode the train to the stop at Gaudi's Sagrada Familia Cathedral. "Wait for it," he said, covering my eyes with the width of his palms when we reached the top of the escalator, then he guided me with his body pressed against my back. When he released me and I gasped at the view, his sense of satisfaction was palpable.

"This is a cathedral?" I remembered visiting many famous churches during my trip to Europe in my twenties. There had been the Duomo in Florence, Notre Dame in Paris, and others I couldn't quite recall. But Sagrada didn't resemble anything I'd ever seen before. "It looks like a cross between an unusual castle and a stunning work of art."

Ryan explained how Gaudi's unique style combined elements of Art nouveau, Catalan Modernism, and Gothic design. "Be sure to take a tour of the Basilica, it will blow you away."

My neck craned upward, viewing the towers stretched high against the blue, watercolor sky while enjoying the sensation of his body lingering against mine.

With one major landmark out of the way, we hopped in a taxi, Ryan checking his watch. "We have about two hours to wander around the Gothic area before..." He stopped short of finishing.

"Before what?" My legs stuck to the vinyl seat, squeaking as I shifted toward him. "C'mon, you can tell me," I pleaded. I had a moment to study his profile while he remained silent, noticing the chiseled cut of his jawline as he pursed his lips to keep from smiling. The faint stubble of a dark beard appearing on smooth, unlined skin. The way his thick eyelashes fanned out, well above the fold of his lid. Every feature seemingly carved by an artist's hands. *Too beautiful,* I thought, not for the first time. I glanced at my manicured hand, now resting on his knee. All the nourishing creams in the world wouldn't stop the lines from betraying my age.

As if sensing my thoughts, his head swiveled to meet my gaze, lacing his fingers through mine and pinning our grip on his thigh. The bulk of his muscle under the jeans tensed as he shifted. "I'm kind of enjoying keeping you in suspense," he admitted, his smile broadening. "You get a little crease between your eyebrows when you're worried, right there." He reached out his index finger and pressed the tip gently to my skin.

"Perfect. I have worry lines." I rolled my eyes.

"Stop. It's adorable. I'd much rather be able to see your expression instead of a face frozen by Botox."

There were some secrets I decided were better to keep hidden. I didn't mention I had some experience with diminishing my crows' feet at the hands of a skilled dermatologist. "Screw aging gracefully," I'd told Madison on several occasions when I was sick of appearing tired, even when I had a full night's sleep. There weren't any gray strands mingling in my dark hair, despite developing streaks of white decades ago. I faintly recalled having perfect skin, but now I never left the house without first applying makeup. Aging, I had learned, was labor intensive, not that I'd come close to becoming a Kardashian. It was about feeling good when I faced myself in the mirror, but seeing myself reflected in the rear-view mirror alongside Ryan, the pressure ratcheted up more than a few notches.

For the next couple of hours, we rode the current of tourists meandering through the twists and turns of the Old Town, Ryan occasionally pulling me into a restaurant to show me a hidden garden or pointing out a cleverly designed mural, which, when viewed from precisely the right angle, well-placed slashes of color revealed two lips kissing. We rounded corners to find art museums tucked inside cave-like stone archways, and modern metal sculptures set against a backdrop of Roman ruins. With each new discovery, I grew more awestruck at the intrigue within this city. From the pleased look on his face, I wasn't sure who was having more fun.

"What's this plaza called?" I asked as we passed through a square which seemed to flow into two more secluded spaces. Encircled by apartment buildings, a modest but charming Gothic cathedral formed the focal point. As in all the plazas, restaurants spilled out onto terraces, tables and chairs clustered under the leafy trees, and servers scurried across the cobblestones in sneakers, bearing plates of tapas. But in this center, artisans waited on customers in makeshift booths.

"It's Placa del Pi," he said. "And this is where you'll find your surprise."

I gestured to the stalls. "This? I'd love to see what they're selling."

Grinning, he glanced at his watch. "Not this, but we have a few minutes, so let's check it out."

I bolted ahead, with Ryan following, then paused at each booth to admire the paintings of Spain, the fine jewelry, and finally, lingering to drool over the pastries and chocolate, all handcrafted by locals. Sounds drifted down from the balconies surrounding the square. A couple's laughter as they sat at a small table two floors above, their wine glasses precariously tipping. Reggaeton music spilling from an apartment, its wooden balcony doors swung open wide. Scanning the facades, I noticed others basking in the sun and a man reading a book while relaxing in a sling-back chair.

Ryan followed my gaze. "You notice it too, don't you?"

I knew exactly what he meant. "There's an intimacy of life here that's lacking at home. We all stay tucked within our houses, but here, it's as if there are no boundaries. And there's something special about this plaza. I can't quite put it into words."

"This place has a rich history, and the root of it comes from the church over there. The Basilica Santa Maria del Pi."

"I can only imagine how it would feel to live here and have a view of the cathedral every day," I mused. "It's like going back centuries to an earlier age but with modern conveniences. Well, mostly modern. There's still laundry hanging out in the open air."

Checking his watch again, he took my hand in his, leading us toward the entrance of the basilica. "It's time. We'd better go in now."

As we approached the carved archway, I noticed a large cardboard sign with the image of a man playing the guitar. "A concert?"

Ryan handed over two tickets to the doorman. "A Spanish guitar concert."

I whipped around to face him and stared at his profile, my mouth gaping open. I caught the glint in his eyes as they peeked in my direction, a hint of a smile breaking on his lips. He couldn't have known that when I'd seen the advertisement for the show during my stroll down Las Ramblas, I'd made a mental note to find the performance. Perhaps it was because I'd watched Vicky Cristina Barcelona on the flight, but the idea of a guitar concert in Spain stirred my inner romantic. The synchronicity between us gave rise to goosebumps fanning down my arms.

Soft, acoustic music played on speakers as I followed Ryan down the center aisle, my sandals slapping against the slick, tiled flooring, echoing against the walls of the chapel. A hushed reverence permeated the thick air, and a faint scent of incense drifted from the tables, where small candles cast a glow in the dim light of the church.

"This isn't a grand concert hall, but I thought you might like a more intimate environment," he whispered as we claimed our seats on the hard wooden bench, three rows from the stage. A lone chair next to a guitar stand sat perched in front of an altar draped in red cloth, while fading sunlight illuminated the colorful stained-glass windows looming high above our heads.

I leaned close, my shoulder brushing against his. "I love it. This church is breathtakingly beautiful," I said, keeping my voice low, scanning the arched ceiling and holy images gilded in gold against ancient stone walls. Compared to other churches I'd seen, it wasn't nearly as ornate, but an ethereal glow bathed the interior, creating the sensation of traveling back in time.

Thunderous applause erupted as the performer appeared from behind a red curtain, and before he took his seat, he gave a gentle bow to the audience. The gray-haired man wasn't any taller than me, round in the middle, and not at all imposing. He kept his head ducked at a slight angle, as if too shy to admit he was the star of the show.

You could have heard a pin drop as he held his instrument and gently plucked the strings. But when he played the first notes, a jolt of excitement coursed through my body, my pulse racing in time with the music. I was mesmerized by his hands—the way his long fingernails plucked at the strands with such lightning speed, they blurred before my eyes. Some songs I recognized as classics; the audience cheering even as he strummed the initial chords.

As the tempo slowed and a deep, soulful melody echoed off the stone walls, I allowed my eyelids to close, surrendering to its seductive power. It pierced through my defenses, finding its way to the depths of my soul. It caught me completely off guard. In a Gothic church, thousands of miles from home, I found myself transported by the music of a renowned maestro, stirring emotions within me I could barely comprehend.

For reasons I didn't understand, Ryan reached for my hand, intertwining his fingers with mine just as tears welled in my eyes. I didn't pull away. I didn't force myself to snap out of the trance. Instead, I savored the tenderness of his touch, the warmth of his presence beside me, and the melodies pulsing through my very veins. It was as if I'd lost a layer of skin, my senses tripling with a new sensitivity—emotions bubbling to the surface. And as the final notes faded into silence, vulnerability washed over me, leaving me feeling exposed.

When I found the courage to raise my lids, I saw Ryan's gentle gaze meeting mine. His slight nod, a squeeze of my fingers conveyed everything—my emotions spilled out like a punctured piñata. It was too much. His other hand reached for my face, brushing a thumb against my damp cheeks. The gesture almost caused a deluge. There was no question I was in trouble. I had to get myself under control.

To my relief, the tempo soon became lively again. Ryan's hands thrummed against his thighs to the rhythm as my feet played accompaniment, tapping against the tiles. Even after the audience begged for an encore and the maestro took a bow, we lingered on the bench while people filed down the aisles.

"Thank you," I said, shifting in my seat to face Ryan. "It was the most perfect surprise. This music, this culture... it resonates with me."

"I can see that. It does the same for me. My mother came from Spanish descent, but her ancestors crossed the pond generations ago."

"Now it all makes sense, the reason you're so drawn to this city." I didn't know how I'd missed the signs before. His olive skin and dark curly hair, his tall, lean body and stunning good looks. He looked Spanish. Maybe it was no coincidence he'd picked me out of the crowd. Freud would have a field day with that observation.

In the glow of the streetlamps, Ryan and I made our way back to my apartment, stopping at a gelato shop we stumbled upon in an obscure alley. I ordered my favorite.

"Chocolate and hazelnut?" he asked.

I held out the cone. "It's a perfect flavor combination. Taste it."

He leaned in, slowly circling his tongue against the ice cream. Droplets of chocolate trickled down the side of the cone, and I nearly melted into a puddle.

"Would you like a lick of my pistachio?"

Tit for tat, I thought. While training my eyes on his, I wrapped my lips around the mound of ice cream, then slowly released it from my mouth with a moan of pleasure. Sure, it was unfair to tease him, but the look on his face was worth it.

"Yum. That's a delicious flavor," I said, licking my lips.

He shook his head. "You're so bad."

"You have no idea." I added a wink. Before he could take this flirting to the next level, I came to my senses. "Jet lag is catching up with me. Walk me back?"

"Where exactly are you staying?"

"It's near the corner of Las Ramblas on Portaferrissa."

"Damn, chica, you're in one of the busiest tourist sections."

"It was the only apartment I could find in the center on short notice. I'm moving to El Born soon for the rest of the month."

"Born is my favorite barrio in the city. You'll love it there. But let's take this street on the right. It's a shortcut."

"Lead the way, because without GPS, I'd never make it back."

We chucked the wrappers on our cones in a garbage bin on the corner after finishing the last bite simultaneously.

"Can we meet tomorrow night?"

"Since my son isn't arriving until next week, my calendar is wide open."

"Oh, you have a kid?" His footsteps halted on the cobblestones. Then, after quickly scanning the street, he hooked his arm through mine, pulling us out of the path of an oncoming onslaught of drunk twenty-year-old guys weaving and stumbling their way down the narrow alley. We huddled so close to the stone wall while they passed, I could feel his breath on my cheek. "How old is he?"

I cringed at the question. Telling a man my son's age inevitably resulted in a look of surprise, followed by math calculations.

"He recently graduated from college. He and his high school sweetheart are coming here for the first time." It was all true, but I simply evaded the actual numbers. I considered adding that I'd been a teenage mother. I waited for a moment, but his face didn't show the usual reaction.

His smile reached his eyes, and there was something about the glint in his gaze I didn't quite understand. "They'll have an awesome experience here. Do you have a good relationship with him?" With the alleyway clear, we resumed walking, and I breathed easier with more distance between us.

"The best." I beamed with pride at the thought of him. "Since he was small, we've been close, and although he lives in New York, it hasn't changed. I made him my top priority, staying in the marriage much longer than I should have. In the end, he was fourteen when we divorced. I must admit, there were times I probably smothered him, but he knew he could always count on me."

Ryan nodded, but he looked past me into the distance where a line was forming outside a tapas bar. "Well done, Sofia." I remembered something he'd said about his childhood when we met. *We weren't exactly like one of those happy families you see on TV.* How dysfunctional had his family been? It didn't seem as though it was the right time to ask, because his tone abruptly shifted. Whatever he was thinking, it was gone in a flash.

When we arrived back at my apartment, I had my key ready to unlock the wooden door. I already knew I wouldn't invite him upstairs, but like any man, his eyes conveyed hope—as if standing at a roulette table, waiting to see where the ball landed. "Goodnight, Ryan. Thanks for a great day."

"I'll pick you up tomorrow night at nine o'clock. There's a place I want to show you."

Before I turned to open the door, he was stepping away.

"Can I get a copy of the tour schedule? You know, just so I'm prepared." I was only half joking.

Throwing his palms into the air, he replied, "Now, what fun would that be?"

We grinned at each other, then I watched him leave until his tall frame disappeared around a corner. This was going to be an adventure. I only hoped I would be able to keep it in perspective, wrapped in a vacation bubble.

Chapter Eleven
Ryan

"I wondered when you'd get back to Barcelona, but seriously, a coffee date? I've waited for months to see you, and this is the most entertaining activity you can come up with?" Maria gave me a coy look from across the table, placed her lips around the wooden stir stick, and proceeded to suck on it. She had never been subtle.

I had picked this cafe to meet because it was quiet. Most of the people in the place were working on their computers, earbuds firmly secured. It wasn't in the center of town. This was important because I didn't want Sofia wandering in and getting the wrong idea, which, given how Maria was dressed, would be likely. With her legs crossed, her skirt had hiked up almost to her crotch, revealing a patch of red underwear. Her breasts were nearly falling out of her low-cut top. This wasn't unusual for Maria, and I couldn't deny she had a way of making me hot, but not now. I'd come here for only one reason.

"So, how've you been?" I asked.

With a head flick, she tossed her hair over her shoulder and broke into a seductive smile. "Fine. I keep myself busy." I knew exactly what she was doing, but I didn't bite. "Busy" meant she was fucking other guys. I couldn't give a shit, but she liked to bait me.

"And you? What have you been up to, Mr. World Traveler?"

"Working, as always."

"God, you work too hard. But you're in Barcelona now, and it's time to let loose a little. How long are you staying?"

"A few weeks? I'm not sure yet," I said, deliberately vague. I had been gearing up to have this conversation for a while. Ghosting her wasn't an option because if we ran into each other by accident, it could get ugly. And since Sofia was here, I knew it had to be done today.

"And you didn't think to text me? Tell me you were coming? I remember when you used to be so excited to see me, but now, I don't hear from you until you arrive?"

Maria had chosen to believe I was into her. I wasn't. I was never that excited to see her. We'd had some fun times, sure, but to me, it was a casual thing. Had I given her a different impression? Or was she just yanking my chain for the hell of it? I realized this was going to be more difficult than I'd anticipated. I took a sip of my coffee and decided to rip the band aid off.

"Maria, I'm not here to hang out with you on this trip. I wanted to do you the courtesy of letting you know in person." It was partly true. Mostly, I couldn't take the risk of running into her with Sofia by my side. Better to have the explosion now, and the way her brown eyes were flashing, I expected the bomb was about to detonate.

"Oh, really?" She leaned back in her chair and folded her arms across her chest. "Now you have something more important to do here?"

"It isn't personal, Maria. We've had our fun, and it's time for me to move on."

Her laugh was so sudden and loud, it caused a group of young people working on their computers two tables away to whip their gaze in our direction. I figured if I stayed calm, she'd settle down. The laughter subsided, but she was still putting on a show.

"Oh, Ryan, do you think I'm devastated by this news?" She ramped up the drama by placing a hand over her heart, her lips pouting. "That I'm in love with you? Oh yes, my heart is broken."

"No…"

"Do you think you're the only guy I'm fucking? You're not even good at it."

I flashed on that saying about a woman scorned. There was no use trying to talk her down and no point disputing her statement, though she'd always said the sex with me was great. Nothing mattered except ending this now and getting the hell out of here before she made more of a scene. So, I humored her.

"I might not have been good at it, but you were. In fact, you probably have men lined up waiting to date you. I know I'm no big deal to you, but I just wanted us to part as friends."

She eyed me cautiously, but her shoulders dropped a few inches. "It's your loss." It was a relief to see her stand. She straightened her skirt, then stepped close so she could straddle my leg. "And let me be clear, we are not friends." If I had anticipated what she was planning to do next, my reflexes would have kicked in faster.

She held up a water bottle, then tipped it and emptied its entire contents all over my lap.

"Classy, Maria. Real classy."

As she stormed out, the group at the other table exploded into fits of laughter. One guy yelled, "Oh, man, what the hell did you do to deserve that?" I threw my palms in the air and shook my head.

A girl, probably college age, chimed in. "You broke up with her, right?"

The third guy interjected, "It doesn't matter what he did. I saw how she was acting. Anyone could tell she was a bitch."

While the debate broke out, I was busy plucking napkins from the dispenser, trying to sop up the water, the flimsy tissue disintegrating into pieces. A female server noticed my efforts, and taking pity on me, she brought me a towel. I thanked her and made a mental note to leave a tip with the bill.

The girl shot back, "That's no way to talk about a lady. The word 'bitch' is so misogynistic."

Guy three argued, "Oh, and you don't call a dude a prick? Besides, she was no lady."

This was getting out of hand. I stood up, still drenched and looking like I'd pissed my pants. I exchanged a glance with the first guy who started all this. We both shrugged in the way people do when they're saying, what are ya gonna do? then headed to the cash register.

As I made my way back to the apartment by metro, I noticed the furtive looks thrown in the direction of my crotch. The wet patch was more obvious under the bright lights. At the next stop, I grabbed an empty seat and threw my jacket over my lap, becoming lost in my thoughts as the car rolled along the tracks. When I'd met Maria in Barcelona, she had been fun and more than willing to hook up whenever I got into town. She wasn't interested in having a relationship, and I had made it clear I wasn't either. But the thing I'd come to realize was younger girls played games. Maria was immature, and yes, maybe a bitch today, but I had chalked it up to her age. I couldn't imagine Sofia ever acting like that, no matter what.

Sofia wasn't the first older woman I had dated, though I had no intention of discussing my past with her. A few years ago, there had been Claire. She was the one who had shown me how satisfying a relationship could be with a woman who had some maturity—some life experience under her belt. We could sit for hours just talking; real conversations about music, politics, philosophy, travel. And when we fucked, she not only knew what she was doing, she was clear about the things she liked and freely expressed it. It was cool not having to guess or wonder what a woman was thinking.

It wasn't heartbreaking when it ended, but I did miss her. She didn't go all drama queen. Neither of us had any illusions it would last, but we had appreciated our time together.

I hoped Sofia and I could have a similar kind of thing now. Uncomplicated yet meaningful. But if I was honest with myself, my attraction for Sofia was intense—more intense than with Claire or anyone else. I would need to be careful and keep to our agreement, for both our sakes.

Chapter Twelve

At ten-thirty in the morning, Barcelona was just waking up when I tore down the stairs, giddy with vacation excitement. The store owners were opening their doors, the streets not yet clogged with shoppers. Chalked signs on the street read "Cafe con croissant 1,95." Even with the euro to dollar exchange rate, this was a bargain compared to Starbucks.

After stopping at the tourist center to collect some maps and brochures, I settled in a tiny cafe and sipped the most delicious cappuccino while poring over the materials, determined to venture out on my own. Ryan had already texted this morning, confirming our date tonight and apologizing he couldn't join me, as he needed to work. Though I didn't tell him, I was relieved to have the day to myself—time to recover from the stimulation of his company yesterday.

A young blond server dressed in jeans, a T-shirt, and sneakers met my eyes as she passed by with a tray loaded with coffee and pastries.

"Everything okay? Do you want anything else?"

My head whipped around at the sound of English. Did I look American? I glanced down at the brochures. They must have been a dead giveaway.

"Everything is perfect, thank you. I'm just trying to figure out where I should visit. It's my first time here." Though Ryan had given me recommendations, today it all seemed like a blur of information.

Her smile was a sweet, welcome sight. "Give me a moment, I'll tell you."

After she'd taken the order to a couple in the back, she returned to my side, bending over the table and pointing a blue fingernail at the colorful map. "Of course, you must visit the places of Gaudi, if you like interesting architecture. He was the genius of the modernist style."

Searching through my stack, she located the brochures of Sagrada Familia, Park Güell, and Casa Batlló, and fanned them out on the table in front of me. I scanned the images of multi-colored tiles, fanciful sculptures, decadent facades, and spires that seemed to reach the sky. Since Ryan had already convinced me about Sagrada, I couldn't miss seeing the rest of his work.

Then she pointed to the area on the map near the cafe. "In the old city, there are many places to see, but you must walk to discover them. The Cathedral of Barcelona is here." Her nail tapped on the image. "It's very close."

"Thank you so much for the information. May I ask where you are from?" With her pale skin and sun-bleached blond hair, it was a safe bet she wasn't from Spain.

"I'm from Russia. I came here about five years ago."

Something Ryan said yesterday reverberated in my mind. "So, you live here as an expat?"

"Of course. There are many expats here from all over the world. You will see, Barcelona is very special."

Before I could ask her more, a customer walked through the doorway, and she turned to him, speaking in fluent Spanish. I marveled at the way she'd picked up the language. Despite several semesters of classes in high school and college, I had forgotten all but the most basic words. Granted, college seemed like a million years ago.

I could have sat in the cafe all morning, watching the people pass by or listening to snippets of conversation while enjoying several cups of coffee. My server didn't seem to mind that I was taking up space, but I couldn't wait to explore, so, after flagging her down to pay the bill, I took her advice and set out, walking through my new hood.

Much like yesterday, the magic of the city seduced me within minutes, discovering delights around every corner. I made a mental note of my favorite spots, although I didn't have a clue how I'd find them again. I walked for countless hours through the Gothic Quarter, still not able to identify which direction I was heading. Even the blisters on my toe and the sunburn blushing on my shoulders didn't deter me.

After winding my way through a maze of alleyways, by some miracle, I found myself in front of the iconic Barcelona Cathedral. My eyes scanned its intricate facade—the stained-glass windows, towers and spires, and hauntingly configured gargoyles. But the action in the square below the steep steps captured my attention. At least three different musicians were stationed around the plaza, and flocks of tourists traversed in every direction. Just when it seemed the scene couldn't get more chaotic, a troupe of acrobats appeared in the center, hurling themselves into the air as onlookers cheered in amazement.

When I followed the path, I discovered medieval ruins around the corner of the cathedral. Roman walls and towers stood crumbling but preserved. It wasn't on a grand scale like the Coliseum in Rome, yet there it was, in the middle of the bustling city—a snapshot of history that had survived through the ages. The ancient stone walls formed a circle, and even the tall trees which were rooted there, their heavy limbs bearing enormous, dark-green foliage, seemed to have thrived for centuries. This spot, I noted, was also a popular place for group selfies, the ruins serving as a backdrop. As for me, selfies weren't my thing (given they made my nose appear absurdly huge), but I took a few shots of the scenery to send to Madison.

Satisfied with my progress and dying for another glass of sangria, I finally spotted a free table in a hidden, tree-laden plaza. Paella was the specialty at this restaurant, although I suspected all restaurants here staked the same claim to fame. I knew I was taking a chance, but I had no idea they would serve my lunch on a plate the size of a car tire.

"This is an order for one?" I asked the server when he delivered the wheel.

He looked at me, perplexed. "Of course," was his only response before he sped back to the kitchen.

The amount of rice alone could have fed a family of four. Still, I wolfed down almost half, devouring the shellfish and efficiently ignoring the eyes staring at me from the heads of five gigantic shrimp. Only a few days ago, I had been drowning my troubles with wine and junk food. I couldn't have imagined I'd feel happy again just sitting on a terrace—dining on paella in the middle of the afternoon. Before I could sink into worrying about 'what's next,' I forced myself to stay in the moment. *Life is short and shit happens, so why not grab every ounce of happiness that comes my way? I reasoned.*

After I stuffed the final bite into my mouth and drained the sangria from the glass, I understood the rationale for the siesta. The warm, thick air left me sticking to my clothes and my eyelids battled to close. I considered it a miracle when I found my apartment, wearily climbing the stairs with visions of a long nap before I had to get ready for... my date? No. My next stop on the tour.

Chapter Thirteen

"Wow. You look... stunning." Ryan's gaze raked over me when I stepped through the large wooden door and into the dimly lit street. Sleep had worked miracles, erasing the dark circles under my eyes. I had leapt out of bed before my alarm sounded, showered, and changed into a flowery spaghetti strapped sundress that nipped in at the waist. My hair was swept up in a loose bun, and I'd thrown a white chiffon shawl around my shoulders.

I returned his stare. "You clean up pretty well yourself." How did this man make a dark pair of jeans and a crisply ironed shirt look so good? I was certain it had something to do with his impossibly long legs and the way his shirt was tailored to reveal the cut definition of his arms. I tried not to gawk, but he caught my eyes roaming his body.

"What?" he asked, but I knew that he knew.

A particularly strong hot flash burned my flesh, as if molten lava was about to explode from the top of my head. Dammit. They came with a vengeance when I was nervous. He probably thought I was blushing, because what would he know about hot flashes?

"Nothing," I answered, fanning my face as if it would stop the inferno. "It's just a warm evening, don't you think?"

To my relief, he didn't have a clue. "Summers in Barcelona are definitely steamy. Ready to see more of the city at night?"

He proffered his elbow, which I gratefully looped my arm into, steadying me as I attempted to walk on the uneven pavement in my too-high strappy sandals. Just as I was about to ask where we were going, I recognized the familiar sculpture and fountains of Plaza Catalunya.

"You see that tall building on the other side of the square?"

I looked past the fountains, noticing the plaza was less hectic at night. Not one pigeon was in sight. I assumed they were asleep, tucked away somewhere, resting up for another day of diving at unsuspecting tourists. "I think I can make it that far. These shoes are totally wrong for Barcelona's streets."

"Cute sandals," he said, glancing at my feet, "but I don't see how women walk in high heels here. Flats are the way to go."

"Clearly. But then you'd tower over me like a giant." My neck craned to look up at him. "I know I'm short, but next to you, I appear particularly height challenged."

Now it was his turn to stare. "Alright, let's give it a different name. You're petite." He shrugged, as if mulling over the word. "Petite and feminine—I happen to appreciate those qualities." He held open the door of the hotel, motioning me inside.

I desperately hoped I could avert another hot flash. "Thanks," was all the answer I could muster, but I felt myself beaming the entire ride in the elevator.

"Stunning. Absolutely stunning." My pointed heels ticked across the tile as we walked to the edge of the tenth-floor terrace. The expansive view revealed the city below, aglow in golden lights against the dark sky from the sea to the mountains.

"I thought you'd like this place." When I swiveled toward him, he wasn't looking at the view but quietly staring at me, his face glowing under the string of amber globes.

Our eyes locked. It wasn't just his proximity making me nervous; I could smell the subtle tones of his cologne. The potent look he gave me, the blue of his irises expanding with the intensity of his gaze—seducing me with his pheromones.

"Um... do you think we can get a drink? I'm so thirsty."

"Cava?" The way he smiled with calm assuredness was almost as unnerving.

I nodded, and we headed toward the bar, passing the high-top tables illuminated with candles and the pots of brightly colored flowers strategically decorating the entire terrace. Above the low thrum of city traffic, the rhythmic sound of house music floated through speakers, courtesy of a long-haired DJ whose head bobbed to the steady beat.

"Do you like this music?" Ryan asked as we took our place in line at the bar.

I wrinkled my nose. "Not especially. You can't dance to this."

"Wanna bet?" His right arm wrapped around my waist, pulling me close and pressing his hand at the small of my back. A lightning bolt shot through me at the feel of his touch, our bodies gently swaying to the hypnotic rhythm.

So, I did what any nervous teenager would do. I made fun of him. "Well, if you consider this dancing, I commend you on your two-step moves."

The devious way he lifted one brow was the only warning I had before he raised my arm and twirled me in a spin. Unfortunately, at that moment, with impeccable timing, the couple next to us hurled together in an embrace and the man's foot stepped backward, his heel landing squarely on my toes. I let out a scream, which sent the man hopping several inches off the ground like a startled rabbit. To onlookers, it must have seemed like we were players in a comedy skit. I would have laughed, if not for my throbbing toes.

"I'm so sorry. Did I hurt you?" His forehead wrinkled in concern and the lines around his eyes gave me reason to think he was about my age.

"No worries, all fine here." My grimace didn't quite convince him.

"Let me buy you a drink." The tall, delicate woman who'd body slammed him a moment ago, now rested her arm over his shoulder and nodded with a look of sympathy. It was then I noticed his French accent.

Ryan caught my eye. I shrugged. "That isn't necessary."

"It's the least I can do. I'm Jean-Claude and this is my wife, Sandrine."

Ryan extended a hand, and I offered our names. I couldn't help noticing the pride in the man's eyes when he looked at her, and the way she slipped her palm to his, their fingers interlocking as if it was inconceivable not to be linked together.

We relented to the insistence of the couple, so, carrying our champagne glasses, the four of us drifted to an open table, Jean-Claude apologizing for the tenth time. I'm not sure what made me ask, but I hadn't seen many couples so in love. "How long have you two been married?"

They smiled giddily at each other, and Sandrine answered, "It is our ten-year anniversary today, so we're on holiday in Barcelona."

My mouth dropped open. I would have guessed they were newlyweds. "How lovely."

Ryan raised his glass. "Congratulations. Happy anniversary."

"And what about you two?" Sandrine was beaming. For a second, my gaze slid to Ryan, whose lips parted slightly as if he was about to answer. I jumped in first.

"Oh, no… it's not like that." I shook my head emphatically. "We are… just friends." I could feel Ryan's stare on my cheek but couldn't bring myself to face him.

Sandrine's scrutinizing eye shifted from me to Ryan. "Maybe you don't know what you are just yet, but there is more than friendship here. It's plain to see on your faces." She turned to Jean-Claude. "Don't you think they make a lovely couple?"

Jean-Claude nodded obediently. "My wife likes to view herself as a matchmaker or love guru. I'm not sure what term you'd use in English, but she's very intuitive about these things."

They exchanged a knowing smile. "My husband is my best friend, and I am his. Friendship is a good foundation for a relationship, don't you agree?"

Ryan didn't miss a beat. "Totally, yes."

I wanted to drop through a trapdoor and disappear. But when I finally peeked up at Ryan, he was smiling. Sandrine had him drafted into relationship status, yet his face held no trace of embarrassment. In fact, he began telling them the story of how we met and our incredibly timed flight to Barcelona.

Another bottle of cava arrived at our table, and while the three of them comfortably chatted, I excused myself to the bathroom. The wine was muddling my brain, leaving space for emotions to surface. Why did I care what they thought?

While I was putting on a fresh coat of lipstick, Sandrine appeared from a stall and joined me at the sink. As she washed her hands, her eyes slid to mine in our reflection.

"I can see how much he likes you, and I think you like him, too. So?"

I handed her a paper towel, stalling for a few seconds before answering. "You're not wrong. But there's more than a few years difference between us." My gaze dropped to the sink. Why did she make me so nervous?

Unphased, she continued. "What has age got to do with anything?"

I scoffed louder than I'd intended, but she lifted my chin with one finger, her eyes radiating a look of serenity as she connected with mine. "Darling, don't dismiss this thing your heart is telling you. Love can conquer many obstacles."

"No, you don't understand. It's not love. Lust, maybe. And believe me, love crumbles under the weight of obstacles."

Her eyes narrowed, studying me as if she could read my innermost secrets. "Listen to me when I tell you, losing love doesn't have to destroy the heart. The heart is resilient. You can love again if you are willing to enjoy the good moments and accept that not everything is meant to last a lifetime. It's life, yes?"

She squeezed my hand. One touch and my eyes began to brim. I brushed my cheeks with my palms and shrugged, stemming the rising tide of emotion. Then she linked my arm in hers and said with a wink, "We'd better get back. Who knows what the men are up to."

"I never would have imagined how much I would love it here," I admitted, as we strolled through the uncluttered center of Plaza Catalunya.

"I know exactly what you mean. It's easy to fall in love with this city." He laced his fingers in mine, holding my hand while we walked, reminding me of Jean-Claude and Sandrine.

I thought to myself, *It would be easy to fall in love with him.* But the definition of insanity was doing the same thing over and over again while expecting different results. Sandrine may have had a point, but my heart had enough cracks and scars for one lifetime.

When we reached the entrance to my apartment, Ryan faced me and held my shoulders in his hands. I looked up into those deep-blue liquid pools and spoke before he could lean in.

"Thank you for a wonderful evening. Everything was perfect." I lifted my sore foot off the ground, easing the pressure. "Well, almost everything."

A gentle smile crept across his lips. Incredibly delicious lips, tempting my resolve. "It was my pleasure." He shrugged, with a hopeful, puppy-dog look on his face. "I could give you a foot massage, if it might help."

I rolled my eyes. "Feet are definitely a slippery slope."

"Alright then," he conceded. "I'm headed to the London office tomorrow, just for two days. Have fun, but be careful. I'll see you when I get back." He released my shoulders and planted a kiss on each cheek. "Ciao."

The absence of his touch sent an unexpected ache rippling through me, then panic bubbled up. Would he return? Was I pushing him away?

Thoughts of Ryan chased each other in circles as I lay in bed, tossing and turning, unable to sleep. I couldn't help wondering what it would be like if he were lying there next to me. I bolted upright, gave myself a stern NO, and padded into the kitchen to make a cup of tea. It occurred to me that it was morning in California. Maybe I could catch Madison before she went to work.

"Girl, it's about time you called." She answered my video call on the third ring, her stainless-steel refrigerator visible in the background. "I only have a few minutes before I have to jump in the car, so fill me in fast."

I pulled in a breath. "There's not much to tell yet, but Barcelona is truly an amazing city. Ryan has been showing me around and—"

"Yeah, yeah, what about Ryan?" Her eyebrows twitched as she tipped the coffee mug to her lips.

"Nothing juicy to report. But we are having fun. Oh, you'd be proud. We agreed on a deal for him to be my tour guide for the duration—no expectations, no mushy stuff—just fun. How's that for carpe diem?"

"Define fun," she said, using air quotes. "If you're not hittin' it with that dude, you haven't reached carpe diem."

"Jesus, give me a little time to warm up. I just got here."

"And think about all the orgasms you've already missed. He's still into you, right?"

I thought about the way his eyes gleamed when he looked at me, our bodies swaying together when we danced last night, the feel of his erection growing against me. "I don't have any doubts about that, but is there anything wrong with getting to know each other?"

"Fine." She gave me a defeated eye roll. "I have some news too." The smile on her face was infectious and I grinned back at her.

"Why do I sense your news is juicier than mine?"

"Not yet, but very soon. I met this guy online, go figure. Roger. Think, Taye Diggs."

"You struck gold, a unicorn among the profiles." One night, when we had nothing better to do, we had scrolled through our dating apps, swiping left on dozens of men. The photos made us laugh so hard, tears streamed down our faces. It was incredible how many guys took selfies in their bathroom, shirtless, no less. And most of them should have kept their shirts on. It had been entertaining yet crushingly disappointing.

"Who would've guessed I'd find a unicorn? And he's a nice guy, from what I can tell. It's still early. I'll keep you posted."

"Just make sure he's single!"

Madison glanced at her watch, suddenly frantic. "Damn. I'm gonna be late. I want details by email!"

I put my cup in the sink and thought about what she said. There was no doubt I was dying to climb Ryan like a tree. Fantasies had been popping up, and like a game of whack-a-mole, I'd been beating them down. But I wasn't sure how long I could keep that up, or if I wanted to. Still, if I crossed the line, he could easily become an addiction. And then what?

Suddenly, I wished I had some poster paper.

Chapter Fourteen

It didn't take me long to pack up on my final day in the Las Ramblas apartment, given there were no closets. My clothes had remained in my suitcase, now tangled in a heap. I gave one last look around my flat to make sure I hadn't left anything behind. A can of cockroach spray sat on the counter. Technically, it was mine, since I'd picked it up in the market, but I hoped I wouldn't have further use for it. Cockroaches freaked me out, because if you saw one, there were hundreds of cousins hidden away somewhere. Yuck.

When I texted the manager for help with my luggage, he told me he was busy handling the check-in for another apartment. I suspected that while it might not be a lie, he probably would have done anything to avoid a second encounter with my bags.

So, I lugged my heavy suitcases down the stairs, cursing myself for never having learned to pack light, all the while knowing I still wouldn't heed this lesson. I located the taxi line around the corner without difficulty, and within ten minutes, I arrived at my new apartment in El Born.

I was ecstatic to find this cozy, two-bedroom flat had been remodeled with modern furnishings and conveniences.

Thankfully, it came with an elevator, and after opening several cupboards, I deemed it cockroach free. These were little victories, but it meant things were looking up. My new home.

The location couldn't have been better; a much nicer section of town. Though directly above the pulsing center of activity, the double pane windows on the balcony doors blocked out the noise from the pedestrian street two floors below.

After unpacking and hanging my things in the wardrobe, I stepped out into the midday sun to investigate my new hood. Charm oozed from every tiny alley, a striking contrast to the Gotico only a few streets away. Though the buildings here were also fashioned out of huge rectangular stone in Gothic style, these held trendy, upscale shops. Stealing glances through the open doorways of bars and restaurants, I made a mental note of the ones that bore a chic interior decor. I loved the romantic ambiance of those tucked inside brick caves like hidden treasures. Others had an airy feel—cavernous establishments with high, vaulted ceilings and lamps dangling from above.

I wanted to share my new finds with Ryan and invite him out for dinner, but it would have to wait until he returned. It was hard to get him out of my mind, our conversations played over and over in my head. As I meandered through El Born, I told myself to stop obsessing—to stay in the moment and let the unique sights and sounds distract me.

Though I wandered for hours, I had become secure in the knowledge I would indeed get lost. But this was my new normal—the joy of discovery my new high. After resting my weary feet in a terrace cafe, sipping a perfect cup of cafe con leche (from a real cup and saucer—not a paper to-go cup) I turned on my GPS and felt a little proud I'd survived another day of exploration. Without a doubt, I could find my way back to my apartment. Alone and directionally challenged; still, my confidence had blossomed.

My spirits ran high all afternoon, anticipating the arrival of my son and his girlfriend. Ben had been less than enthusiastic when I offered to share my apartment. "No offense, Mom, but this is supposed to be a romantic holiday for Callie and me."

I didn't say as much, but it was hard to make peace with the fact he was all grown up now with a life of his own. Gone were the days when it was only the two of us, when he was content to vacation with his mom. It occurred to me it might be easier to accept his metamorphosis gracefully if I had a life of my own, one which included romantic holidays. There hadn't been any romantic holidays since the first few years of my marriage, and that seemed like a million years ago.

Ben called me at four o'clock to say they'd arrived. "I'm running out the door to get some groceries, but we're so excited to see you. Please come for dinner. I'll be cooking."

The sound of his voice made me smile into the phone. "I can't wait, sweetie. Should I bring anything?"

"A bottle of wine would be good. I'll text you the address. I think we're close to where you're staying."

At eight-thirty, I tucked said bottle of wine and a fresh loaf of bread in my newly purchased Barcelona tote bag and headed out to find their flat. It turned out, their apartment was only a few streets from mine in El Born. Although it didn't stop me from getting lost, winding through the alleyways several times before climbing the narrow stairs of the third-floor walk-up. Ben greeted me at the top of the landing with an embrace that warmed my heart.

"No elevator here?" I puffed out, my lungs protesting.

"Nope, unfortunately. But hey, it beats the gym."

"Let me look at you." I held him by the shoulders. "Oh my God, that beard! It's so long now." I grabbed a tuft of the wiry hair and gave it a tug. "I'm still getting used to the whole mustache/beard thing." Though he'd inherited his dad's hard-set jaw and my nose and eyes, he had his own unique style; a trendy gentleman's haircut, skinny jeans, and leather jacket—even when the weather was balmy. A mom's pride aside, he was damn good looking. He topped out at almost six feet, the same as his dad. In the last few years, his body had matured, gaining a set of broad shoulders and a muscular torso.

"It's not the first time I've heard that. Callie's been after me to get a trim. She's over there." He gestured inside, and I peeked in at the miniscule kitchen, barely room for two people.

I squeezed past him and spotted Callie washing dishes in the kitchen. Her face lit up the second she saw me. "Sofia!" Callie dried her hands on a towel and threw her arms around me. "We're so excited to see you here." I hugged her back, immensely grateful we'd become close. She was like the daughter I never had; a sweetheart, who was devoted to Ben. Her fashion style complimented Ben's, yet she was authentically herself—bold, beautiful and, most of all, kind.

Backing up a foot, she studied me for a moment. "You look amazing. Did you change your hairstyle?"

My brows pinched together, my answer more like a question. "No...?"

"I can't put my finger on it, but there's something different about you."

Ben brushed past us, carrying a plate of olives to the table. "Yeah, Mom, you look happy. Why? I mean, you just lost your job, right?"

"That's true," I confirmed. "But there's nothing like a vacation to make you forget your life has imploded." The last thing I wanted to do was burden them with my troubles, so I changed topics. "How do you like your apartment?"

"It's not luxurious by any standards, but we got it for free through a friend, so we're not complaining," Callie said. "We only have basic cookware, which sucks for Ben."

Ben whirled around the kitchen, searching through drawers and cabinets. "Not a problem. I can be resourceful when I have to." He pressed a clove of garlic with a dull knife and began mincing, while Callie found mismatched wine glasses in the cupboard. We jostled for space as she passed me the bottle opener, and after several yanks, the cork popped free.

Ben stopped chopping long enough to shoot me a sideways glance. "I could have done that for you, Mom."

"I have opened a few bottles of wine on my own since you've been gone," I teased, throwing an arm around his shoulder. An unexpected wave of nostalgia tugged at my heart, and the back of my eyes prickled. "I've missed you so much."

When he met my gaze, his eyes were soft. His sensitivity, I thought, was one of the many things I'd always loved about my boy. "I've missed you too," he said, dropping the knife on the counter to wrap me in a sideways hug. Out of the corner of my vision, I saw Callie smile and extend her hand, offering me a glass.

I swiped at my cheeks and gratefully grabbed hold of it, passing the next one to Ben. "I think we need a toast. Here's to your first European adventure." The sound of our glasses clinking shifted the mood, and Ben shooed us out of the cramped space. Callie and I obliged, settling on the chairs at the wooden table where we could watch him work.

"So, what have you been up to so far while you've been here?" he asked.

I was sure he expected the question to be answered with a simple accounting of my travelog, but since there had been nothing simple about my trip, it was hard to gauge how much to tell him. While he delivered the small plates of tapas to the table, I filled them in on the unlikely coincidences, careful to tread lightly. Ben had cast me in the immaculate conception version of Mom—and according to his psyche, that didn't include dating or, God forbid, sex.

Callie wasn't shy though. "I can't believe you actually ran into him on the flight to Barcelona. How random is that?" My son was noticeably silent. She added, "Do you have a photo of him? Better yet, his Insta account?"

I scrolled through my cell and found the selfies we had taken on the first day. "We're not friends on Instagram, but here are a few pics." I passed the phone to Callie.

Ben shot me a look. "What happened to what's-his-face... Ron?"

"Yeah... that didn't work out." I let my explanation hang in the air, ignoring the way he tapped his fingers on the table, waiting for more. It wasn't my job to explain my love life—or lack thereof.

"Dang, he's cute. You scored," Callie said, then passed the phone to Ben.

I instantly regretted putting Ryan on display when I saw my son's expression become a scowl. He resembled his dad when he didn't like something; his brows pinched together and his eyes narrowed. "How old is this dude?" he blurted out.

I bristled. "Old enough."

Callie, my ally now, broke in. "Ben, stop. Your mom is a grown-ass woman. Quit being such a baby. She's entitled to do what she wants."

"Mom, I'm just worried about you," he said, softer now. "You've been through enough crap with men, and well... he looks too young for you." He looked at Callie, expecting validation, I supposed, but she glared at him. She also must have kicked him under the table because he yelped, then his hand reached for his shin.

"What?" he said to her. "I just don't want her to get hurt again. You know how these young dudes are."

Oh, the irony. But then who better to advise me on how young dudes behaved than another "young dude?"

Just then, Callie tipped her nose up and sniffed. "Ben, is something burning?"

"Fuck." He bolted for the stove and plucked the pot off the burner. "I think the soup is a gonner."

Callie followed him, hugging him from behind, her voice gentle as she reassured him. "Aww, babe, I'm sorry. It's fine though. We have enough food."

I loved how they could disagree yet always be in each other's corner. They had figured this out all on their own, and I visualized them growing old together, unlike me—divorced, single, and probably growing old alone.

Ben served the rest of the meal, I poured us more wine, and we talked about their trip. On their itinerary were all the places I'd traveled at their age, plus a few more. They told me how the countryside in Belgium popped with the brightest greens, purple flowers in bloom everywhere. I contrasted it with the Black Forest in Germany, which wasn't on their list, reminiscing about the humongous pints of beer the servers delivered at the Hofbrauhaus in Munich. I didn't mention how my friends and I got so drunk, we finished the evening holding each other's hair while the other vomited.

I liked how he viewed me as a cool mom. I had ventured out of the States—had sought the adventures they were now experiencing. My impulsive trip to Barcelona was becoming a kaleidoscope of changes, layered with experiences I hadn't predicted.

I think we were all relieved to drop the topic of Ryan, but when we'd finished dessert—a delicious, homemade flan—I wanted to show Ben I wasn't ignoring his feelings. "Honey, I appreciate your concern, but I'm okay. I know what I'm doing. Can you just be happy your old mom gets to have a little fun?" I reached across the table and squeezed his hand. He gave it a squeeze back. That was enough for me.

"So, when do you meet up with him again?" he asked.

"Ryan is in London right now, but he emailed me with plans to get together as soon as he returns in a couple days. He's meeting me at the apartment when his plane lands. So, we'll see."

"You're glowing, Sofia. When you talk about him, you light up," Callie said.

I shifted uncomfortably in my chair. "I just appreciate having someone to show me the sights. He seems happy to do it, and he's a nice guy. That's all."

Before the evening ended, we made plans to take a tour of Gaudi's Sagrada Familia Cathedral and have dinner together.

"Your eyes are glazing over, sleepyhead," I said, tousling Ben's hair. "It's time for me to leave."

"Jet lag, I suppose, and jumping from country to country. I'm fading."

When Callie nodded in agreement, I scoffed. "You guys are far too young to be worn out."

"And you're far too young to be dragged down by us. Go party, but be safe," he said.

After hugging Callie at the door, Ben and I trudged down the stairs, then he walked me to the corner. "Just follow this street until it curves. Turn left, and you'll see the main avenue." Fortunately, he'd inherited his father's internal compass. "We'll see you tomorrow," he confirmed, planting a kiss on my cheek.

I ran a hand down the side of his jaw, and for a split-second, I saw an image of his sweet, boyish face. It swept me back in time, when that three-year-old boy considered me the center of his universe. "Get some rest, son." I folded him in my arms, then... reluctantly let him go.

As I walked through the alleyway, I saw myself at Ben's age, random memories bubbling up from the archives in my brain. A time when the future held unlimited possibilities. I had been bold then, fearless even. How had I become this person? Did it happen over time, or was there a moment when I decided to hang a 'closed for business' sign on my heart? Was there a year when I gave up on my dreams, or were they slowly eroded over time? *There has to be more to my life. This can't be how it ends*, I thought.

I stopped in the middle of the alleyway and stared at the scene surrounding me. The terrace umbrellas gleamed with strings of twinkling lights, restaurant tables lining the long cobblestone street ahead. Latin music drifted from the open doors of bars that were only now filling with partiers at midnight. Girls in short skirts and high heels stepped precariously over uneven streets, giggling as they made their way to the clubs. Couples walked arm in arm, occasionally embracing, their backs against the stone facades, stealing kisses in the dark.

Once... long ago, I resembled those young lovers, oblivious to the inevitable heartbreak. Although those memories were cloudy and had distorted over time, I could hear my younger self crying out—telling me not to forget the pieces of me I'd left behind.

I swiped my palms across my damp cheeks and continued toward my apartment, then I felt a smile creeping across my lips. A shift had already begun. Like a Rubik's Cube, the pieces were moving—rearranging into a new design. The pulse of the city stirred something in me, churning things in every direction the way a wave scatters the sand in an underwater cloud. Vague recollections of the dreams I once had drifted to the surface.

Was it worth the risk? Since I didn't have poster paper handy, the pros and cons ricocheted like a ping-pong tournament in my mind. It was as if there were two cartoon characters perched on my shoulders, each shouting their opposing opinions. The loudest one said, *You've been through enough hurt. Keep your guard up.* Then I heard Sandrine's words; *Don't dismiss this thing your heart is telling you. Love can conquer many obstacles.*

I covered my ears with the palms of my hands, trying to drown out the voices. Instead, I listened with my heart. Only then did I know what to do.

Chapter Fifteen

"How was London?" I asked as soon as Ryan stepped through my doorway.

On the surface, it was a straightforward question, but any woman would know there were layers hidden beneath. As in, *Were you meeting up with some other girl in London? Are you the kind of dude my son was worried about? A player? Are you still good with our arrangement? And finally, Why are you interested in... me?*

I had spent the last few days thoroughly enjoying every-thing Barcelona had to offer. I'd seen all the sites on my list, tasted amazing food, and shared precious moments with my son. But I'd also had an epiphany of sorts. If I was going to crack open the door to possibilities, I had to be certain it was safe.

"London was cold." He quickly scanned my apartment and commented, "This is a great place. Good find." Then he pulled me into a hug so tight it squeezed my ribs—an intimate and warm embrace, as if he'd come home to me waiting for him a thousand times. "It was raining, but I was stuck in meetings anyway."

After releasing me, he rocked back on his heels and his eyes raked over me, gliding from my head to my feet. "To be honest, it's good to be back. I... missed—" His unfinished sentence hung in the air. I saw the rise of his chest when he inhaled, then cleared his throat before speaking as though recalibrating his words. "You look amazing."

I beamed a smile. Noticing the way his gaze drank me in, I was glad I'd dressed to impress. Prepared for an evening out, I was wearing a short black summer dress with a daring, slanted neckline which highlighted my breasts. Okay, yes, I wanted to look seductive—I wanted to see that look on his face.

"I need to change before we head out. My clothes have been sticking to my skin all afternoon." Ryan pulled off his jacket, placing it over a chair. "The flight was delayed, so I thought I would come here instead of going to my apartment. I'm desperate for a shower, do you mind?"

"Be my guest. It's down the hall." I waved a hand, gesturing in the direction. "There are clean towels in the cupboard."

This wasn't awkward at all, I told myself as I cleaned up the kitchen, still able to hear the water pouring from the shower through the crack of the open door.

I tried not to think about him stripping off his clothes, his body sleek and wet and glistening. By the time he emerged from the bathroom, I had scrubbed the dishes in the sink squeaky clean several times. He appeared in the kitchen, droplets falling from his dark curls, a fresh tailored shirt clinging to his muscular frame where his skin remained damp.

"There. Better?" He spread his arms out wide, and I took advantage of the opportunity to inspect further. Indigo jeans hugged his narrow hips, brown leather loafers, and matching belt. The combination, along with the dress shirt, created a casual-chic effect, as if he'd put some effort into dressing for the night out. He looked so damn hot.

"Yep. Better. You clean up nicely." He smelled good, too. A mixture of body wash and something else, like a spice with tones of oak. It could have been his deodorant, but I knew if I used the identical fragrance, it wouldn't smell the same. Whatever it was, the way it mixed with his natural scent was intoxicating.

"Let's head for the center of El Born, if you're ready," he said.

I slung my handbag over my shoulder and took a deep breath. "Ready."

His hands gripped my waist, and an involuntary shiver ran through me. "Wait, you can't wear your purse like that in this town. Thieves can snatch it in an instant."

"Oh. Right. I forgot." His chest was so close. I wanted to press my face against it, to breathe in the scent of him.

He pulled it over my head, the strap across my body, then lifted strands of my hair and placed them neatly over my shoulders.

"There. You're good now." I caught his gaze traveling down the strap to where it nestled between my breasts. He cleared his throat before he spoke again. "Dinner first?"

I wondered what was second, but tonight, I told myself to stop worrying about what came next.

I sensed something different about the way we talked between bites; the mood breezy and light. We sat on a terrace, sharing a bottle of wine and plates of tapas. I had grown to love the pots of steaming mussels, the grilled squid, and especially the pan con tomate, which basically consisted of toasted baguettes rubbed with olive oil, garlic, tomato, and salt.

But more than anything, I loved his company, seeing his smile across the table, and the way his eyes lit up when he looked at me. I couldn't tell if there was something different about him or if it was me—somehow more relaxed and confident in his presence.

"I have an idea. Let's take a taxi to the clubs at the beachfront," he suggested after handing his credit card to the server.

"Am I dressed okay for a club?"

"You're perfect." Pushing away from his chair, he winked at me. "Maybe I'll let you see my dance moves."

I couldn't keep a straight face. "Oh, you mean you have more than a swaying two-step?"

He rolled his eyes, then took my hand as we walked to the taxi stand. "So little faith in me," he replied, his tongue pressing the inside of his cheek.

When we arrived in Port Olympic, the scene was in full swing. Girls in micro dresses and six-inch high heels lined up to enter the clubs. I was glad to have chosen a figure-flattering dress and a pair of mid-heel sandals that wouldn't send me tripping over the cobblestones. As much as I would've liked to appear as elegant as those twenty-somethings, a face plant on the ancient streets would not have been attractive.

As we waited to enter a club, I caught sight of the marquis above the entrance: Carpe Diem. Hand to God, I couldn't have scripted the night any better if I'd tried.

I was relieved to find a mixed age crowd in this line. Ryan took my hand and steadied my steps as we descended the stairs into the restaurant transformed into a sultry nightclub. The DJ's blend of hypnotic house music filled the room, and people swayed with the rhythm. Scantily clothed women performed atop the pedestals, which held ornate bronze statues. Their perfect bodies gyrated like Las Vegas showgirls, only slightly obscured by the billowing mist from a hidden fog machine.

"This is some scene!" I yelled into Ryan's ear over the sound of the music. "I've never seen anything like it."

Ryan nodded; his eyes transfixed on the dancers. I couldn't blame him. They were stunning. He met my gaze again and led me through the crowd to the bar. The dance floor blended into every bit of free space within the large room. From the tables to the hanging beds reserved for the VIPs, people danced freely with drinks in their hands. Apparently, a partner wasn't necessary, only a desire to get swept into the driving communal pulse.

I kept an eye on Ryan as he stood in line to order cocktails, but the music distracted me, feeding my urge to dance. While deep house didn't fit my style, this set had undertones of an African beat with a smooth, sensual rhythm. When he returned with two mojitos, I took one from his hand. "Let's see your moves." I hooked a finger through his belt loop, pulling him to me.

He laughed, a melodic and sexy sound that poured through me. I felt the rumble as our bodies moved together, his free arm wrapped around my waist. Our steps fell into sync, the delicate touch of his fingers tracing my spine, guiding my every move. I lay my cheek on his shoulder, lost in the scent of him, in a hypnotic trance as we swayed to the beat. My reserve crumbled as his grip tightened around me, bringing me flush against him. And then there was the warmth... Oh my God, the warmth of him. Sparks of heat rose from the places where our skin touched.

By the time the song ended, every inch of me pulsed with a driving drumbeat. I downed half my drink and handed him the glass. "Where's the restroom?" My voice trembled. No one had made me feel this way—ever.

"In the back, to the left." He gave a nod toward the entrance. "I'll wait for you there."

Halfway to the bathroom, I turned and glimpsed him nearly swallowed in the crowd. Horrified, I stopped and watched as a young woman pounced on him—her breasts falling out of a dress with a V neckline to her navel. She wrapped her arms around Ryan's neck, gyrating against his body, inviting him into more than a dance. I couldn't turn away; my eyes riveted on them. He struggled with the burden of her dead weight pressing against him—stumbling drunk—until, at last, he pried her hands away and stepped back, his face contorted with fury. Before he could spot me, and before I saw something I'd regret, I sped to the back of the restaurant and threw open the door to the restroom.

I filed in line behind other women, focusing my attention on the ornate mirrors and a sink the size of a bathtub where water poured from the mouths of brass lion heads. One look in the mirror and I saw the flush of my skin, my pupils dilating as the green of my irises fanned out. There was no use trying to calm down. Not with this electric current pulsing through my body.

Everything will be fine, I told myself as I came out of the stall. *He couldn't be interested in the bitch who'd moved in the moment I was gone.* But what if I wasn't here? I barely knew the man. Doubts infiltrated my brain like unwelcome guests as I washed my hands and stared at my reflection. What was I doing here? Glancing at the young, smooth faces of the other women in the mirror, I felt ridiculous. I should tell Ryan to forget the whole thing. Call off our arrangement. I took a deep breath before I stepped out into the wide entryway, my eyes searching for him.

Out of nowhere, hands grabbed at my hips from behind, stopping me in my tracks. My head whipped back, expecting to see Ryan. But it wasn't Ryan. A surge of panic ran up my spine. A young, dark-skinned man spun me, hooking his arm around my waist, binding me to him.

"Guapa! Do you speak Spanish? English?" His breath reeked of tequila, and he staggered on his feet, swaying against my body. "You are so sexy," he rasped.

I pushed both hands on his chest and tried to break free, but he held me tight in his grip. "Back off! Let go of me." He didn't seem to care I was shouting, my voice swallowed by the din of music. Maybe it was the noise or the drunken chaos in the club, but people were oblivious to my protests. I frantically searched my distant memory for the self-defense moves I'd learned in college. It must have been only seconds, but time blurred with the rush of adrenaline spiking through my body.

In the dim light, I saw Ryan's tall frame emerge at the man's side and tower over him. Relief flooded through me as his large hands gripped the guy's shoulders, digging into his shirt. If a look could kill, Ryan's fierce gaze would have knocked the guy out cold.

"Let go of the lady NOW and back the fuck off, or I will throw you across the room." Ryan's voice reverberated with a deep and ominous sound. His shoulders lifted against the tensing muscles in his neck.

My captor craned his head up and cringed when his gaze met Ryan's, his eyes flashing with rage. The man released me like he was recoiling from a blazing flame. "Hombre, relax. I didn't know she was with you."

His grip only tightened, shoving the man's back hard against a column of stone, and for a split second, I thought I saw his fingers slide toward the attacker's throat. I gasped. The guy went limp, fear sparking from his eyes.

"Alright man, chill," he choked out. "I'll leave, but you gotta let go of me."

Ryan's lips pressed together in a thin line, the muscles in his jaw twitching as he hesitated. I wanted to call out, to say something to make him stop, but my voice stuck in my throat. People peeled away from the dance floor to gawk at the scene. I heard voices shouting, and out of nowhere, two burly bouncers rushed in just as his fingers released their grip. It didn't take more than a second for the guy to slip away and disappear into the wave of dancers.

Abruptly, Ryan pivoted as though only now remembering my presence behind him. "Are you okay?" The veins in his neck still bulged, and instead of anger, I saw panic flash in his eyes.

Then, a bouncer the size of a truck was looming over us. "What just happened here?"

Ryan's gaze briefly shifted toward him. "That dude attacked my girlfriend."

"I'm fine, really. No harm done." I reached out a shaky hand, stroking the length of his arm. Instinctively, I softened. "Ryan, thank you, but I'm alright now."

His shoulders dropped a few inches, and he released a long breath.

"My colleague followed the other guy, but you two need to leave." The bouncer's tone was a little too threatening.

"Fine by me," Ryan replied. "C'mon. Let's get some air."

He secured his fingers through mine, and we passed through the dance floor to a crowded patio, squeezing around people, mostly twenty-somethings, dancing to music blaring through speakers. We dodged lit cigarettes and tipping cocktail glasses, and then I saw her again. She was standing right in our path, hands on her hips.

"So, this is the bitch you're with now?" She swayed on her impossibly high heels and the drink in her hand spilled in a thin stream onto the wooden deck. A laugh burst out of her. "I guess I was too hot for you. Look at her, is she your auntie?"

I wanted to drop through the floor—to disappear. But she had no idea what she was in for, because Ryan's blood was still boiling.

"Get the fuck out of my way, Maria." He pushed her aside with a swipe of his arm at her hip. "And don't ever come near me or speak to me again." Even over the music, his voice boomed. Once again, we became the center of everyone's attention. I heard drunk guys making obscene comments, the muttering of some girls who may have been her friends.

The huge bouncer was heading right for us, but Ryan swept me out of the terrace, and after a few stairs, we emerged at the edge of the walkway illuminated by lamps lining the promenade. Beyond, the wide beach stretched out to the sea; an oasis of calm compared to the utter chaos we'd left behind. Figures came into focus, only faintly visible in the distance. I could just make out groups sitting on the beach, a man playing his guitar, lovers entwined in an embrace.

"Let's go for a walk." Ryan turned and faced the water, then stepped onto the sand.

"Wait." I bent and slipped off my shoes, losing the grip he had on my hand. "Ryan, I have to ask..." I paused. There were so many questions running through my head, I didn't know where to begin. But he kept walking... silent.

Experience had taught me it was better to wait until someone calmed down before trying to have a conversation. So, I walked with him, the cool sand squishing between my toes. We had made it halfway across the wide expanse before he stopped, his gaze fixed on the distant, dark horizon.

"Sofia, I am so sorry about that."

I wondered which part he meant.

He ran a hand through his hair. "I never would have brought you to this club if I knew Maria was going."

"Who is Maria?"

His whole torso heaved with a breath. This couldn't be good. "She's a woman I've dated on and off here." He rushed to fill in the rest. "It was never anything serious, just someone to… hang out with. I told her it was done—over, full stop. I guess she's pretty pissed. She was drunk and said some awful things. I'm so sorry you had to hear her. It won't happen again."

For several moments, I was speechless; questions still swirling—until one popped to the surface. "When did you break it off with her?"

"A few days ago. Right after you arrived."

"Was it because of me? If that's the case—"

He interrupted me. "No. Well, partly. I mean, I was planning to tell her anyway. I really was done. She seemed fun at first, but as I'm sure you could tell, her crazy is a ten out of ten." He took a breath, studying me. "I didn't want anything to interfere with our time together, so I made certain she was out of the picture."

"Apparently, she's not taking it well."

"She dumped a bottle of water on my lap when I told her." A smile tipped the corner of his mouth.

My first reaction was to laugh. Then it struck me. He saw her in person? And finally, I questioned why I cared.

I turned away from him, walking toward the sea, an uncomfortable silence hanging in the air between us. "Okay, I get it. We both have a past, and it was unfortunate we had to run into yours tonight." After a few beats, I added, "I'm not mad. She's just a kid who's acting out. I can handle it." His shoulders dropped a few inches with relief. "But there's the other, um... incident." The way he slammed his palm against his forehead, I guessed he'd forgotten how we ended up on the patio. "You seemed enraged in the club, out of control. Will you tell me why?" I realized it sounded like a line a shrink would say, but I was sure there was more to this story.

We were walking again, the hard sand along the shoreline under our feet.

"When I was in high school... a girl I knew got caught up in a dangerous situation." He drew his hand through his hair, inhaling a long breath. His voice was soft as he chose his words carefully. "I witnessed a drug dealer pounding on her and arrived just in time to pull the guy off. But not soon enough to prevent the bruises and bloody nose."

Images of the scene flashed through my mind. "So, this man attacking me triggered the memory?"

"I haven't felt that kind of anger until tonight. Seeing you in danger... I couldn't bear it if something happened to you."

"Now I understand. While I appreciate your intervention, I was prepared to knee the guy in the balls." I lifted a tentative smile.

"So, you're telling me you can take care of yourself?"

"If it's just a drunk dude at a bar and not an angry drug dealer, then yes." I may not have been as entirely confident as I sounded, but I needed to change the trajectory of the evening. I wouldn't allow that asshole to spoil the mood. Ryan had to ask if I was okay twice more before I convinced him.

At the water's edge, the waves calmly lapped on the shore, the air still and balmy. With each step, our feet left behind prints, only to disappear when the water rose again.

"Feeling better?" I asked. He nodded. "Good. Because this place is too beautiful to waste. Did you see the full moon?" I pointed to the sky, the orb casting a shimmering beacon of light over the dark waters.

Ryan halted in his steps, then pivoted toward me, closing the distance between us. His body gently pressed against mine, sending shards of heat where he touched me. One hand glided along my cheekbone, and he threaded his fingers in my hair. I waited in anticipation, our faces inches apart, my feet sinking into dampness as the tide ebbed at the shore. *Just be in the moment*, I told myself. Every fiber—every nerve ending—vibrated with hunger for him, and this time, running from the inevitable was inconceivable.

With my shoes dangling at my fingers, our eyes locked in an unwavering gaze, the tension slipping away, dissolving like grains of sand carried out to the sea. My view became telescopic, blocking out the sound of random voices and the music playing in the distance. In the silence of our private bubble, he bent his head and brushed his lips across mine with a gentle caress, then laid his cheek against my face. I heard his breath in my ear before he tilted his chin, and finally, his mouth was on mine, hot and wet. And, oh God, the taste of him; sweet, with a hint of rum and sugar. My lips melted into his and parted as he deepened the kiss, caressing my tongue with his. A tingle stirred deep in my core, a potent desire rising out of the ashes, claiming my body.

When he broke away, his head cocked to one side and the emotion I saw in his eyes made my breath stop in my chest. "You have no idea how long I've been waiting to do that."

My fingers released the shoes, and as they dropped to the beach, I wrapped both arms around his neck. Standing on my toes, I brushed the tip of my nose along his jawline and invited him in again. I didn't know how long we stood there, our tongues dipping and caressing while the world swirled around us in the dark. I let the moment envelop me without thinking, singularly focused on the taste of him and the feel of his hard body pressing against mine.

When he released me, a silent voice inside protested.

"Maybe it's time to get you home," he said, tucking a strand of hair behind my ear.

I nodded, and we traced our steps back across the beach, my legs still trembling. Never had a kiss actually made my knees buckle.

When we reached the doorstep of my apartment, he held me in silence, both of us hesitant to break away. We exchanged expectant glances and another kiss I didn't want to end. My thoughts spun around and around, teetering on the precipice. I wasn't sure how to manage this unfamiliar territory—no free-falling allowed and no expectations. When

I made my decision to wait, I released my arms from around his waist.

"I'll see you tomorrow, right?"

"Of course. I have some surprises planned. Let's meet up first thing in the morning."

"Oh really? More surprises? What should I be wearing?"

"Bring a swimsuit, towel, sunscreen, and some sneakers. Better add in a light jacket in case it gets chilly. I'll take care of the rest." He gave me a wink, then headed down the street.

When I closed my apartment door, I exhaled a long breath I hadn't realized I was holding, then slid against the wood until my bottom hit the floor. My hands held the sides of my face while my thoughts began racing. Breathe. One, two, three, four. After a few calming breaths, I gathered myself up off the floor. The after-effects of being in the moment were brutal. I only hoped I could survive whatever tomorrow had in store, because I knew we had crossed a threshold. There was no going back. And the thing was, I felt more than ready to find out what came next.

Chapter Sixteen

Weaving through the alleyways of Born, I had to take two steps for every one of Ryan's just to keep up. "Are you ready to tell me where we're going?"

"Not yet." He side-eyed me, grinning in that mischievous way of his. "But I promise you'll have fun today."

"It better be worth getting up at eight o'clock," I grumbled, half joking.

"Do you need coffee? Because we can stop and grab—"

"No, it's fine. I had a cup in the apartment, but thanks. I should warn you, I'm not much of a morning person."

"Really?" His lips curved into a smirk. "I'd never have guessed."

My only comeback was a "harrumph."

By the time we climbed the steps to the train station, I was wide awake. While he purchased tickets from a machine, my eyes darted across the grand hall. It looked like something straight out of the movies. The ceiling loomed high above, forming three enormous domes carved in intricate designs. I spun in circles, taking in the stained-glass windows embedded not only in the facade but in the entry to the terminal and even the ticket booths. Passengers crisscrossed the marble floors, sprinting to catch their train.

Ryan found me meandering around in a daze. "What kind of station is this? It looks like a 19th century cathedral."

"It's Estacion Francia. The stained glass gives it that effect. As far as I know, they remodeled it in the early 1900s and again, more recently. Quite a work of art, isn't it?" He gestured with his hand to follow. "Our train is probably arriving now."

I hung onto the edge of his backpack while we made our way to the platform so I wouldn't lose him in the crush of bodies. Sounds echoed in a loud din of voices, speakers announcing the schedule, and metal wheels screeching. There must have been at least twelve lanes covered by a glass and steel archway. A blast of air whooshed through my hair as the cars slowed to a stop, smelling of oil-soaked rails.

We hopped in a car halfway down the platform, claimed two window seats, and tossed our backpacks in the overhead bin. The view of the tracks through the glass stirred memories of the many trains I'd boarded when I was last in Europe. As it lurched out of the depot, visceral sensations sent me back in time and the years slipped away. I was twenty-five again, setting off on a new adventure.

"Where are we now?" I asked only ten minutes later.

"On the outskirts of Barcelona, the scenery is industrial here but just wait. It gets better."

The sun streamed in the tinted windows, momentarily blinding my view of Ryan seated across from me. He pulled the Ray-Bans from atop his head and placed them on my face.

"There. They suit you… in a cute way." He raised an eyebrow. The amused grin lifting a corner of his mouth made me doubt his compliment. I twisted in my seat to see my reflection in the glass.

"Holy crap, these things are huge on me. I look like a giant fly."

"You're adorable."

"Right," I said, fluttering my eyelashes and handing him back the glasses. "So, now will you tell me where we're going?"

"Vilanova, to start, but it's not our final destination. It's about forty or fifty minutes down the coast."

I settled for his answer and watched as the landscape flew by. Soon, we were speeding high above the sea along the edge of a cliff.

"The view from this height is breathtaking." I pressed my nose to the glass, marveling at the contrasts of the deep blue water against the forested hillside and white houses perched on the precipice.

"If you're enjoying this, I'm confident you'll like what I have planned."

I narrowed my eyes at him but knew better than to ask more questions. Ryan liked to keep the mystery alive. As a rule, I wasn't a fan of surprises, but with him, the element of suspense was intoxicating. He hadn't let me down yet.

Once we were in front of the station at Vilanova, he whistled for a taxi and ushered me inside. Within minutes, we arrived at the port where small and mid-sized yachts docked, rocking gently in the sea. There wasn't a cloud in the sky, and the temperature was growing hotter by the minute. I felt the sun's rays burning my skin and searched my bag for sunscreen.

He loped ahead and approached a man standing at a dockside office. I didn't understand a word they said but suspected we were joining a group tour. Ryan motioned with a wave of his hand, and I followed them down a ramp. It was when we stopped at the edge of the wooden pier that I noticed Ryan held a set of keys in his palm. Realization dawned on me in an instant and my mouth gaped open.

"We're going out on a yacht? Out to sea? Just the two of us?"

He raised his arm and pointed to a sleek craft bobbing with the tide. "She's a beauty, right? A sixty-footer." My gaze landed on a white luxury boat with black trim.

"But... how? When...?" My eyes must have widened to the size of saucers because he mimicked my surprise, his eyebrows shooting up. "Is it yours?"

"I wish. I do plan to have one someday, but this belongs to a friend. He's happy to let me borrow it for the afternoon."

I followed Ryan's lead, stepping into the little boat while grasping his hand for balance. As the dinghy chugged through the water and drew closer to the yacht, the tiny motor whining and gurgling, I caught sight of the name painted in a calligraphy scroll. *Carpe Diem.* I tilted my eyes to the blue sky as if to say, "Are you kidding me?" The universe wasn't messing around. It hadn't been gently tapping on my shoulder, it was dropping frigging boulders on my head.

"Come aboard," he said when we pulled alongside the enormous boat. Ryan grabbed hold of a rope at the rear, and I stepped out carefully, grateful to have worn my sneakers for traction.

"This is over the top incredible. I never imagined…" My voice trailed off as I stared at the inside of the cabin, plopping my backpack onto the leather seat. "I've never been on a yacht before. Well, apart from group tours, but never on something this nice." I whirled to face him. "Do you know how to drive this thing?"

He pursed his lips, stifling a laugh, which came out sounding like a raspberry as the air escaped in a rush. "Do you honestly think I'd bring you out to sea if I didn't? Come, let me show you the layout."

His hand wrapped around mine as he led me from the helm at the top to down below on the main deck. It was basically a sleek, modern apartment with an engine attached. I plunked down on the black leather swivel chair in the lounge and gave it a spin.

"So, this is how the rich folks live?"

"Moderately rich, I suppose," he called from the galley. "For our purposes, it has everything we need, and I brought provisions." He unloaded plastic bags from his backpack, stowing everything in the refrigerator. A few moments later, we continued the tour; him leading me down a spiral staircase. "This is the bathroom, or head, as they call it."

I peeked around the corner to find a sink and toilet, plus a large, jetted shower. "Good to know I won't have to pee out in the water. This is definitely classy." He side-eyed me. "What? The smaller boats don't have bathrooms. Just saying."

I knew he was playing when he rolled his eyes, but when he opened the next door, my mouth hung open once again. This was no joke. There, in the middle of a room with sea view windows, was a king-sized bed covered in decorative pillows and fitted with what appeared to be fine Egyptian cotton linens.

I swallowed. "In case we need a nap?"

Ryan cocked an eye and gave me a look. One that said, really?

I was trapped on a boat with a man who undoubtedly had a plan. The thing was... the plan was growing on me. This was the ultimate romantic setting, unless I became seasick. It was a distinct possibility, but I didn't need to disclose that just yet.

With Ryan at the helm, we crept out of the port, slowly at first, and only picked up speed once we hit open water.

"Go sit up front. You'll have the best seat on the ship." His voice boomed in the air, blasting over the roar of the engine and the wind whipping past our faces.

Unsteady on my feet, I tried to appear graceful, navigating my steps while the boat tilted and swayed. But when the hull bounced off the swells, I landed with a thud on the large lounge bed, arms and legs splayed wide to catch my balance. Glancing behind me, I saw him belting out a laugh. I stuck my tongue out at him, then adjusted my position and struck a pose for his benefit.

After a few minutes of bouncing on the open sea, I got the hang of it. Taking hold of the metal railing, I relaxed into the rocking motion, occasionally ducking the spray of cool water as it shot in the air. Under the sun's rays, the deep waters reflected the most beautiful shade of turquoise blue, becoming lighter and laced with frothy white waves as it neared the shoreline.

From this vantage point, the view was even more spectacular than from the train. Wide, golden beaches stretched one after the other, bordered by small towns and jagged cliffs rising high above the sea.

"Which beach is that?" I yelled to him, pointing to a large stretch of sand with a port alongside the point of a rock formation jutting out from the shore.

"Sitges. We can stop there if you like."

"Later maybe. I'd prefer to see more of the coast first."

"You got it," he called to me and shot a thumbs up. "Are you enjoying yourself?"

My head bobbed with a nod; a silly grin plastered on my face. I grabbed my hair into a ponytail as the wind whipped strands in all directions and realized my cheeks were aching. I hadn't stopped smiling since we stepped onboard.

It seemed like we had traveled for miles before the engine slowed and the boat came to a stop. This far out at sea, the shore appeared as a thin line. Ryan hopped down to the rear of the craft, pushed a button and released a chain, which sent the anchor deep beneath the hull. While I relaxed on the sun deck, he disappeared into the galley and returned with a tray, balancing a bottle of white wine and an array of Spanish tapas.

"What's all this? You packed a picnic?"

He handed me a chilled glass. "Just a little something to tide us over until we stop in town later."

I gratefully sipped the cool wine, then piled my plate. We ate lunch side-by-side in companionable silence, wrapping the cheese and serrano ham with hunks of baguette—our gaze drifting to the occasional seagull cruising across the sky. *It's so easy to be in his company*, I thought, as I relaxed into the rocking motion of the sea.

Ryan's voice emerged as a whisper, almost reverent. "It's so peaceful, right? There's nothing like being out in the open waters to take your mind off everything else."

I rested my neck on the top of the couch, took in a big breath of the salty sea air through my nose, and released a sigh. "This is absolutely perfect. I can't imagine a better way to spend the day." I shifted my head and shaded my eyes to see him. "Or anyone I'd rather be spending it with."

His eyes softened when he smiled, the shades of blue in his irises glimmering in the sun's rays. But it was the hunger in his gaze—it ignited my body in a thousand tiny explosions. It seemed like an eternity since a man had looked at me that way. His thumb brushed against my lips, the sun disappearing behind his torso as he hovered over me. Our breaths mingled—his lips a whisper away, my pulse pounding in my ears. I urged him closer, until his lips were caressing mine in a long, deep kiss. I pressed my mouth to his, showing him how much I needed this.

When we came up for air, my chest was heaving, sweat trickling into my eyes. "I'm so hot," I panted.

He laughed. "Yes, you certainly are."

"Well, yes, you're making me hot, but the sun is brutal. Can we go for a swim?"

"Sure, but give me a second." His gaze trailed down to his groin, and I couldn't help but glance at the evidence of his arousal, too.

"No worries, but I wouldn't bet on that going away any- time soon." I pressed my lips together, trying not to laugh. "You might need some cool water."

I scanned the surface of the sea and didn't see any boats within eye shot. "Swimsuits or skinny dipping?" I asked, shocking myself as much as him, judging by the look on his face.

"Definitely skinny dipping."

We raced each other, stripping off shirts and shorts, then sneakers. I trained my eyes on the horizon. My bra and underwear went flying somewhere into the lounge. The white parts of our bodies that had been sheltered from a tan flashed bright in the daylight. I didn't want to think, or have time to become self-conscious, or wonder if my butt looked too big (since it was the biggest patch of pale skin on me).

"Ready? I'm going in!" Perched a little too high for com- fort, I gathered my courage and jumped feet first into the inky blue below, sinking briefly under the water. When I surfaced, Ryan was standing on the edge of the deck, his statuesque body silhouetted against the azure sky. I stared unabashedly at the sight of him, and from somewhere deep in my throat came a purr.

"Here, catch." He threw me a floatation ring, and as I swam to grasp it, I heard a loud splash. He popped to the surface and shook the droplets from his curls.

Paddling my legs, the cool water grazed my naked body. It felt utterly delicious and sensual, and... liberating. In that moment, I abandoned my inhibitions—surrendered myself to the current. With my eyes closed, I floated weightlessly on my back; the breeze hardening the tips of my breasts. I felt the sea swoosh around me as Ryan swam to my side—then, the warmth of his mouth on my nipples. I sank into the delicious sensations, softly moaning sounds of pleasure. He placed the ring under me—my bare skin splayed out in plain sight, caressed by his hands and the silky salt water. The sheer bliss was almost too much.

My lids fluttered open, and I tilted my neck to peer into his eyes. "Hi there."

"You have beautiful breasts. I wish I had my camera to capture you like this. My God, woman." He shook his head, moisture glistening on his curls. "Do you realize how fucking beautiful you look right now?"

Embarrassment, self-consciousness, or insecurity bubbled up. I wondered how this man saw me so differently than I viewed myself in the mirror. But I reminded myself not to dismiss the proverbial gift horse.

I felt my face beaming. "At the risk of spoiling the moment, is my mascara running?"

He dipped his head and coughed out a laugh. "No, you're fine."

I shifted and placed the ring between us, both of our elbows resting on it while we floated on the motion of the tide. We kissed—a sweet, salty, delicious kiss. I wanted to stay there forever, drowning myself in the taste of him. Our legs fluttered long strokes against one another below the water. My body surrendered to the surge of need pulsing through my core.

Finally, I brushed my lips against his ear and whispered, "I'm ready."

Chapter Seventeen

Below deck, sheer curtains muted the light streaming in the windows. My gaze slid to the king-sized bed, to the watery shadows dancing across the sheets. Heartbeat racing, I stood before him—water pooling around my feet and heat fanning through my belly at the sight of his bare skin; the whisper of soft hair leading a trail down to his groin. Slowly, I released the big, white, fluffy towel, letting it drop to the floor, along with my modesty and worry. It was the way his eyes drank in every inch of me, the look of pleasure on his face that unhinged me. I froze, anticipation gripping my insides in a fury of anxiety and lust as his footsteps slid against the wood planks, moving toward me with deliberate intent.

Inches apart, my skin tingled, as if his proximity sparked a field of static electricity. I was only vaguely aware of the sound of the water lapping at the sides of the hull and the gulls cawing in the air. The roaring noise in my ears drowned out everything else, thumping in tandem with my pulse.

I couldn't think. I didn't want to. I only wanted to feel—to lose myself in this moment.

Just when I couldn't bear one more second without his touch, he pulled back a fraction. "Are you alright? I mean..." He gestured tentatively toward the bed.

"I'm fine. Or I will be when you get your body over here." He had no idea how fine I was now, or how much I needed this.

"Are you on, er... I have condoms." His fingers scraped through his hair. "Jesus, I hate killing the mood. It was so perfect."

"No need. We're safe." This wasn't the time to have a conversation about menopause. "And from where I'm standing, it's still perfect."

As if a light had flashed to green, he lunged, his arms capturing me, his body warm and hard against mine, his lips and tongue claiming my mouth. The rush of excitement spiking through me overpowered any logic or reason. I wanted him, no longer caring how this might complicate my life.

"I've been waiting so long to kiss you... to touch you," he breathed out against my ear, sending shivers across my skin.

Closing my eyes, I let the tips of my fingers study his form, trailing across his broad shoulders, down the bands of muscles on his back and the perfect round curve of his ass, before my palms drifted to his thighs. "And you have no idea how I've wanted you to."

Then, neither of us spoke. Words weren't necessary, because our hands were discovering each other; our chests rising and falling with synchronized breaths. I inhaled the scent of him—a dizzying mixture of the sea and his familiar pheromones permeating my senses.

With every kiss, every sound I uttered, he grew harder against me. His voice whispered low in my ear, calling out my name like a song. Every nerve ending on fire, I gasped as he pressed me to him, the fine sprinkling of hair teasing my nipples—my neck arching at the feel of his warm lips pressing against my pulse. Finally, with one fluid movement, his arm wrapped around my waist, whisking me onto the bed.

I lay on my back, staring at his gorgeous face only inches from mine, and slipped into this dream; a fuzzy state of reality where the edges of the lens became blurred and the only sharp image was the man at the center of my focus. His imposing frame hovered over me, dwarfing me in his shadow, while I imprinted every inch of his body to memory. The smooth texture of his skin, the broad angle of his chest, the cut of his jawline, the bulging muscles on his arms now twitching with the force of his weight.

When my eyes slid back to his face, I took in his expression—an intense, heated gaze penetrating deep inside me. It was as if he'd punctured a hole through all my barriers.

His eyes, oh, those eyes. Iridescent blue irises expanding, revealing everything to me—layers upon layers flashed in those eyes. They invited me into an intimate, hidden place within him, drawing me in with a magnetic force. I didn't even try to resist. As if sinking into them, I plunged headlong into the deep end of the pool, weightless and free... surrendering myself to him.

The silky softness of his skin brushed against mine in lunges and dips, his lips feathering kisses as he roamed over every sensitive peak and valley with astonishing precision.

My back bowed under his touch, the pads of his fingers driving me crazy with need for him. My voice filled the air with sounds of pleasure; sounds strangely unfamiliar to my own ears. I'd never felt so desired. It was the catalyst I needed to release all my inhibitions. Parts of me I thought were dead rose from some deep burial ground inside, bursting to the surface with the force of a volcanic eruption.

Silently, he showed me how much he wanted me—the color of his irises darkening to a deep shade of blue, his hips pinning me to the bed. He laced his fingers in my damp hair; our lips pressing, teeth crashing with blinding, urgent need. The taste of his hunger made my core tighten with an irrepressible desire to feel him inside me. As if deliberately making me wait, his lips left a trail of kisses down the curve of my neck to my breasts—indulging his thirst for what felt like an eternity. The slow, delicious torture had me gasping for air, impatiently pleading for more.

"Please," I breathed out, then sucked in air as he rolled my nipple between his teeth. He responded with a low growl that vibrated on my skin, intensifying each sensation. His hand slid down my stomach... to the inside of my thighs... then between my legs. I exploded in tiny fireworks where he touched me, swept away by a force more powerful than the sea itself. Time became undefinable, his caresses infinite. Our voices blurred and melded together in whispers and moans. His words tickled my ears, telling me I was beautiful and oh, so soft.

In one swift move, I curled myself around the bulk of him, tumbling him onto his back, drinking in the sight of his body—so strong, so masculine, so beautiful. I indulged in the feel of his skin, tracing the outline of his muscular torso with my fingertips—over the curves and ridges. My eyes locked on his body, mesmerized by this perfection. A sharp inhale expanded his chest, his neck arching as I teased a trail down his abdomen... then took hold of him in my hand. On a breath, he whispered, "Ah... Sofia." I watched as a look of pleasure washed over his features, felt his hips tensing to meet my touch, sensed his heartbeat racing—my own keeping pace with his.

Somewhere amid the kisses and half uttered cries, I lowered myself onto him—melting into the sensations—until I was just need and want and longing. We rose and fell with the rhythm of the ship for what might have been hours—building and slowing until neither one of us could hold back any longer. The sound of our explosions blasted through the tiny cabin, carried on the breeze to the infinite sea.

I vaguely registered the distant caw of seagulls as my heart rate slowed and my surroundings came into focus again. We lay on those luxurious sheets in a tangle of arms and legs, transfixed by the motion of the yacht's gentle sway. Mesmerized by a shared gaze, as if we'd discovered something incredible and needed to hold on to it or it might disappear. I reached a hand to his forehead, wiping away the mixture of sweat and salt.

"That was..." My head was spinning.

"I know." He wrapped his fingers around mine and tenderly kissed my palm. "Never in my life."

"Me, either."

"We might have to do that again. Just to make sure."

My cheeks lifted with a giddy grin. "You think?" Then I felt his erection growing against my side. "Now? Jesus."

"How about we hit the shower first?"

"What, no jacuzzi onboard?"

Untangling ourselves, skin now sticky and damp, we made our way to the giant shower. I let the warm water flow through my hair and trickle down my body. The saying, you wash my back, I'll wash yours, took on a whole new meaning in the jetted stall. He pinned me against the tiled wall, and with the steam billowing against the glass, we confirmed the first time wasn't a fluke.

When we emerged from the bathroom wrapped in fluffy towels, my stomach rumbled, announcing that he had awakened more than my appetite for sex.

"I'm starving, are you?" he asked.

"You read my mind."

We rummaged through the fridge, piled our plates with fruit and cheese, and carried them to the sundeck. It wasn't long before the warm air prompted us to lose the towels. The sun beat down on our naked bodies as we sprawled out on the seat, my head laying against his thigh, his hand stroking my hair.

"You certainly fulfilled your promise." My eyes swung to look up at him; the silhouette of his head framed by the sun. "I am having a fun day. Thank you."

His tight abdomen bounced when he chuckled. "Believe me, the pleasure is mine. Do you want to dock at Sitges and tour the town? Maybe get some lunch?"

"Soon. I'm more relaxed than I have been in ages. Let's enjoy it a little longer."

"I totally agree," he said. Come here." Lifting me to him, he wrapped me in his arms. I leaned my back against his chest with a contented sigh, and an unexpected laugh barked out of me.

"Madison would be so proud of me."

"Who is Madison?"

"She's my bestie. The woman responsible for convincing me to go on this trip, and... to give you a chance."

"Smart friend. Remind me to thank her sometime!"

"So, is this what your life is like? Glamorous yachts, vacationing all over the world... shagging unsuspecting women senseless?" I angled my neck to peer at him.

"First, I don't think you were altogether unsuspecting, but I'm glad to hear I drove you senseless." He bent and kissed my forehead with now familiar affection. "I am blessed, no doubt. I enjoy my life, but it's not all fun and relaxation. Too much of the time, my work is intense. I deal with multi-million-dollar companies, and my firm expects me to make the right decisions. One wrong move, and the financial consequences could be catastrophic."

"I can't imagine living with the pressure. Don't take this the wrong way, but you seem young to be holding a position with that kind of responsibility. How did you advance in such a short time?"

"I went straight through college and got my MBA without a break. Luckily, some highly influential people picked up on my talent, and, well, one day I was entry level and the next, I was rocketing through the ranks."

"I do appreciate a man who is driven, although I can see why it would be hard to maintain a relationship."

His eyes narrowed, and I could tell he was contemplating his words before answering. "I have been laser-focused on my work, as well as my interest in travel and experiencing other cultures, but as I mentioned before, something is missing." Hesitating, he stroked my hair, tucking a lock behind my ear. "Something a little more meaningful, but... I don't know... maybe I haven't been ready." He didn't look at me then. It wasn't my business to press him for more, though I was curious.

"And what about you? Has your life been wrapped up in your job?"

"It was, but now... my perspective is shifting. Maybe I'm doing things in reverse compared to you, but I think it's time to do more living and less work. Anyway, my future is unknown at this point. But I'm on vacation, so, I'm taking a break from thinking about my career. Today, I'm in total bliss."

"Then I'd like to keep you in that condition. It's your turn to drive the boat."

"You can't be serious."

His smile crinkled against my ear. "Don't worry, I'll guide you."

Reluctantly, we pulled on our clothes. It was my suggestion. I suspected Ryan would have navigated into the port stark naked. It was exhilarating steering the large vessel through the open sea and into the choppy waters churning in the afternoon wind. I stepped back when we arrived at the harbor in Sitges and he took the wheel, easily sliding her into an empty slip.

The hours slipped away as we explored the quaint, pristine village and ate a late lunch on the terrace of a seaside restaurant. We held hands across the white tablecloth, sipped cava sangria, and stroked each other's legs under the table. Mostly, we played. A comfortable easiness settled between us.

I learned he had a silly side. While his jokes were more silly than funny, he kept me laughing all afternoon. Now that I'd given up fighting the losing battle to defy our attraction, I could relax and simply be myself. Even if we had nothing more than these moments today, I told myself I would be grateful for this little slice of heaven.

I hated dropping off our yacht when we arrived back in Vilanova just as the sun was setting, feathery pink clouds fanning across the darkening sky.

"Are you sure we can't keep her?"

"You're adorable." He looked at me with such sweet eyes, my heart melted. "We can take her out again someday, or maybe when I get one of my own."

I stilled. Someday? Someday was far beyond the time-frame of our vacation. Someday wasn't part of our plan. I had to keep this in perspective. Expectations would lead me down a dangerous path. But the moment was so perfect, I didn't want to spoil it with a debate.

On the ride back, we both drifted off to the clacking sound of our car speeding along the tracks—my cheek resting on his shoulder, his head relaxing against mine. Somewhere in my sleep, I heard his phone ping, but I was way too comfortable to lift my head until the wheels squealed to a stop, jolting me awake. I opened one eye in time to realize we had arrived at Estacio Francia.

"Baby, we have to get off the train now."

I yawned and sighed audibly, then realizing what he'd said, the low rumble in his voice when he called me, "baby," I grinned and met his gaze. "Do we have to?"

"C'mon, sleepyhead, I'll carry our backpacks."

When Ryan retrieved his phone, the muscles of his jaw tightened as he glanced at the screen.

"What's wrong?" I asked.

He shook his head; tucked it away. "Nothing."

I suspected Maria hadn't let it go, but she was his problem, not mine. I knew he didn't want me in the middle of it. This was the advantage of having no expectations. The attachment I was developing for Ryan was another matter.

He followed me up the stairs when we arrived back at my apartment. "I have to grab the travel bag I left here the other night," he said, once we walked in the door.

I flipped on the light switch and spun around, suddenly wide awake. "You aren't leaving me tonight, are you?"

"Do you want me to stay?" He slid forward, his body hard and warm against my own. His lips swept across mine, teasing me with feathery kisses.

My fingers twisted in his shirt, pulling him close—while my foot kicked the door closed.

Chapter Eighteen

"Hey, sleepyhead."

"Mm." I felt Ryan's lips on my neck, planting kisses down to my collarbone. I cracked one eye open, instantly blinded by the light pouring in the window. "Did I mention I don't do mornings? What time is it?"

"Eight o'clock. I have to work today."

Blindly, my hand searched for his arm and grabbed hold of it. "No." I pulled it around my body, pinning him against my backside. He laughed, his breath tickling my ear.

"Believe me, I don't want to go, but if I get some work done now, I'll take you to an event tonight. Sound good?"

"Fine." Releasing his arm, I rolled over to face him... I didn't sleep with guys. Or rather, I didn't wake up next to guys until after numerous dates, when I was convinced my morning breath, smeared makeup, and unruly hair wouldn't deter them from ever seeing me again. Had I worried about this when I was in my twenties? Maybe a fraction, but as the years went on, mornings became maintenance intensive. Low light was my friend. Morning light, not so much.

"Wow. I can't believe I slept so soundly," I said, holding my hand in front of my mouth.

"Spending a day on a boat will do that."

My eyebrows twitched just above my fingers. "Right. It had nothing to do with you keeping me up half the night."

"You're welcome," he said. I swatted him with my other hand, and he grinned. "Hey, I'm paying the price too, and you get to go back to sleep."

He moved my arm away and planted a kiss on my lips, despite my protest. I watched as he raised himself off the bed, then began slipping on his clothes. *Popcorn should be served with this show,* I thought. Because seeing him naked in the morning light was even better than in the dark.

"What's your plan for today?" He shrugged into a shirt. Damn.

"I thought I'd hang around and wait for the next show. Watching you get naked is my favorite sport."

"Funny, but getting you naked has become my favorite sport. I'm planning to practice later."

Oh so casually, I stretched and let the sheet fall away, turning onto my stomach. The pained moan he released was my reward for the tease. "I'm not sure what I'll do today... without my tour guide," I breathed out, channeling my inner Marilyn Monroe.

His hands cupped my ass, his face hovering over my check, his voice low in my ear. "You are so bad. Two can play this game. I'll up my score later." His palm slapped my ass—I yelped—and he met my lips with one last kiss before heading for the door. "Yesterday was epic, by the way. I can't wait to see you later."

Butterflies swarmed in my stomach. "Me too. Now go to work so I can get some sleep."

After I heard the front door close, I pulled the pillow over my face and squealed, "Oh my freaking God, what is happening here?" Then I talked myself down, my voice muffled by the thick filling. "Just calm down. Everything is under control. It's a temporary endorphin high and it will pass." *No wonder I haven't felt this way in a long time,* I thought—endorphins were more addictive than heroin. *Considering all the addiction support groups, there really should be one to treat this.* I made a mental note to check online.

This could lead down a dangerous path. I had to focus on something else. When I finally left the apartment, I headed for the big clothing stores, because nothing beat retail therapy. I wrestled my way through the crowds at Zara and Mango, finding the fashion there to be far more stylish than at home. Granted, it didn't take much to beat TJ Maxx and Target. My bags multiplied as I found treasures in the smaller shops too. At this rate, I'd need to buy another suitcase.

Apparently, running from the endorphin addiction, I'd smacked headlong into a shopping addiction, and I was riding the biggest high of all: vacation clothes shopping. I grabbed items off the rack like it was a Black Friday sale; the dressing room strewn with a pileup of must-haves. One way or another, I was going to look dazzling tonight.

By the time I returned to my apartment, exhaustion hit me like withdrawal symptoms. I sprawled out on my bed with my laptop, surfing the internet. Between Facebook, event websites, and local publications, I learned there were so many things happening every night in Barcelona, it would take months, maybe years, to exhaust the options. I felt giddy at the possibilities.

While I scanned for live music and concerts, I ran across a website with events for expats, which, according to their homepage, also welcomed foreigners passing through town. It lit a sparkler in my brain; my curiosity piqued. This could be my chance to catch a glimpse of what it's like to move to another country—peek behind a curtain I've always craved to be revealed.

The event was at an upscale restaurant/bar. I book-marked the page and texted it to Ryan, asking him if he'd be up for going. He shot back a thumbs up emoji, then wrote he would pick me up at eight, which was perfect, since I needed time to become "dazzling."

I strolled into the event linking arms with Ryan, confident, secure, fabulous. But if I had known how the evening would unfold, I would have opted for a quiet dinner at home.

"Sofia Drake," the hostess repeated, then ran her finger-nail down the list. "Ah, I found your reservation for a table. Glad you could join us. People are mingling at the bar right now. You'll see the designated area for this event."

"You'll call us when our table is ready?" Ryan asked.

Her eyes shot open wide, apparently realizing we were together—a couple—not just two people lining up for separate tables. "Oh, I didn't notice... um, yes. I see now. Reservation for two."

"Was that awkward?" I said to Ryan as we made our way to the bar.

He replied with a shrug, but I couldn't shake the feeling that everywhere we went, people were adding up one plus one and questioning the answer.

The restaurant area flowed into the bar under high ceilings, which gave way to a spectacular view of the city through the enormous windows. The modern decor oozed elegance.

We easily found the group milling around the lounge, and given my heels, I was more than happy to find a couple of free seats.

I considered the length of my dress as it hiked up my thigh, wondering if it was too short, but the look in Ryan's eyes reassured me—his gaze traveling up my leg to the slit at the thigh.

"Gorgeous. You have great legs, but you must know that, right?"

I had worn my new, off-the-shoulder, cobalt-blue dress, which clung perfectly to my curves with the help of some side rouching.

His gaze held me steady, and I beamed. Seeing myself reflected in his eyes, I felt beautiful. "Thank you. Feel free to keep the compliments coming."

"Definitely. What would you like to drink?"

"A gin and tonic?"

Before I could finalize my decision, voices speaking English drifted through the multilingual chatter, catching my attention. A group of four peeled away from the crowd's center, heading toward the empty space beside us. I sized them up quickly: two men, two women, all carrying that relaxed confidence of people who'd found their groove in a foreign city.

"If you need help finding an apartment, I know a great agent here," said a tall man whose British accent sounded like it belonged on the BBC.

The woman beside him looked polished—crisp blouse, designer bag, the kind of shoes that whispered money. "That would be a lifesaver," she replied, her nasal East Coast drawl cutting through the ambient noise. "I've been bleeding cash in an Airbnb since I got here a few weeks ago."

"You're going to love it here!" The third woman practically glowed with enthusiasm, her smile infectious and genuine.

I found myself leaning in to catch their conversation, glancing between speakers. When the enthusiastic woman suddenly turned toward me, I felt heat creep up my neck—caught in the act of shameless eavesdropping.

"Hi! I'm Antonia," she said warmly, gesturing to the others. "This is Sylvia." She turned to the tall man with an apologetic wince. "I'm so sorry—your name again? My memory's been terrible lately."

"No worries at all, it's Phillip." His smile was easy and genuine. He nudged the fourth member of their group. "And this is Harry, our resident listener."

Harry raised his hand with mock resignation. "Someone has to balance out Phillip's gift for conversation."

Phillip chuckled, the kind of laugh that spoke of years of friendship built on comfortable teasing. "And what should we call you two?" He looked between Ryan and me as Ryan turned in his seat to join us.

"I'm Sofia, and this is Ryan." I took the lead while Ryan offered a friendly nod. "Are you all expats living here?"

Sylvia's hand went up. "Newest member of the club—just moved from Manhattan a few weeks ago. These two have been Barcelona veterans for years."

"Is this your first time here?" Antonia asked, her curiosity genuine.

"My first visit, though Ryan's practically a regular. I'm already smitten with the city. When I found this event online, I thought it might be nice to meet people who've actually made the leap to live here."

Sylvia leaned forward, her eyes lighting up. "Oh, honey, you've found the right crowd. This group is full of wonderful people from everywhere who've made Barcelona home. And let me warn you—this city has a way of getting under your skin. You might find it harder to leave than you expect."

"I can already feel the magic working on me. Going home is going to sting."

Phillip's eyebrows raised with interest. "I actually know someone who helps with apartment hunting, if you ever decide to take the plunge. We're all in the group directory, so it's easy to connect later."

"I'll definitely keep that in mind." I glanced at Ryan with a grin. "I'm really glad we decided to come tonight."

He squeezed my hand, the moment cut short by a sound so shrill, it could make eardrums bleed. "RYYYAAAN-NN." Miniature sneakers thundered across the wood floor—a child-sized figure practically flying through adult legs, dark hair fanning in all directions as she jettisoned straight for Ryan and attached herself to his legs.

"Dawn! Wow, you're so big now." He bent and scooped her into a hug. His eyes scanned the room, landing squarely on a couple hastily heading in our direction.

"Hello, Corrine." Ryan shifted, releasing Dawn. "I'm surprised she remembers me. It's been over two years?"

"Yes, well, she is a very precocious girl." Corrine patted her daughter's head, which might have seemed like a warm gesture except for her glacial tone—her expression vaguely... hostile? She instantly reminded me of the Lilith character on the show *Frasier*. Her eyes briefly darted toward me, sizing me up in a nanosecond, then disregarding me altogether.

"I'm eight-years-old now," Dawn announced, holding up eight small fingers.

The silent pause that hung in the air held untold stories and old resentments.

Ryan broke the tension, or at least the silence. "This is Sofia. Sofia, Corrine." His hand gestured in the space between us. I mustered a faint, "Hello." Dawn waved at me, but her mother's lips pursed in a tight smile that was more of a grimace.

Random thoughts popped into my mind like bubbles escaping. Age? Probably about thirty-three. Looks? Dark hair like her daughter—cute, but she didn't seem to care much about her appearance (no make-up, slacks, and a forgettable blouse). Was she always this abrasive, or was she reacting to something that happened between her and Ryan? Had they been in love? Who was this guy by her side? A new boyfriend, or perhaps the girl's father? The next question felt like a knife piercing a wound. Why was Dawn so enamored of Ryan? His affection for her was sweet, but it made me wonder....

The forgotten man next to Corrine gently nudged her. I had a hunch he was used to being invisible. "Oh, right." Corrinne said. "This is Dan." The man squared his shoulders and straightened so he appeared slightly taller, which made little difference since he stood only a few inches higher than Corrine.

"Excuse me, little one." A server in a black dress carrying a tray full of plates weaved around Dawn bouncing on her tiptoes like a pogo-stick. The air was so thick with tension, even Dawn's excitement didn't make a dent.

"We just had dinner. What are you doing here?" Dawn asked Ryan, her hands patting his knees as if they were the timbales in her very own Tito Puente concert.

I couldn't help noticing how his eyes softened when he looked at her, his voice lilting in a playful tone. "We're here to go bowling, silly girl."

Her head tilted for an instant; her little eyebrows scrunched together. She erupted in giggles when she got the joke. "There's no bowling alley here." He made a goofy face and tickled her belly with the tip of his fingers. She squirmed with delight.

"We had an early dinner, but now it's time to leave." Corrinne's voice was the cold bucket of water thrown on this party. "We should get her to bed." Corrine turned to Dan for corroboration. He simply shrugged. Apparently, Dan was more of a listener than a talker.

"Oh, I talked to Evan and Tanya," Corrine said to Ryan. "They must be still around here somewhere. You should find them. Evan was wondering if you were in town. He needs a partner for paddle."

His tone clipped, Ryan simply answered, "Thanks."

Corrine took hold of her daughter's hand. "Say goodbye to Ryan, dear." Dawn waved with her free hand, her grin fading into a pout.

"Good to see you, Corrine," Ryan said. But he said it in the way people do if they bump into a former teacher that had made their life a living hell, yet poking the bear wouldn't be smart, so you let it go.

She returned the obligatory, "Good to see you too, Ryan." Her face pulled taut with a constipated smile, she nodded at me, which was only the second time she'd acknowledged my presence. Then they headed for the exit—Corinne dragging Dawn out by the arm. It took considerable effort because every few feet, the little girl stiffened her body, craning her neck to cast a glance back at Ryan.

Dan shrugged and muttered, "It was nice to meet you," though we all knew it wasn't true. Corrine called out his name and shot him a threatening stare. His short legs scissored in a power walk to catch up to them.

"That wasn't awkward at all," I mused. Ryan shifted in his seat and when his eyes met mine, I lifted an eyebrow. "You don't have to explain anything to me, but I am curious."

"Corrine is from the Bay Area, too. I'd heard through mutual friends she'd moved to Barcelona, but I haven't had contact with her in years." He raised a finger to signal the bartender, who was busy shaking a cocktail, the ice rattling against metal. "Running into old girlfriends is never comfortable, but Corrine has a way of taking difficult to the next level." He shook his head. "Small world. Especially here among the expat group."

"Dawn certainly looked happy to see you."

"Her, I don't mind running into." There it was again. His expression brightened. "She's such a sweet kid, but when we broke up, Corrine prevented me from seeing Dawn anymore. Said it would be too hard for her, but I suspect it was too difficult for Corrine. We didn't end on the best of terms."

"Makes sense, I guess. It's like losing people in a divorce—family and friends polarize. They pick one team or the other. Kids get caught in the fallout."

"We never lived together, just dated for eight months or so. At the time, I assumed Dawn gravitated toward me because her father was rarely in the picture." His attention shifted again to the bartender. "I really need a drink about now. Anyway, I just hope Dan is filling that role for her."

Before we had the chance to order drinks, the hostess approached me. "Ms. Drake, your table is ready."

Scanning the room, I found the expats scattered in the crowd, absorbed in conversations. I hopped off the stool, wondering if I dared ask Ryan any more questions. The affection he had for Dawn only enhanced my view of him, but it also summoned old ghosts—of loss and my dried-up ovaries.

I could pose the question casually; Ryan, what are your thoughts on children? Do you see yourself having a few of your own someday? But what would be the point? We were having a vacation fling, nothing more. So, I mentally swept those worries under the rug, leaving a baby-sized lump protruding from underneath the checkered carpet, and quietly closed the door.

We followed the hostess to a booth near the window with an expansive view all the way to the sea. At first, he was quiet, apart from when the server appeared and he ordered a bottle of wine. I fidgeted in my seat, pretended to check my handbag for some mysterious lost item, then gazed past the glass at the winking blanket of lights below. Even before he changed the subject, I had decided not to ask anything more. We didn't owe each other explanations or the details of past relationships.

Once we'd ordered our food, the dust seemed to settle. Talking about our time in Barcelona had us both smiling again. Ryan laughed at the delicious sounds I made as I devoured each new dish the server presented, and I poked fun at the way he methodically took the shrimp meat out of all the shells before taking a bite. We settled into a surprisingly relaxed conversation, given the unexpected twist just an hour before.

"You got caught having sex your very first time?" I held a napkin over my mouth as I coughed out a laugh.

"It was mortifying. The coach spotted us under the bleachers. He threatened to kick me off the football team but let me off with a warning. I think he found it amusing." Shrugging with a grin, he then turned the tables. "Your turn. Most embarrassing sexual experience." He raised his wine glass, then took a sip.

It didn't take me any time to remember. "University parking garage. My boyfriend and I were in the back seat of his Chevy when two police officers—male, unfortunately—knocked on the window and told me to get dressed, then ordered me out of the car. Talk about mortifying! They wanted to make sure it was consensual."

"Was it?"

I pulled a face. "I was a grown adult, quite obviously enjoying myself. We just didn't have any other private space when the moment of desire struck."

He smirked. "Guess it wasn't so private after all."

"Ah, youth." I sighed, my mood shifting, once again remembering the age gap. "Well, your memories are a lot fresher than mine. My college days seem like ancient history." I felt myself crumbling inside, my hopes caving in. I stared out the window, into the darkness—the encounter with Corrine and Dawn rushing back, daring me to ignore the truth.

Ryan's fork clattered to the plate. "Sofia, stop. If I don't care how old you are, why should you?" I opened my mouth, trying to conjure the words to describe how it made me feel, but it was too painful to tell him. "Look, I know it bothers you, but I don't give a damn about the age difference. I see a bright, compassionate, beautiful woman when I look at you." He shook his head, a wry smile breaking on his lips. "Who also happens to be incredibly sexy. And I'm sure I'm just scratching the surface." He groaned, and the space between his eyebrows crinkled. "I can't even think straight when I'm around you."

I stared at my plate, poking the last of the potatoes with my fork. How was it the only man who seemed to value me was so young? He saw past the crow's feet and smile lines—he saw beneath the exterior. He saw all of me. It took my breath away.

"You make me feel the same way. I can't promise to ignore our age difference, but I haven't run again, right?"

He acknowledged me with a squeeze of his hand, but I realized I hadn't ever told him my age. My policy was, if they don't ask, I don't tell. Hell, even if they ask, I usually don't tell. I didn't want to be labeled or imprisoned in a box marked with a number, and anything over forty was an ominous box. Though he didn't appear to care, I couldn't take the chance. Not tonight, anyway. I'd finish this ride with him, and with any luck, he'd never have to know.

We passed on dessert, and rather than socializing with the group, we spent the rest of the evening together, just the two of us huddled in our own private world. The clock was ticking on this vacation, so there was no time to waste.

Chapter Nineteen

When I was growing up, I dreaded the final week of summer vacation—when carefree days and lazy mornings were about to be replaced by alarm clocks and classrooms and homework. I felt that way now, as the last days of my vacation went by much faster than I liked. Ryan stayed on the job, inventing new things for us to do every day, probably because it served as a distraction from the inevitable.

We spent lazy afternoons at the beach and drank delicious sangria at the chiringuitos on the sand, packed with tourists. The vacation vibe there was in full swing, a non-stop party. There were magical nights in the alleyways of the Gothic quarter, perched on the steps near the cathedral, transfixed by Spanish guitar music.

One evening, we stumbled upon a group of people sitting in a plaza listening to a man with a guitar singing mournful flamenco songs. We parked our bottoms on the ground to watch the impromptu show. Since the night Ryan had taken me to the concert in the cathedral, this music had become one of my favorite things about Spain. The sound of the guitar seemed woven into the fabric of the city, whether emanating from speakers in bars or resonating in plazas where street musicians played.

Everyone clapped in time with the music and another man joined in the song, but it was less a duet than a conversation set to a melody; a question followed by an answer—an interaction they knew by heart. Before long, a couple got to their feet, heels clacking on the stone; arms high, fingers snapping. It wasn't a performance—it was a way of life, a story passed from one generation to the next.

Ryan explained this was a tradition born in the south of Spain. Each time I heard the music, I felt the sounds resonating through me, striking a chord, bringing me to life. Out of all the countries I'd visited, none had touched my soul the way Barcelona did. For so many reasons, the thought of this trip coming to an end filled me with dread.

We avoided the topic, until one day Ryan said, "What time is your flight on Monday?"

Panic rose from the pit of my stomach. "Early afternoon." It was already Friday, and I needed to prepare my mind and my suitcases.

We sat at a candlelit table at the port, watching the golden hues of sunset cascading on the water, just as I'd done the night of my arrival.

"I wish I could fly back with you, but I have to go to the London office before returning home," he said, his voice catching slightly on the words. The silence that followed felt heavy, charged with everything we couldn't say. The waves lapped against the boat hulls like a heartbeat, while tourists' laughter drifted from nearby tables—sounds that seemed to mock the ache building in my chest. The evening air wrapped around us, warm and intoxicating, and I found myself desperately trying to memorize every sensation—the way his presence beside me made everything feel possible. I wanted to capture this moment, the heady feeling of a balmy summer night, lock it in a bottle to carry with me through the fog-shrouded streets of San Francisco, where I knew the cold would seep into my bones and these evenings with him would fade in the wind.

Ryan was the first to break the silence. "Let's go out of town this weekend, up the coast, where it's quieter."

"Where? How far?" I asked.

"It will only take a few hours. I'll rent a car so we can tour the area. It's called Costa Brava."

I considered this for a moment. I wasn't sure if I wanted to leave Barcelona during the last few days. He noticed my hesitation.

"It's gorgeous there, I promise. Have I steered you wrong yet?"

I smiled. "Okay, Mr. Tour Guide. You're on."

My eyes slid over to Ryan, tucked in the driver's seat of our gray sports car as we headed out of the city. The color of his eyes seemed luminescent against the reflection of his light-blue sweater, creating a striking contrast with his black hair. This morning, I noticed his curls had grown during the trip—less styled, more casual. His tousled vacation look was growing on me.

"What?" he said, side-eying me.

"Blue is your color. You're extra cute today." I didn't want to admit I was memorizing every detail of him, storing him in my mind to retrieve when this was... over.

"You're extra cute today," he argued.

I came back with, "No, you're extra cute." I held up my hand. "Nope. It's settled. Can we have some music?"

He relented and clicked the play button on his phone. "Is this okay?" Crisp sounds of classical violin music poured through the car speakers.

"It's beautiful. I never figured you for a classical music kind of guy."

"There are a lot of things you don't know about me."

"I have you trapped in a car. Spill it. I really want to know more." It was true. Despite, or maybe because, our time was ending, I wanted more of everything with him.

"Okay, you asked for it. I play the violin. I used to play in a symphony until my work had me traveling so much."

I stared at him. "You're joking."

"Oh, you have so little faith in me?"

"Okay. What's this piece?" A test I had no answer sheet for.

"Bach, Violin Partita 3 in E major."

"Can you play this?" My mouth hung open in disbelief.

"I have, but this one is particularly difficult."

Once the traffic cleared, we sailed down the freeway. I adjusted my seat back and closed my eyes, the music seeping in through my pores. The solo violin sounded so emotional, as if it were telling a story of pain, sorrow, joy, and excitement. In my mind, I visualized ballet dancers on tiptoes, my muscles reflexively moving in time with the dance.

The tracks transitioned seamlessly through the rest of the partitas, then into a concerto, the full orchestra booming at high volume. I stole glances at his face, his transfixed expression; his head bobbed, and his index finger moved above the steering column like the baton of a maestro.

"What an incredible high it must be to play in a symphony—one voice among many, merging in perfect harmony to create a single, breathtaking masterpiece."

Ryan pushed a button on the steering wheel, lowering the volume. "I'm glad you're enjoying it. Not everyone appreciates the complexity of classical music." I sensed his smile radiating at me, even with my eyes closed. "It's a metaphor for life. The rise and fall, the intensity and the quiet. The hope and despair." A faint strain in his voice told me there must be more behind his observation.

Who was this man? I tilted my chin and stared at his profile as the car whizzed past endless white sand beaches. "It sounds like you know something about life's ups and downs."

The muscles along his chiseled jawline tightened. "You could say that."

Silence. The tension hanging in the air made me wonder if I should have asked.

I stayed quiet and let my palm glide over the fabric of his jeans, coming to rest gently on his thigh. The tense bands loosened, relaxing under my touch.

With his right hand on the top of the wheel, he navigated around the car ahead and drew in a deep breath. "I was sixteen when life started throwing me curve balls. As I mentioned the night we met, my family didn't resemble those happy families depicted on television sitcoms. My parents fought constantly, and I wasn't sure why until the shit hit the fan. All I knew was that my dad worked all the time. My mother complained he was never home. My sister was fourteen then—"

"Wait, you have a sister?"

"Had a sister. Jennifer, she..." His voice broke on the last syllable. "She couldn't cope with the stress, eventually turning to drugs. Cocaine, heroin, and who knows how many others." Out of the corner of his vision, he checked my reaction.

My stomach twisted in a knot, but I remained calm, encouraging him with my voice. "Go on," I urged softly.

"She overdosed and died at fucking fifteen." He shook his head, his grip tightened on the wheel. I stifled a gasp, swallowing hard against the lump in my throat. "Ironically, it happened at the same time the board of directors of my father's firm accused him of embezzlement. I always thought of it as karma, because he was the reason she was so fucked up. Anyway, his high-powered lawyers got him off. I still don't know to this day if he was guilty. It was a shit show. The family fell apart at the seams, and there was no one there for me to talk to."

My heart clenched. How did he make it through such pain? I knew that many families fell apart after a tragedy, a death. "Where are your parents now?"

"They both live in the Boston area, but I only have occasional conversations with my mom. I haven't seen my dad in years. But it's fine. He wasn't much of a father."

By the way his jaw tensed, the muscle bulging on his neck, I didn't believe for a minute it was fine.

"Were you close with your sister?"

"My sister and I were tight until she started using drugs. Being the older brother, I wanted to fix the problem—to make her stop. I tried everything, but nothing I did mattered. She retreated into her own world. That's what made it so tough to lose her, but in many ways, she was gone long before she died. My mom was my rock, but when Jen passed and my father almost went to jail, she was barely hanging on. The divorce nearly tipped her over the edge."

"Wait. Was she the girl you had to save from the drug dealer?"

He nodded.

It all made sense now. The anger, the panic. I ached for him—for that young boy and the scars he still carried inside, but the last thing he needed was my pity. I let my hand rest on his shoulder, showing him I was still there, while we both fixed our eyes on the road ahead.

"So, you started acting out?"

"Yep." The word drawled out his mouth like a petulant teenager. "I stayed away from drugs. I wasn't stupid. In fact, I managed to keep straight A's in school. But I guess my anger drove me to take a lot of risks. At least, that's what the shrinks told me." He shot me a sideways glance, finally breaking into a tight-lipped smile. "I started stealing. That was how I got high. By my senior year, I had advanced to auto theft and turned pro."

"Why am I not surprised?" I quipped, partly to lighten the mood.

He almost looked proud of himself now. "By seventeen I had developed a business, buying and selling car parts. Seems like I was destined for my line of work, don't you think?"

"It is ironic. Always a success story, are you?"

"Well, until I got caught. Since I was a juvenile and my father had friends in high places, the court sentenced me to counseling and house arrest."

"And so... the shrinks."

"A succession of them. I suspect I caused a few to leave the business," he snorted. "In retrospect, I was a tough case, pretty closed off. It was an extremely hard road back, but I found one shrink who stuck with me. She didn't allow me to push her away. I believed she really cared about what happened to me, and eventually, I let her help me."

Silence filled the vacuum sealed car; I hadn't noticed when the music stopped. Loosening my seat belt, I carefully leaned into him. My mouth hovered near his ear. "Thank you for telling me. It can't be easy to relive those memories." I kissed his cheek, the curve of his smile lifting on my lips. "You are what we shrinks call resilient. But I imagine you have some scars, probably hidden where no one can see."

His left hand raked over the top of his head, threading through the loose curls. "I suppose so. That chapter of my life is locked up tight so it doesn't poison me again. I haven't talked about it in a very long time." Silence hung in the air for several moments. "I don't know why I spilled my life story to you."

"Maybe because I'm a good listener? And maybe because it was time to let it out. Talking about old wounds is cathartic... healing."

"Okay, now I'm convinced you're a shrink." His gaze slid sideways at me. "Your turn. Tell me something I don't know about you."

"Uh-oh. I'm not sure if we want to go down that road. It might get depressing."

"As much as my story? Doubtful. Now spill it."

The traffic funneled down to one lane, and I waited while Ryan gunned it to pass a slow-moving car. I shifted my weight, sinking into the seat cushion.

"My youth wasn't as dramatic as yours, but my family life wasn't stable either. My mother left my dad. At ten-years old, I didn't understand why my dad was just... gone. Even a kid knows when their parents fight, but I begged them to fix it. To a child, it's simple. You say you're sorry and make up." My voice cracked at the memories rushing back.

I cleared my throat. "Anyway, I guess it was worse than I thought back then. My dad had quite a temper. You never knew what might set him off like a landmine exploding. Years later, I learned he was having an affair, which is ultimately why she left him."

"Did he hurt you?" Ryan blurted out the question. I recognized the fearful look in his eyes and rushed to reassure him.

"No, never. Actually, my dad and I were close. We still are. He was great to me, loved me dearly. Strangely, he remains the only man in my life who has really understood me. He accepted me completely and unconditionally. Despite his flaws, which came from his messed-up childhood, he knew exactly how to be a good parent, intuitively sensing how to guide me with reason instead of force."

He took his eyes off the road long enough to send a glance my way, the corners of his mouth ticking up. "Something tells me you were a handful."

"Now, why would you assume that?" I tried my best to sound offended, then gave up. "Alright, yes, my family would undoubtedly tell you I was a tad rebellious, strong-willed, and quite determined. I always had a plan, and I didn't let anything derail me. My mother used to say I should have been a lawyer, because of the way I could argue my case. I was five at the time."

"Seriously? I guess you've given me fair warning."

I couldn't help feeling the tiniest bit proud to shift his view of me. Stubborn streak aside, I wanted him to know how all the parts of me formed the whole person I had become. On the surface, it could appear I'd allowed life to bulldoze right over me, but I hadn't always been this way.

"Back then," I continued, "I fought for any cause I deemed worthy. I was a feminist before I'd heard the term, and certainly an activist. It might surprise you to know I spearheaded petitions, staged student walkouts, and gave a speech to the city council—all for causes related to injustices, racism, and equality." Somewhere in the recesses of my mind, I wondered when I'd become accustomed to defeat—settled in order to survive.

"I'm impressed." He nodded, then placed his attention on the road. "Did you have any downfalls? Because those are noteworthy attributes, in my opinion."

"Boys. I suppose Freud would have an explanation, given my father wasn't always around. And I got fired from my first job right out of high school for trying to mount an insurrection against the bank that employed me."

"On what grounds?"

"I went to the state labor board because of unfair practices in the workplace. They didn't appreciate it, to say the least. Lessons learned." I shrugged.

"You really don't have a dark side, do you? Although, I am wondering about the boys." I saw his brows twitching, even as he kept his eyes straight ahead. The traffic slowed to a crawl on a stretch of windy road.

"Hah. I'll fill you in sometime. Maybe. There is one more thing."

His gaze slid toward me for a second. "What?"

"I haven't had a serious relationship with a man since I was married." I rubbed my clammy hands against the fabric of my pants.

"Nothing?"

I shook my head. "Only one that lasted six months, and it turned out to be anything but serious." Without thinking, I blurted out the question I hadn't intended to ask. "And what about you?"

"There've been women in my life, but I'm not sure I would put any of them in the category of a serious relationship."

The traffic jammed and slowed to a crawl. There was no telling if it was an accident up ahead or simply too many cars heading for the coast. Ryan pumped the brakes until we came to a full stop, finding ourselves stuck behind a long line of cars crawling at twenty miles per hour through hillsides. In the distance, the sea reflected deep blue against the cloudless sky. Ryan's thumb thrummed on the wheel, choosing his words.

"I suppose it's been hard for me to trust anyone enough to let my guard down. I went through hell when I lost Jen, and obviously my coping skills weren't great. When you're in a serious relationship, there's a reasonably high risk of getting hurt. And coming from a substantially dysfunctional home, I didn't grow up with a lot of faith in matrimonial success."

"Ah. The no free-fall policy," I said.

"Yep." A faint note of laughter tinged his voice. "My last girlfriend became frustrated because I traveled so much. It's not easy to have long-distance relationships, but if I'm honest, I'm not sure I really cared. Does that sound weird?"

Calculations spun in my head. If I only considered his words, it was pretty clear he remained detached from women, and I'd tag him with a huge red flag. But my experience with him was so different. The way he looked at me seemed anything but detached. But then, our agreement created a zone of safety.

Without meaning to, my response came out like a cross between a psychotherapist and a woman who was fishing for an answer to a question she shouldn't ask. "It isn't weird, especially when your career has been the focus. It doesn't sound as if you were invested in that relationship. Though from what you've told me, you haven't let yourself become attached to anyone. It's possible you'd react differently if you found someone... someone special who gave you the motivation to care. Someone you could trust. You just haven't met her yet."

For a moment, he took his eyes off the road and pierced me with a look. Coupled with a cheshire cat smile, his expression told me more than I was ready to handle. A hot flush of heat rose straight to the top of my head.

I turned the air vent directly at my face and fixed my gaze on the car ahead. I really shouldn't have fished. "Um... so, are you going to tell me where we're heading, or do I have to guess?"

"We'll be exploring the calas and villages along this coast."

"Calas?"

"They're like small coves, inlets from the sea with calm water."

Ryan downshifted the gears as we snaked along the narrow roads leading into the hills, the pine trees and dramatic coastline below reminding me of northern California—minus the frigid air. Finally, we rolled into the driveway of a large hotel with white and blue striped awnings.

A man in a uniform walked briskly to the car with a luggage cart. I guess we looked like Americans, because he spoke in English. "Can I help with your bags?"

"Thanks, buddy, I've got it." Ryan tossed the keys into his hand and passed him a bill, then added, "We'll be heading out soon, so you can leave it nearby."

Before we entered the hotel, I wandered to the edge of the cliff, taking in the spectacular view of the sea and the calas below. "Absolutely stunning!"

"I thought you'd like it." His dimples popped with a broad, satisfied smile. God, I could never get enough of that smile. But... I wouldn't have that chance, would I?

As it turned out, our room was equally stunning. Far from the rustic motel style I was used to, this enormous suite with high, wood-beamed ceilings screamed elegance. A free-standing fireplace stood in one corner and a wet bar in the other. The sun streamed in through the floor-to-ceiling windows, illuminating the soft beige colors. Ryan opened the sliding door, and we stepped onto the balcony to find a distant view of the sea past the trees.

"I'm not sure I want to leave this hotel room. This is amazing, really." I laced my arms around his waist and looked up at him, a giddy smile pinching my cheeks.

"In hindsight, maybe I should have had the valet put the car in the parking lot." His voice was low, suggestive, and I knew exactly what he'd do next. I wrapped my arms around his neck as he scooped me in the air, heading for the king-sized bed.

We ended up in an urgent tangle of arms and legs and deep, sweet kisses. Sometime later, we lay between the white sateen sheets; my body draped over his, limp and sated, his chin resting on the top of my head. I rested my cheek on the rise and fall of his chest, swallowed up in the heaven of an afternoon delight.

"It's not that I don't want to go exploring, although I think you're to blame for the detour, I'm just not sure I can move, let alone walk."

"Mm," he purred, the tips of his fingers stroking up and down the curve of my back. "You feel so good. How is your skin so soft?"

I raised my eyes to his, my chin on his chest. "Because I'm a girl?"

He laughed, his belly bouncing against mine. "Alright, on the count of three, we get up. Ready?"

I nodded. Sometime after ten, I cooperatively set my feet on the floor.

Chapter Twenty

The sun was still burning high in the sky when we set off to explore, my arm hanging out the window, the wind blowing my hair in all directions. I controlled the tunes, my favorite salsa music blaring on the speakers as the car zoomed through the turns.

We'd left the hotel prepared with swimsuits under our clothes, so the minute we landed at the first beach, we sprinted across the burning sand, weaving around the summer crowds, then peeled off the layers and plunged into the sea—our skin instantly finding relief in the cool water with a simultaneous sigh, "Ahhh."

Ryan took off like a rocket, his arms and legs powering him past the shallows where the children splashed like baby dolphins. I nearly became the object of target practice when a water gun fight broke out between two older boys. I half ran, half swam out of the line of fire, my legs propelling me out further, into deeper water.

Ryan was floating on his back when I caught up with him. "Have a look."

I flipped over, legs scissoring to keep me afloat, my gaze trailing along his sightline. Tree-lined cliffs encircled the cove; dirt trails etched into the hills leading to look-out points. "Oh…" I breathed out a sigh. You weren't wrong. It's beautiful here."

His gaze shifted to me. "As I said, have I ever let you down?" He moved with easy strokes and captured me in his arms. Suspending me above the surface, his lips met mine. We kissed until a passing boat kicked up the waves, the salty water splashing up our noses.

"Way to kill the mood," I coughed out.

I paddled until my feet found purchase on the sandy bottom. When I caught my breath, I wrapped my arms around his shoulders. "You are the best tour guide in the entire world."

"Be sure to leave a five-star review on Yelp, please."

I raised a smile, my face nestled against the curve of his neck. "You've earned a solid ten. Honestly, this has been the best vacation in my life."

He pressed a finger to my lips. "Shush. It's not over yet."

I knew what he meant. Neither of us wanted to admit it was coming to an end.

Ryan packed our afternoon itinerary with enough activities to keep us distracted. When the heat became overwhelming, we stopped at another cala and doused ourselves in the cool water. For lunch, we dined on fresh fish at the water's edge and watched the boats motoring into a tiny harbor. As we strolled along the seaside promenade, he lined up behind a row of bouncing children to buy me an ice cream cone—just because he knew it was one of my favorite afternoon indulgences. By day's end, I wished we had a week to spend on this coast.

We returned to the hotel exhausted and slightly sun-burned, with just enough time to shower and grab a drink at sunset. Sitting side-by-side at the edge of a terrace high above the sea, we watched as the expansive sky transformed into a light show. As if painted by a master artist, a special gift for our last night, splashes of gold and crimson streaked across the horizon.

"Did you special order this sunset?" Despite this beautiful setting, a heavy cloud descended over me, my voice sounding too perky. It didn't take a psychologist to see right through me. It was the last one we'd see together. I swallowed against the knot in my throat.

He shot me a smile that didn't reach his eyes. "Well, I have to keep my customers happy."

I realized we were both terrible actors. "Okay, then. What's next?"

"Are you hungry?"

My stomach growled. "Starving."

He signaled the server, and soon, small plates of tapas filled the top of the table. Twinkling lights illuminated the towns below like a diamond necklace draped along the coastline, the sea disappearing into the blackness, punctuated by the occasional glow of a boat passing. In the cala directly below, sailboats rocked in the harbor next to a brightly lit promenade dotted with restaurants.

Even from a distance, I could tell the mood was festive; children chased each other through the crowds, lovers walked hand in hand, vendors presented their wares to passersby. I had come to love the concept of promenades since I'd been in Spain; a place to stroll and enjoy the simple pleasure of listening to the waves lap gently on the shore—feeling the balmy breeze of summer on my skin—breathing in the scent of the sea and the smokey essence of burning fire pits where slabs of fish sizzled over the grill.

But at our table, the mood had grown somber. We ate in silence; our gaze fixed on the view.

"Do you like the food?" Ryan asked.

"It's delicious." I plucked another mussel from the pot, slurping the juice from the shell. Then I wiped my hands on the napkin. "It's just... well, it's our last dinner together. Our last night."

"Why? There's still Sunday night before you leave."

I shifted in my chair. "When we return tomorrow, I'll need to be alone. I have to pack up—which, believe me, isn't going to be easy, considering the extra things I'm bringing back—but also, I want some time for myself." I knew this was non-negotiable.

Ryan looked like I had shot him with a taser.

"This was our agreement, remember? Vacation fun and done." I couldn't meet his gaze, or I'd break into a million pieces. Instead, I poked the shells in the iron pot.

"Is that what you really want now?" The sharp edge in his voice caught me off guard.

It was agonizing to see the hurt look in his eyes; a reflection of the pain I felt. "It doesn't really matter what I want."

The server came over then, but Ryan waved him off before he could say a word. I finished the wine in my glass, and he reached for the bottle, topping off mine, then his.

"What if I want to re-negotiate our deal?"

"You're proposing to be my tour guide in San Francisco?" I said, more flippantly than I should have. God, I wasn't handling this well at all.

"Sofia, you know what I mean."

I fought the urge to leap out of my chair—to run. "And you know it can't work. What would your mother think of me? What would your friends say?"

"Look," he began, "I'm just saying we can see each other when we're back in San Francisco. Don't make this a big deal, just go with the flow."

"What? Continue the fun with no expectations? I need some structure to pull that off. This vacation has been the structure—the container. I don't know if I can handle it when we're home."

"No. I can't accept this ending."

My head shot back at the resolute tone, the intensity in his voice. Observing my silence—my shock, his voice softened, his expression pleading.

"I can't just let you go. Please, Sofia, don't make any decisions now. We'll meet up when I return and re-evaluate. Okay?"

I pressed my eyelids shut, imagining all the possible scenarios at once. He was right. Despite the foreboding warning bells sounding off in my head, I wasn't ready to let him go, either. Straightening myself in the chair, I finally said, "Okay. Deal. Now, can we please return to our room?"

"My thoughts exactly."

There are moments in your life when you want nothing more than for time to stand still—to capture the memories like fireflies in a jar, where there's no chance of ever losing them. This night with Ryan was filled with a string of those moments. We savored every minute, every touch, every gaze into each other's eyes. Maybe because we both knew there might not be more nights like this.

We undressed each other with reverence, each of us drinking in every detail as if committing the visual memories in a photo album to be retrieved later. I lost track of time as our lips pressed together in long, slow, delicious kisses. Hours passed. I had no idea how long we spent in each other's arms, forcing ourselves to stay awake. By the look in his eyes, his goal was the same as mine—to experience every sensation of pleasure, as if in slow motion. While sometimes, our wild, fast-paced, headboard banging sex had been what we'd both needed, tonight was different. Rather than speeding down the highway with a pressing need to reach a destination, we were in no rush as we took the scenic route.

I let my hands roam over now familiar peaks and valleys. His mouth zeroed in on the sensitive spots he knew would quicken my breathing. We spoke in a shared language of utterances and sighs and gazes that conveyed unspoken truths. The intensity of our intimacy split me wide open. The thought of giving him up caused a burning sensation to rip through my chest. I could hang on, but at what cost down the line?

By morning, my eyes were red and puffy—not only from the lack of sleep. Several times, I'd had to slip into the bathroom, close the door and let the water run so he wouldn't hear my hiccupping sobs. But he knew.

Though his eyes were tinged with a melancholy shadow I hadn't seen before, he tried his best to show me more of the coastline on our route back to the city. And I tried to summon the interest to care about sight-seeing. We both knew we were faking it, and by the time we were cruising on the freeway, the only sound was the purring of the engine.

"This is too hard," I said as he dropped me off at my apartment. "I can't invite you to come up."

"I know."

Standing at the side of the car, he crushed me in an embrace—our arms tethering us together until I didn't know where my body ended and his began—neither one of us rushing to part. I ran my fingers through his hair, then slid my hands down his back. He held my face in his palms and kissed me. I barely registered the swarm of people passing by; the horns honking in the street.

When we finally broke apart, I managed a weak smile, but my voice was husky. "See you in San Francisco."

He nodded. "Have a safe flight. Text me when you arrive."

Neither one of us said goodbye. I simply turned and carried my bag to the apartment.

Chapter Twenty-One

T he transition back to reality was like moving from a world full of color to one so shrouded by clouds it became a muted shade of gray. Literally and figuratively. Freeways replaced quaint cobblestone streets. Instead of dining on terraces teeming with life, I ate alone at my kitchen table. The bland, suburban neighborhoods paled in comparison to the stunning architectural facades I'd been gazing at only a few days ago.

Since I'd returned to reality, the previous month seemed surreal now. Even today, one week later, as I sat in my breakfast nook having my morning coffee, I was still untethered. I wondered how long jet lag lasted, though I knew it was only partly to blame.

An endless loop of memories, especially of our last night together, played like a slide show in my mind. I relived the way his skin radiated with warmth next to mine, how his dark eyelashes fluttered when he slept, the feel of his breath gusting in my ear when he called out my name.

Most of all, it was impossible to forget who I had become when I was with him—uninhibited, passionate, free. I didn't know whether to be embarrassed or to send him a thank-you card. Either way, he'd opened the floodgates. Now what?

Madison's text pinged while I was searching for my stash of chocolate—my drug of choice.

> **So, are we still on for tonight? I can't wait to get the details of your trip.**

> **Of course! Looking forward to it.**

> **Awesome. Meet you at our spot on the Embarcadero, 8:00.**

The day passed as if in slow motion, in stark contrast to the way time slipped by in a blur while I was on vacation. I finished unpacking and doing the laundry, but the clock had barely moved. It was only noon. Flopping back down on the bed, I opened my laptop and pored through the emails from Ben. They had left Barcelona soon after we'd met to go sight-seeing, then continued to France and Italy. I clicked on the picture of Ben and Callie in Venice, having dinner at a trattoria overlooking a canal. The orange and red awning, the gondola drifting in the background, reminded me of a photo of myself during my first trip to Europe.

The memories came flooding back, but it was the fresh memories that rose to the surface and made me smile. A few weeks ago, I never would have imagined the adventure Barcelona inspired. That Ryan inspired.

To commemorate the trip, I spent the afternoon organizing my photos, anticipating Madison's curiosity. By the time I got ready to meet her, I was so engrossed in the sights and sounds of Barcelona it was difficult to get excited about a night out in the city.

I stood on the tip of my toes and searched for Madison, peering around heads in the crowded restaurant bar. The buzz of my phone vibrated against my hip, and when I dug it out of my purse, I found her text.

I'm in the parking garage, Be there in 5.

As a couple got up to leave, I rocketed across the room and claimed the coveted seats with a waterfront view; the bay gleaming through the floor to ceiling windows.

When Madison found me, I was staring out the window, watching the sailboats bob in the harbor, a lemon drop martini in hand.

"Look at you, Sofia Drake. World traveler. You've got a whole new vibe goin' on." She swung her hand in a circular motion, as if sizing up my aura.

I jumped up, surprising her with a bear hug. "God, I missed you!" When I released her, I noticed she was dressed to kill. "Let me see, give it a twirl."

She twirled on the toes of her five-inch stiletto heels. The kind that made my feet scream just looking at them. Her signature skin-tight animal print dress hugged every voluptuous curve.

"You never can tell who you might meet at a bar." Her face broke into a coy smile as she scanned the room before lowering herself into the seat across from me.

As if on cue, a handsome server appeared at our table. "What will you ladies have?"

She cupped a hand to her mouth and muttered in my ear, "Besides him?" Turning her attention to the young man, she said innocently, "I'll have a vodka tonic."

I raised my glass, still almost full.

When he was out of earshot, she said, "He certainly is cute. I think his name tag said Tony?"

"Madison, he looks to be barely thirty." At the sound of my words, I winced. Ryan was only thirty-five.

"And your point is?" Her acrylic fingernails clicked against the tabletop. When I didn't respond, she continued. "Catch me up on your wild ride in Spain. But first, I want to hear about Mr. Gorgeous."

"You were right. The trip was amazing, exactly what I needed. And so was Ryan." I paused and looked out at the boats bobbing in the estuary. How could I put into words the effect this man had on me? How he had changed me. "Ryan was... quite a surprise. I never expected a guy his age to be so mature, so sophisticated. Not to mention he romanced the pants off me—literally."

"Thank you, Jesus," she said, her head tipped to the ceiling.

I felt the heat rise, my face turning pink. "Once we got started, girl, we didn't stop."

"Did you get a UTI?" She was giggling now.

"How did you know?"

"It always happens when a woman suddenly increases sexual activity. It sucks to be female sometimes."

"Thank God for the farmacias there. They fixed me right up. But I need to get your take on my dilemma."

The server delivered her drink order, and she settled back in her chair. "This sounds serious."

I took a long pull on my cocktail. "Based on your suggestion of going for carpe diem on this trip, I only agreed to hang out with him if we kept it limited to the vacation. No expectations, no strings—just fun."

She nodded slowly. "Okay, I get that. So how did you end things?"

I let out a painful sigh. "There's the problem. We couldn't quite put the lid on it. He wants to re-negotiate our deal when he gets back, and I don't know what to do."

"Where is he now?"

"He's working in London, but he should be home soon."

With perfect timing, my cell phone vibrated against the table. Ryan's photo was on the screen, along with a video chat request. Immediately, my heart jolted, performing backflips against my ribs. "Should I answer it?" I blurted, my finger already on the button.

"Yes!"

"Hi. What a surprise. Are you back in town?" I asked, holding the phone in front of me and turning up the volume with my thumb. The sight of his gorgeous face sent tiny fireworks pinging through my body.

"Hey there, beautiful. No, I'm still in London, but I couldn't wait. I wanted to see your face again. I've missed you."

That did it. I dissolved into a puddle. In the screen's corner, I glimpsed my image, grinning at him like a teenager. "It's really good to hear you; see you, too. Although your voice is a little muffled, hard to hear you with this noise."

"I can tell. Where are you?"

"I'm having a drink with Madison." I rotated the phone, positioning it so he was facing her.

"Hi, Ryan." She waved at the screen. "Sofia was just telling me what a great time she had with you in Barcelona."

"Nice to meet you. Sofia told me you two were besties. Has she given you the juicy details yet?" His low, rumbling laugh tumbled from the speaker, then he cleared his throat. "I mean, how she skippered the boat across the high seas with ease."

I rolled my eyes just as Madison peeked over the phone at me. "No, but I'll drag it out of her."

"Juicy details? What on earth could you mean?" I looked into the camera again and pulled a face.

"There it is. That's one of your looks I've missed. The innocent, playful one. There're others too, but we'll get to that later. I've gotta run to a meeting. Later, hon." He signed off with a wink, and I puckered a kiss, wondering if it was too cheesy.

"Wow, you weren't kidding about a face that could melt a girl's panties. Though he doesn't seem too young. He looks... seasoned."

I shrugged. "Probably that's the reason I fell for him." Then I realized what I'd just said.

"Oh, girl... you are in trouble." She drew out the syllables in the last word for emphasis.

"I mean... I..." I sunk my face into my hands with resignation. "I am in trouble, aren't I?" I groaned. "In my defense, can you blame me? He's... He's everything I've ever wanted."

"Uh-huh, and?"

"Which leads me back to the dilemma."

"Girl, there's not a chance in hell you're going to walk away from that man, at least not yet. The way you two look at each other, I'm getting a contact high just being near your energy."

"Yes, but it's like coasting down a river when you know Niagara Falls is at the end of the ride."

"The point is, you're on a great ride—maybe the best one of your life—and life doesn't come with a guarantee. People die in freak accidents; couples divorce after they've promised forever. Especially at our age, when we've lived enough to know loss, isn't it better to embrace the good times while we can?"

I let my glance slide around the bar, at the two-to-one ratio of women versus men. Most of us were looking to connect with someone, be it a man or another woman, and it was so damn hard to find. "In theory, you're totally right. But I feel this man's heart, and what we have is deeper than just good times. This is a hundred steps ahead of what I bargained for."

"So, what's the alternative?"

She waited while I considered this—swirling the taste of the dilemma in my mouth like a connoisseur at a wine bar.

"Okay. I'll live in the moment—my new mantra. I won't run. I'll just enjoy him while I can and not project into the future."

"You mean you'll resist trying to control what you have no power over and ride this wave?"

A cringe lifted my cheeks. "Yes...? This won't be easy, you know that."

"Many good things in life don't come easy, but they're part of the magical tapestry. They shape who we are, who we become at the end of the journey."

After slugging half my drink, I added dryly, "Or they kill us. We'll find out which way this goes."

"Oh stop," she said, swiping her hand in the air. "Speaking of risks, remember I mentioned having a date with a new guy?"

Thinking back to our conversation, I nodded. "Yeah, what happened to him?"

"His name is Roger, and he's turning out to be a surprise, too. He's a nice guy—and I don't mean ugly and boring nice—he's handsome, tall, and has a good build. Which is why I didn't expect him to treat me so well. He invites me out on proper dates—with advance notice—keeps in contact almost every day, and seems to enjoy my company. Oh, and he's not married."

My thumb shot in the air. "Yay! That's an excellent start. He sounds like a gentleman. And?" I arched an eyebrow.

"And... He's exceeded my expectations in the bedroom. For that matter, all over the house," she added, cackling out a laugh.

"So, where is Kevin with all of this?"

"I ended things with him, and just to make sure I stick with the decision, I've put him on the 'do not disturb' list on my phone."

"How'd he take the news?"

"I'll leave out the expletives. Suffice it to say, he was angry. He told me I'd never find any man as good as him." She shook her head, letting out a bitter laugh. "The nerve of that guy. I held my ground, though. This time, I'm not turning back."

"I'm proud of you, and happy. It means you're valuing your worth." Then, realizing I had only an empty glass to toast to her success, I raised my hand in the air, summoning the server.

After I gave her the travelog of Barcelona, Madison dragged the juicy bits out of me. It may have been after the second drink took effect. Or possibly it was the third. "Do you know the old saying? It's not the size of the ship, it's the motion of the ocean? Well, it turns out that size—and rocking with the motion of the ocean is the ultimate combination." I might have snorted a laugh watching her busting out in laughter, clutching her stomach.

"I'll put that experience on my bucket list." When she finished giggling, she said, "Okay, I'm calling Tony over. Let's get you a glass of water, then I think some food is in order."

A few minutes went by before Madison thought to ask, "You've only told me about Ryan and your trip. What are your career plans now that you're back?"

"I have no idea. It's barely been a week and I'm readjusting."

"Huh. I never thought I'd see the day when you didn't already have a plan in place."

I shrugged. "Maybe I'm evolving, or simply my mind is still in Barcelona."

Later, Madison snaked her arm around mine as we walked to the garage. "Barcelona sounds amazing. I hope we can travel together next time. I could use an adventure."

"Definitely. Let's plan a trip. Without a doubt, I will go back there. The city made quite an impression on me."

"Are you sure it wasn't Ryan who did the impressing?"

"Well, it was a magical combination." A smile crept across my lips, and I laid my head on her shoulder. "Oh dear, what am I going to do with that one? He's danger personified."

She bumped her head against mine. "You are going to enjoy every minute with him—that's what you're going to do."

"That's it, huh... just have fun?" I asked, as if I didn't know the answer. "Well, this will be different. I've tried not having fun for so long, I'm not sure I remember how."

Madison clicked the fob on her keychain, and a beeping sound echoed through the garage. "Oh, I think you've already refreshed your memory just fine."

"You might have a point." My entire body vibrated every time I visualized him. I was obsessed with thoughts of his return. "Hey, you're good to drive?" I called out to her.

"Yep, sober now." Madison froze mid-step, then her feet shuffled backward. Her head whipped toward me, and I saw the fear in her eyes, beads of sweat breaking out on her face. Taillights flashed. A black car swung out from the space next to hers. Before I could say a word, her fingernails were digging into my arm. "That's Kevin's Mazda." The wheels screeched against the pavement as the car tore down the exit ramp.

"He's stalking you?"

Her chest heaved with a heavy breath. "It wouldn't be the first time. When I tried to leave him before, he chased after me, begging me to come back."

"Madison, look at me." Her eyes reluctantly swung away from the empty parking space. "Has he ever hurt you?"

She shook her head. "I'll be fine. He's probably checking to find out who I'm with tonight. He got the answer."

"Nevertheless, I'm following you just in case he's waiting. I suppose we can't call the police because technically he hasn't done anything to report. But when you get inside, make sure to set the alarm and lock all the doors, okay?"

She nodded. With a few deep breaths, she steadied herself and headed for her car.

"You're sure you don't want to come to my house tonight?"

"No, but thank you."

"Call me if you need anything, please. Even in the middle of the night."

I gave her a hug before we parted, and when we reached the street, I tailed her car until she was certain he wasn't following.

When I arrived home, I received a text from Ryan. He'd be on a plane home in two days.

Chapter Twenty-Two

In California, owning a car was as essential as having a roof over your head. It was the land of freeways, where people might spend upward of four hours or more in their car every day. It was basically a second home, where, in addition to the work commute—we ate on the run, took naps, studied, caught up with friends via Bluetooth, applied makeup, shaved, changed baby diapers, put the baby to sleep, and, sometimes, had steering wheel-banging sex.

But the residents of San Francisco led a different lifestyle. If you owned a car, you had to pay almost the cost of your rent to keep it parked in a garage, yet you only took it out if absolutely necessary. The streets were jammed with traffic, and if you were lucky enough to find a parking space, you'd be so shocked at the hourly rate, you wouldn't be able to enjoy your time out in good conscience.

All this to explain that when Ryan and I agreed to meet in Nob Hill instead of in my suburban neighborhood, I took an Uber. It was a simple decision, as his apartment was close to all the restaurants and scenic parts of town. That was probably the only simple decision we'd have to make that night.

As the sun set over the bay, I hopped into the back seat of the Uber, my stomach clenching with anticipation. I wondered absently if meeting Ryan on our home turf would be different from Barcelona—would we be different? Maybe we had just been two people caught up in the city's magic. These swirling questions weren't helping me to relax.

The driver navigated to his address on Nob Hill as a white layer of fog rolled in from the sea and blanketed the city, bringing with it an icy wind.

I called his cell, shivering. "I'm here."

"Great, be right down in a second."

Waiting on the corner, I scanned the dark street lined with opulent two-story Victorian homes. Many, I'd learned, were divided into several apartments. My eyes fell on his six-foot-three frame as he appeared from a door and shut the metal gate behind him. Instead of shorts and a polo shirt, he was now bundled up in a black wool coat and a cashmere scarf. I also looked like I was dressed for the arctic, in a matching black coat, scarf, and my dressy boots with the three-inch heels. Although, on these hills, hiking boots would have been the better choice. Ah... San Francisco summers.

The fluttering in my chest reduced to a quiet stir when he engulfed me in his arms, his whisper soft against my ear. "I'm so happy to see you."

"I'm so happy you're back."

He lifted my face with a nudge of his chin. "Let's catch a taxi."

"Did you have something special planned, because if not—"

"Well, um…" he mumbled.

I said, "It's fine," at the same time he said, "Whatever you want…"

We laughed, but something was off. Mine too high pitched. His staccato. Ryan explained, "I thought I'd take you someplace special for dinner, but what do you want?"

I cleared my throat. "It's just that I don't want you to have to play tour guide. We're home, and I'd like to see what it feels like to be… normal?"

"Normal?" he echoed. I wasn't conveying myself clearly, because my feelings were about as clear as the thick shroud of fog hanging over us.

"Maybe that's not the right word, but we're transitioning back from vacation mode, so let's just have a relaxing evening. You've impressed me enough. You don't have to keep it going."

He nodded like he understood, but did he? "Okay, how's Italian? I know a good trattoria nearby."

"Perfecto!" I said, aware it was Spanish, not Italian, but whatever.

While we walked, I asked, "How was London?"

He rubbed the tips of his fingers against his temples and grimaced. "Not as much fun as Barcelona, for sure. There was a glitch, and I almost didn't close a deal. It took some finesse and a fair amount of legal counsel to come to an agreement with all the parties involved. It's a matter of creating at least the illusion the merger will benefit both companies."

"But somebody gets hurt in the process, don't they?"

We both watched as a car blocked the road, vehicles stacked up behind it, motors revving. A few angry drivers honked their horns. But the car stubbornly waited for a coveted parking place while an SUV inched forward and backward, the driver trying to extricate his large vehicle out of the too-small space.

"Anyway," he continued, "it's an unfortunate side effect in business, but I try to mitigate the damage. That's why I'm usually able to close the deal."

I tried to imagine him in the middle of a boardroom, wrangling in the world of high finance. It was so foreign to me, but based on what I knew about him, it wasn't hard to visualize him as a powerful force. He'd already proven his skills at negotiation with me.

"This is it," he said, guiding me through the door.

Inside, the warmth was a welcome relief. The scent of pizza baking in a fiery oven emanated from the kitchen. Red checkered tablecloths, wood furniture, and candles made the place feel cozy.

"It's perfect," I said.

We ordered wine, and in the style of Barcelona, we chose a few plates to share. I noticed now how we didn't argue over simple stuff, like I'd experienced with my husband. We compromised—always a little give and take on both sides. Being with Ryan was easy.

I finally relaxed, and if his laughter was any gauge, he was too. Mostly, we reminisced about our trip.

"By the way, did you ever resolve things with that chick... Maria?"

He wiped the pizza sauce off his mouth, revealing a grin. "I don't think 'resolve' is the right word. I blocked her number because she kept texting. One day, when you and I were on the beach, I saw her with another guy. Let's just say it was clear she'd moved on. For her, it was all about ego, not about me."

"Is there any chance we might run into another 'Maria' here in town? I'd like to be prepared this time."

He cocked his head, realizing my question held several layers. "No, Sofia, there isn't. And what about you? Any crazy stalkers I should be aware of?"

I assured with a firm, "No." We could have delved into our histories, but there was no point to an exercise in cross-examination right now.

"Dessert? Or jet back to my place?"

"How about dessert to-go and we head to your place?"

"Deal."

"Have you noticed we sail through negotiations pretty well?"

His cheeks lifted with the broadest smile. "Why do you think I didn't want to let you go?"

I matched his smile and raised him with a sexy stare. "I thought it was the sex."

"Yeah, that too." He arched an eyebrow. "We're just really good together."

I leaned in and kissed him then, in front of the whole restaurant. I didn't care who was watching or judging.

He purred against my lips. "Nice."

Chapter Twenty-Three

It shouldn't have come as a surprise, but as soon as I stepped in the door of his apartment, my jaw dropped. I scanned the expansive great room where a massive glass dining table rested on polished wood floors, accompanied by eight black leather chairs. The adjoining living room was configured in a conversational enclave, its sculptured coffee table set between contemporary, cream-colored sofas, which clearly weren't from Ikea.

I shed my coat, hanging it on a brass hook by the door. My heels clicked on the wood as I wandered over to the bay windows, where the lights of the cityscape glittered in the distance.

"Impressive view, not to mention the apartment." I had a twinge of envy when I considered my modest home. The one I'd painted myself and still held the mismatched furniture purchased from a second-hand store.

"I'm glad you like it." He turned to light a series of tall candles on the mantle. "I'll give you a tour."

I followed him down a hallway but stopped as I glimpsed the large, framed photographs. "Did you take these?"

"Photography is one of my hobbies." Pictures from around the world lined the walls. He named them while I pointed. "Machu-Picchu, that's in Peru, and then there's Vietnam, Africa, Fiji, Japan...." The list went on, each location more exotic than the last.

"I can only imagine being able to see all these incredible places." Now I envied more than his apartment. His world had already stretched so much farther than mine. I walked from one photo to the next while Ryan plugged in his phone to the speaker and chose a track of mellow instrumental music.

The rest of the apartment was just as jaw-dropping. I commented I'd need a GPS to find my way back if he wasn't leading me. He wasn't surprised. I drooled over the kitchen and its modern design. There was enough room for two of my kitchens in the space.

He made a point of showing me around his master bedroom, which, by any standards, was enormous. I noted the king-sized bed with its dark gray linens—definitely a man's color scheme, then strolled into the generous walk-in closet. It held more suits than I could count, plus rows of shoes.

"Now I have kitchen and closet envy."

He shrugged. "What can I say? I like cooking—and clothes." His arm draped around my shoulder, guiding me toward the hallway.

"Wait a minute, are these family photos?" I broke away and moved to the dresser, leaning close to inspect each one.

"Your mom?" I pointed to a portrait and he nodded. "You resemble her, don't you think? She's beautiful." Her features were refined and perfect, like his.

"That's what most people say."

"Are these your relatives?" I asked, handling a framed eight-by-ten photo of a large group huddled to fit within the camera's view.

"That was taken at a family reunion; my mother's side."

"Everyone looks so happy, but you said—"

"Looks can be deceiving."

I turned to glance at him. His smile was noticeably absent, his jaw set tight. "Do you have any of your father?"

"No." He stepped back several feet away from the dresser.

"Your sister?"

"No."

I waited, but silence followed his emphatic answer.

"I'm sorry I asked. It must still be a sensitive subject for you."

"No worries. Let's head to the living room and break out the wine."

He led the way; an icy chill hanging in the air like the vapor trail of a ghost. I should have known better than to poke my nose into his family's wounds.

When I'd settled onto the couch, I noticed a guitar leaning against the wall in the corner. "Do you play the guitar as well as the violin?"

"Yep."

Okay. Ignoring his change in mood, I tried to sound upbeat, to maneuver this night back on track. "Did you intentionally set out to be great at everything you do, or were you born fated to possess more talent than most people could only dream of?

"Sofia, I have to be good at everything. I don't have a choice." He claimed the space next to me on the couch. I studied his expression, trying to read his thoughts, while he hesitated for a few beats. "It's hard to explain, but when I was growing up, the bar my parents—my father—set was extraordinarily high. My therapist said," he paused for emphasis, narrowing his eyes at me, "I may have internalized those expectations a little too seriously. But you aren't much different, are you? You must have worked hard for years to become a psychologist."

I shrugged. "Yes, but I never experienced that kind of pressure and certainly didn't excel at everything I tried. In fact, I was so bad at sports I had to endure the humiliation of being the last one picked when teams lined up at school."

"Aww, sweetie, that must have stung. But you never played an instrument? You seem to have an ear for music."

"My grandmother had a piano, and as a child, I loved to create dramatic pieces on the keyboard, pretending I was composing the most beautiful songs. But I never had lessons. My family couldn't afford them. When I was a teenager, my dad paid for a guitar teacher, but honestly, I didn't have the patience. Plus, the neck of the guitar he rented was too big for me to get my fingers around it. I gave up."

He placed my hand on top of his, dwarfed in comparison. "You do have small hands. They're lovely, so delicate and feminine."

I stared at his hands, his long and slender fingers. Those hands that had proven to be so skilled at making me writhe until I was out of my mind. I wanted—no, needed to feel them touching me again.

"Stay here while I'll get us some wine," he said, releasing my hand. He moved across the hardwood floor to the wet bar. With a click of a remote, the lights dimmed, and soft, ethereal music drifted through the room. The confidence in his stride as he moved toward me made me squirm in my seat.

In an instant, the sight of his naked body standing on the edge of the yacht flashed through my mind, along with about a dozen other images. The way he had been so gentle yet at times had overwhelmed me with a power I'd never experienced with any man. Suddenly, my insides turned molten.

"Here, I think you'll like this. It's one of my favorite cabernets." I was already flushing, or hot flashing, when he handed me the glass. No doubt, the wine would make it worse. With the first sip, the complex, rich flavor poured over my tongue, and I didn't care about flushing anymore.

"This is delicious."

Our eyes locked, and the room blurred, blocking out everything except the man who gazed at me with intention. He leaned in, grazing the sides of my face with his fingers, his thumb skimming the ridge of my bottom lip. Slowly, he brought his face close, his breath warm on my cheek. My lips parted, and I absorbed the heady scent of him as my eyelids fluttered shut. I barely breathed, waiting while his mouth trailed against my skin. The anticipation built until finally, I lunged for his mouth, and… our teeth clanged with so much force, I felt it reverberate through my jaw.

"Ouch!" We said in unison, hands flying to our mouths.

"Is your tooth okay?"

He felt around with his fingertip. "I think so. Yours?"

"It's fine. I'm sorry," I moaned. "Guess I got a little excited. Let's slow it down."

"No, your enthusiasm is great. Okay, get ready. I'm going to kiss you."

That did it. I doubled over with laughter. Tears streamed down my face; my arms wrapped around my aching stomach muscles. He joined me, and then we were rolling around on the couch, half laughing, half aroused.

"You… should… have… seen… your… face."

"Oh, God. Please warn me next time," he said, his laughter trickling down to a chuckle. "I do love the way you kiss me." He pulled me in close, looking more aroused than amused now. "We're usually extremely good at it. You have the softest lips, so full and sensuous." He ran a fingertip across my bottom lip, and then his mouth sealed over mine, proving his point. Thank God.

A smile lifted the corners of his lips, then he kissed me again, and again—until we were shifting on the couch, every inch of his hard body pressed against mine, only pausing when he set our wine glasses on the coffee table.

I heard the sound of my voice moaning, our arms and legs tangling, Ryan pinning me under his weight. But the next sound I made wasn't what either of us expected. The yelp I let out sent him reeling back.

"What? What happened?"

"Your elbow is pulling my hair."

"Oh, sorry," he mumbled, adjusting his position. "How about we move to someplace more comfortable?"

I blinked. "I'm not sure how long I should stay, since I didn't even bring a toothbrush with me." My voice sounded altogether shaky and unconvincing. "Does this still feel... right to you?"

We were back in the real world, not encased in a vacation bubble, and things seemed different. Different good or different bad, I wasn't sure. Yet, I had promised him I wouldn't run.

"Stay with me this weekend. I have an extra toothbrush somewhere, and we can get you a change of clothes tomorrow. Give us time to adjust to the changes, please."

If the resolute way he looked at me wasn't enough persuasion, the tips of his fingers were stroking my shoulders, then circling the crest of my breast. I leaned into his touch, and my head rolled back as he planted kisses down the curve of my neck.

"Hmm... you have a point. But..."

Ryan stopped. Dammit. I needed to make up my mind. He tipped my chin with a finger, turning my face to his.

"What's wrong? Tell me."

"I could get used to this. I mean... you have a way of seducing me that makes leaving difficult. What if I like this—you—a little too much?"

He stared at me.

Okay, let's try this again. I took a deep breath and rambled on. "I'm not sure I can continue to do this with you and stay... detached."

"Who's detached? I'm pretty certain our connection has been growing, especially since the day on the yacht." He leaned forward, elbows resting on his knees, his fingers steepling over his face, thinking. "I'm skilled at a lot of things, but sometimes I suck at comprehending the emotional language of women."

I couldn't help laughing, though I did feel bad I'd confused the poor guy. "You're a man. It's a standard competency deficiency."

He pretended to swat my leg. "Give me a break here. I'm trying."

"And I'm not doing a great job communicating. Maybe we just need some time to reconnect in our new environment. And most likely, I should stop overthinking this. But I'm still not sure what this is now."

"Come," he said, taking my hand and leading me to the bedroom. "I want to hold you, and that damn couch isn't cooperating."

Ryan adjusted a switch, and the lights dimmed while I climbed on the bed. It felt so soft, like floating on a cloud. Ryan was on his back, both arms wrapped around me as I nestled into him. For a while, I listened to his breathing and the ethereal music playing softly through the speaker. I kept my eyelids shut tight, except when I peeked at him to see if he had his eyes closed. He did.

His fingers intertwined with my hair, delicately allowing each strand to glide through them in a rhythmic motion. I inhaled the scent of him the way one does when sniffing a glass of wine before the first sip, savoring the layers of oak with an undertone of spice and something uniquely Ryan. He smelled familiar... comforting. And at once, I knew we would be okay.

A low purr came from deep within his chest as he nuzzled my cheek with his stubbled chin... and then his lips were on mine, causing the most delicious sensation to trickle through me. I didn't want to think or evaluate anymore—I just wanted him.

Shifting, my legs straddling his hips, I unbuttoned his shirt and let my palms slide against his skin, while my eyes drank in the sight of him. My fingertips outlined the muscles in his chest... then the ridges of his cut abs... and down the trail of wispy hairs until I reached his pants.

I was struggling with the buttons on his fly when his hands replaced mine, easily ripping them open. Our gaze locked while he shrugged off his shirt, then his pants.

I sat on the bed and leaned back, grinning up at him. "You left me the easy part." My mouth went dry as I hooked my thumbs on the elastic and tugged. A ragged sound escaped me, and if I could've formed words, I might have told him just the sight of his body nearly brought me to tears. The beauty of him was overwhelming, and tantalizing as hell.

"My turn." His voice, deep and seductive, sent shivers across my skin. He disrobed me with ease, unfastening my bra with an impressive one-handed maneuver. A low growl rumbled in his chest as his gaze landed on my breasts, grasping them in his palms before lowering his face. At the warmth of his mouth, I unraveled, the sensation fanning down my belly. I rolled my hips, inviting his fingers to strip off the last of my clothing.

"Sofia…" His whisper caught on my lips, the heat of his skin pressed against mine setting off a wildfire, and every inch of me literally burned for him. Reason and doubt disappeared. All I could think of was what I wanted to do to him. How the weight of his body descending on mine gave me the luscious sensation of powerlessness, of being taken.

We moved as one, our bodies tumbling across his massive bed, all hands and lips and heat. And oh, the delicious, sweet taste of him laced with wine. The pad of his finger skimmed over the curve of my hip. My fingers curled in his dark hair, and I arched my body into him, rising and falling in perfect rhythm.

It didn't matter if his elbow pinned my hair again or if I grew sore in tender places. I became lost in my desire for this man. Lost in the sheer strength of him, the way he flipped me over with a toss of his hand. Lost in his eyes, the way they could see my every emotion and anticipate my every need.

Thoughts tangled in my mind, and words slipped out of me in breathy gasps before I could stop them. "I definitely like you too much."

His hands wound in my hair, his lips soft against the base of my throat, and the sigh he made rushed straight to my heart. When he lifted his gaze to mine, the look in his eyes split me open. "I knew I was going to like you too much the night we met. I wasn't wrong."

It was several hours later before we lay panting and spent. My body, limp and sore, draped over him. I rested my head on his chest, listening to the sound of his heartbeat returning to normal, my gaze transfixed by the glow of the candles on the dresser. The cool breeze billowing through the sheer curtains sent an involuntary shiver across my skin.

"Are you cold?"

I curled myself around him and nodded against his skin. Enveloping me in his arms, he held me close while he bent and reached for the fallen bedding. My thoughts swirled, memories of the last several hours chasing themselves in hot circles. I couldn't remember ever having sex like this, each time better than before. No doubt, this was a slippery slope. The thought of leaving his side was incomprehensible now.

"Hey," he said softly. "You okay? You're awfully quiet."

I tilted my head to look at him. "I'm fine, just a little amazed—maybe confused."

His eyes narrowed. "I get the amazed part. I'm blown away too at how we are together." He blew out a breath and ran a hand over his stubbled jawline, then shifted so he was facing me. "But why confused?"

My brain was still mush from the whirlwind, and I scrambled to find the words. Finally, I let out a long exhale. "I'm not so good with the unknown, the unpredictability. I'm really trying to live in the moment, but... it's like being on the most amazing ride at Disneyland, one you want to stay on and get in line over and over again. I'm not talking about the, It's a Small World ride, I'm talking about the Indiana Jones ride. But you know the park will close sometime, and those Mickey Mouse guards are going to throw you out."

At first, he looked at me like I was speaking an unfamiliar language—which I was, because it was the language from a female brain. But realization quickly dawned on his face.

"Now that you mention it, being with you is kind of like the Indiana Jones ride. There definitely is a lot of screaming." An adorable, playful grin erupted on his lips. Then he leaned down and kissed my forehead. "Sofia, the park reopens 365 days a year, so you can always go back for more. I'm certainly not going to throw you out. In fact, I'm giving you unlimited season passes."

I rolled my eyes. The metaphor was working better than I thought it would. "You know what I mean. Just promise me one thing."

"What?"

"Promise you won't ghost me. We haven't known each other for long, but this became intense fast. If you have something on your mind, just tell me. I'm a big girl."

An unexpected, incredulous look flashed across his features. "Why would I? If anything, I should be asking you not to ghost me. You were the one playing hard to get."

"Yeah, well, now that you have me…"

He placed a finger on my lips. "Shush. No ghosting allowed between us. If you think I'm that kind of guy, you don't know me well enough yet. Don't you realize how happy I am to have you here with me? I want you to stay. In fact…"

He pulled me to him, our bodies pressed together, the heat of his skin causing a tsunami within me. I felt him lengthening against my belly and his lips on mine. I stifled a giggle, trying not to say something cheesy about Indiana Jones.

Chapter Twenty-Four

My eyelids tentatively blinked open, registering the rays of light pouring in through the sheer curtain. I glanced at the clock on the bedside table. Nine o'clock. We'd maybe had four hours of sleep? I looked at Ryan lying next to me and wondered if I'd disturb him if I got up to pee. Besides, I desperately needed that toothbrush before a morning kiss. I gaped at his face; those luscious lips slightly parted with soft breaths. *He must be exhausted and jet lagged*, I thought. Carefully, I slid away from his side and padded quietly to the bathroom.

In bright daylight, the mirror provided a revelation I wasn't prepared to see. My hair was more disheveled than Medusa, and my makeup had smeared, leaving black smudges under my eyes. I searched for lotion and a tissue, then found a brush at the bottom of my purse. Ryan had left a new toothbrush on the counter, thank God. After I'd finished freshening up, I heard a knock and reflexively threw a bath towel around my body, knotting it in the front.

"Can I come in? I really have to pee."

I reached for the brass handle and swung it open. "Don't you have another bathroom in this gigantic apartment?

He rubbed the sleep from his eyes, standing naked in the doorway. "Yes, but this one is closer, and I wanted to do this." His arms captured me, bringing me flush with his body, his lips on mine.

"Mm, good morning to you, too."

"You taste minty fresh," he said, his voice raspy.

"I highly recommend it, and thanks for the toothbrush." I winked at him and motioned him into the bathroom. As I sprinted back to the bedroom, the sound I heard made it clear he hadn't closed the door behind him. I envied the way guys didn't care, while I practically bolt-locked the damn thing.

When he came in and found me sitting on the bed, the towel firmly wrapped around me, he pulled a face.

"What?" I asked.

Then, unexpectedly, he grabbed me by the hand, guiding me until we were positioned in front of a full-length mirror in the corner. Standing behind me, his fingers took hold of the towel and tore it loose, letting it fall to the floor. I looked at my reflection and winced as the bright light revealed the dimpled patches on my thighs, the loose skin on my arms, and the round part of my belly that, despite the crunches, never seemed to flatten.

He pressed his chest against my back, wrapping his arms around my shoulders. "Why the fuck would you want to hide this beautiful body under a towel? I've seen you covering yourself with towels or bed sheets the minute you get out of bed. In case you didn't know, I love seeing all of you."

Is this what I looked like to him? Didn't he notice my flaws? "Far be it from me to argue with a compliment," I said, "but there are parts of me that don't seem exactly beautiful."

In our reflection, I saw the way his eyes scanned my body, taking me in at the same time his fingers traced over my skin. "This part here…" His fingertips skid along the inside of my thigh. "Is so soft. I could nestle my face in these thighs and live there."

I snorted a laugh. "But that part is also saggy."

He ignored me and ran a palm over my belly. "This is one of the most feminine places on your body, and it leads to this…" His fingers dipped between my legs and I let out a gasp, which abruptly became a disappointed moan when his hands abandoned that spot, sliding up my torso. In our reflection, I watched as he palmed my breasts, a look of adoration splashing across his features. "And these beauties drive me insane, so full and round and soft."

"They used to point up instead of down," I replied, but his hands felt so good… who was I to argue with his appreciation?

"Don't you get it? Perfection is bullshit. We all have things we dislike about our bodies. And I'm glad your breasts hang naturally, not like those fake tits. Nice to admire but much less personal to feel… and hold." He was rolling my nipples between his thumb and forefinger, sending ripples of intense heat down to my core.

Just as my breathing became ragged, he reached down and grabbed my butt with both hands. "And we haven't even gotten to how this round ass makes me want to—"

"Okay, okay. I get your point. Women judge themselves harshly, and a good part of that is because we compare ourselves to supermodels, thinking that men want those kinds of bodies."

"Some guys are superficial, and all males are visual. We might gawk at those model types, but when it comes to getting down to it—it's about the person we're in bed with—at least for me. I love more than your body. I love the way you respond to my touch—the feeling of your soft skin brushing against mine—how you sense what I like, and... how our rhythm falls in sync. I love seeing you naked, not because you're just some random body but because of the way you make me feel when we're together."

My chest rose with a breath, my heart doubling in size with... love? Nope, it was gratitude. It had to be just gratitude.

I stared at my reflection. Instead of focusing on the saggy bits, I saw the parts of me I liked—and then, the entirety of me. I smiled at him in the mirror. "Okay, no more covering up. You want naked? I'll give you naked all day long, dude."

The look in his eyes turned smoldering hot. He swiftly maneuvered me back to the bed... then proceeded to show me just how much he liked my parts.

"So…" I said in my sexy, afterglow voice while stroking a line down his chest with the tip of my finger, "what are we doing today?"

He drew me in tighter with his arm wrapped around my waist. "First, we're cooking breakfast."

"We? I assumed guys did breakfast."

"Ah, but this is a joint project—a bonding experience."

"Um… I think we bonded very nicely already."

"Good point. And yes, we did. More than nicely." He rolled onto his side and faced me. "Sofia, I don't know what you are doing to me, but please don't stop. It's incredible being with you."

I ran my hand through his tousled hair and gazed back at him, wondering how, in all these years, I'd never found a man like him. "I won't stop if you don't."

"Deal. Now, what do you want for breakfast?"

"I usually eat light, but for some reason, I'm starving this morning," I said, jabbing his side with my elbow.

"Me too. Omelets? It happens to be my specialty."

"Would you make me a cafe con leche the way they do in Spain? God, miss those."

"I believe my machine can manage it." He was on his feet, pulling open a drawer. "I can't wait to see you in sexy lingerie, but this will have to do for the time being." He tossed a dark-blue t-shirt on the bed, leaning in with a quick kiss.

I pulled it over my head; the shirt falling softly over my thighs, and breathed in the smell of him—the scent now burned into a primitive part of my brain. There was something so seductive about the way a man smelled—masculine pheromones. Oh, how I'd missed that during my endless relationship drought.

"As much as I enjoy wearing your clothes, I'll need to go back to my place to shower and grab a change. What's the plan for today?" I asked again, scooting onto a stool.

Ryan slid a steaming cup of coffee with milk across the tall table. "How would you feel about seeing a Barca game? Some of my friends are getting together at a sports bar to watch it on the big screens."

"What's a Barca game?"

He set the pan on the gas stove, spun around, and leveled an incredulous stare at me. "What's a Barca game? Woman, how long were you in Barcelona? They are world famous for their soccer, or futbol, as they call it."

Blanching a little, I confessed, "I have to tell you, I'm not much of a sports fan, but I'd be happy to go with you." I raised the cup to my lips, purring. "Mmm." It came pretty darn close to the coffee in Spain. "Hey, if it's about Barcelona, I'm in. Sounds like fun." As an afterthought, I added, "Would it be okay to invite Madison? Maybe she can bring her new boyfriend."

"Of course. It would be nice to meet her." He slid a plate to me; a perfectly formed egg omelet, then kissed my cheek. "Bon appétit."

Sometime later, after dissuading him from throwing me back on the bed, I managed to climb into my clothes. I called Madison on my way home in the Uber.

"Sure, I don't have any plans for today, and I'm dying to check out Ryan."

"Do you want to see if Roger can come?"

"Wait a minute. I'll ask him."

"He's with you now?" I laughed. "I guess we're both having a busy weekend."

His response boomed through the speaker. "Watching sports on a Sunday? Babe, you're my dream girl."

Madison giggled. "We're in. Text me the details when you get home."

"Will do." I touched the screen to end the call, wondering if this was moving too fast. Meeting each other's friends was next level relationship stuff—the thought was more than a little unnerving. Were we in a relationship? The definition was still unclear, although neither of us planned on seeing anyone else. How would Ryan's buddies react to seeing us together—to him dating an older woman? I only hoped a two-hour window would give me enough time to do a beauty makeover that would shave off a few years.

Ryan's text popped up as I was pulling into Sam's Bar and Grill, telling me he was already inside. He'd offered to pick me up, but I'd declined, and since this bar was outside the center of town, I was sure to find parking in the lot. If he came to my home, I'd feel the pressure to clean when, really, I had to stay focused on getting ready. Turns out, I'd needed every second of those two hours, most of it spent in my closet plucking clothes off hangers, then checking myself in the mirror. My bed was littered with rejects by the time I walked out the front door, and my head throbbed from anxiety.

But as my car pulled into the lot, I had convinced myself (mostly) I had nothing to worry about. I'd settled on my butt-lift jeans (which, I determined after some contortionist moves to check my backside, didn't make my ass appear enormous), and a racer-back t-shirt, which flattered my curves and broad shoulders. Boots and a black leather jacket topped off the outfit for that carefree, badass look.

A knot tightened in my chest as I swung open the door and scanned the room for Ryan, surprised to find the restaurant jammed to capacity. I never understood the immense popularity of sports, yet seeing this crowd literally on the edge of their seats waiting for the next game-changing move, I suspected I was in the minority.

Granted, the bar was filled mostly with men, some wearing their team's t-shirt bearing a logo of either Barca or Real Madrid. The air was thick with the odor of beer and fried food. The crowd erupted into cheers as the announcer's voice poured through the five screens. Barca had apparently scored a goal. At least I knew it was a goal, not a touchdown, but beyond that, I was completely lost.

I hadn't moved from the doorway when I caught sight of Ryan standing, waving his arm high in the air. When I squeezed through the maze of tables and reached for his outstretched hand, he gently pulled me into a hug. This one gesture instantly eased my anxiety several notches.

His voice rose above the din with an introduction. "This is Sofia." Three faces nodded in my direction. Almost imperceptibly, the men's eyes widened simultaneously. "Sofia, this is Raul, Johnnie, and Sam."

I barely managed a quick "Hi, good to meet you" before the guys were back on their feet, laser-focused on the screen. I used the moment to study the three men.

Sam, a Black man roughly Ryan's height, had the broad shoulders and unhurried movements of someone built like a linebacker—powerful but gentle, with an easy smile that came naturally. Raul's spiky haircut framed warm caramel-toned skin, and his lilting Spanish accent reminded me of the dancers I'd met at salsa clubs—lean and quick-moving, with friendly, alert eyes. Johnnie looked like he'd stepped out of a college brochure—clean-cut blond hair, trimmed neat on the sides—until you noticed the intricate tattoo sleeves winding up both arms, telling a different story entirely.

All three appeared to be about Ryan's age. When the scene settled down, Ryan motioned for me to sit in the chair next to him.

"The match began a half hour ago," he explained, "and as you can see, it's a night game in Barcelona. Barca already scored a goal against Real Madrid. They're bitter rivals and have been battling it out for years."

I stared up at the screen with an irrepressible grin. He added, "They're playing at Camp Nou, on the outskirts of town."

There it was—the city that had captured my heart. Spending Sunday afternoon in a sports bar just got a lot more interesting. "Go Barca!" I raised a fist in the air. "Is that what you say? Or is there some special cheer for soccer?"

A laugh burst out of his lips, spraying a fine mist of beer on my jeans. He grabbed a napkin and patted down my leg. "Ah, that's my girl. You can cheer however you like, as long as it's for our team." His gaze trailed off to the bar where servers were filling their trays. "Let me get you a drink. Is a beer okay?"

'My girl.' It had a nice ring. "Of course... a hefeweizen, please."

Then it was just me and his friends, and with a lull in the action on the screen, an awkward silence fell over the four of us. The sweat pooling in my armpits threatened to drench my shirt. I considered slipping back into my leather jacket, but given the temperature in the bar, I'd look like a crazy person.

Sam broke the ice, his voice gentle, inquisitive. "Ryan mentioned you two bumped into each other on the plane. How did you like your first trip to Barcelona?"

"Loved every minute. It's probably my favorite city in Europe. Barcelona is the kind of place you can lose yourself in and no matter how much you explore, it will still surprise you." Beneath the table, I ran a sweaty palm down the leg of my jeans. "Have you been there?"

"Yes, several times. I have to agree with you." He smiled at me then, and there wasn't a trace of the scrutiny I expected to find. "I travel a lot. Ryan and I work together, but Barcelona is one of the most chill places to visit."

On my right, I sensed Raul's and Johnnie's eyes on me. I plastered a smile on my face and casually shifted toward them.

"Do you speak Spanish?" Raul asked.

"Very little, I'm afraid, but the Spanish I learned in college came back to me in bits and pieces while I was there. The basics are useful to a point, but I'll need to brush up, maybe take lessons."

Silence. A pause in the conversation wasn't a good sign. I rambled, filling the empty space, the words spilling out of me like I was pumped up on five Red Bulls. "You would think I'd be fluent, given that I listen to salsa music all the time. I catch some expressions in the songs but can't piece together the meaning. And of course, we live in California, where they speak Spanish almost as often as English, and I have many Latino friends."

Johnnie piped up. "You dance salsa?" Skepticism oozed from a smile that wasn't a smile at all. He might as well have said, "You just had a baby?" This guy immediately sent my hackles rising.

"Yes, for a few years now. I took classes here in San Francisco from a fantastic teacher." By the expression on their faces, I'd caught all of them off guard. "What I love about salsa is the friendly atmosphere. People come to enjoy the dance and socialize. A lot of my friends are from that world." Raul was smiling now, and I got the sense his first impression might be changing, the needle shifting from maybe to yes. "Do you guys dance?"

Sam raised a finger. "It's hip hop for me."

"I can get down to that music, but it tends to be all about the bumping and grinding in the clubs," I replied.

He nodded in agreement, then Raul chimed in. "I dance salsa, but I'm from Columbia. We do it a little differently there."

"There is a difference, I agree. I'm accustomed more to Puerto Rican style, which I guess migrated through the States to New York and Los Angeles." This was progress, finally.

"Not me," Johnnie declared emphatically. "I'm way too white to risk bustin' a move." The other two burst out laughing. "You know, Ryan doesn't dance much, either." His tone, the message behind the words, sent off warning bells.

"Oh, he can if he wants to. I got him out in a club in Barcelona, but it was house music, so nothing too technical." Take that, Johnnie know-it-all.

Just then, Ryan set a beer on the table in front of me. "Here, babe, it took forever since the bar was stacked. Did I hear you outing me?"

"Johnnie says you don't dance, but I think you've been holding back on your friends."

"Hah. Don't overestimate me in that department."

I raised an eyebrow and lowered my voice to a whisper. "You can't be perfect at every single thing. It wouldn't be fair."

He fixed me with a hot, penetrating look. I half expected him to kiss me right there in front of the guys.

Madison's squeal broke in, killing our moment, a cascade of braids fanned my cheek as she dipped her head next to mine. "Finally! We had a hard time spotting you. This place is a zoo. I never dreamed soccer was so popular."

Roger stood beside her, and despite her five-inch heels, he still made her look short. I saw the appeal; he was a unicorn among dating profiles. A handsome black guy who, by the size of his imposing frame, may have been a football player in his youth. She hadn't mentioned his age, but I guessed him to be in his early forties. She was beaming.

"Madison, this is Ryan." I gestured with my palm. "And you must be Roger. Hi, I'm Sofia."

"So pleased to meet you, Sofia. Madison says you two are besties." He lifted a brow in my direction. The men exchanged a firm handshake. Ryan introduced his friends while she and I traded a nuanced glance, layered with questions already percolating.

"Have a seat, you guys. We saved a couple of chairs," Ryan said.

"What's the score?" Roger asked Ryan, but his eyes swept around the group.

"It's still one to zero, Barca," Ryan answered. "They scored in the initial twenty minutes, but things have slowed down. Do you follow soccer?"

While Roger explained that although he liked the game, football was his passion, having been a middle linebacker in college. Ryan revealed he'd also played college football. Because, of course he had. It was evident in his build, but while Ryan was lean and muscular, Roger had a bulkier frame.

When I peered around Ryan, I saw his friends had shifted their focus to the screens. Madison sat next to me and, across from her, our guys were reminiscing about their football days. To my relief, the conversation flowed as though we were two couples who'd known each other for ages. We only paused long enough to check the action on the screen, the crowd erupting into a frenzy when a goal was in sight.

While the guys were distracted, Madison nudged me with her elbow and said into my ear, "I approve of Ryan. You're worried, I get that. He's young. Despite the number, he has an air about him, as if he has an old soul. And I can see the way he looks at you. He likes you—a lot. His eyes go all glassy with a warm and fuzzy expression when he thinks nobody is watching. Like a puppy dog."

"I trust your instincts. It's a relief, because I like him—a lot. Too much, I'm sure."

"What about his friends?" she asked, throwing a glance at the guys. They were chugging their beers, completely engrossed in the screens.

I sucked in a breath between my teeth. "It wasn't easy, but I might have won over two of the three. I wonder what they're going to say to Ryan during the post-game debriefing when I'm out of earshot."

"I'm not sure it will make a difference to him either way."

"Don't underestimate the power of friends. Look at you and me. We pretty much rely on each other's judgement to keep us headed in the right direction."

Madison snorted a laugh. "But they're guys. They give a one sentence comment and lose interest. Then it's on to sports, business, whatever. They're not worried about who's dating who."

I kept my voice low when the round of cheers died down. "Roger seems like a good guy. You may be on to something there. And he's definitely hot."

She grinned, and we realized the guys were no longer watching the screens—they were tuning into our conversation, their eyes pinning us both simultaneously.

Roger leaned back in his chair and crossed his arms against his broad chest. "Ryan, if I know women—and I think I do, insofar as a man can know women—it's a pretty safe assumption they're talking about you and me."

Ryan's gaze bored into me like a laser, only uttering, "Hmm." I held his stare and upped the game, shooting him a hot, smoldering look. His eyebrow rose in response. I raised mine, adding a wry smile. We didn't need to speak a word, yet it was as if we'd had an entire conversation.

Madison responded to Roger with a wink and a Cheshire cat grin, cooing at him. "Only good things, baby. Don't worry." She climbed into his lap, curling her arms around his neck. I'd never seen her appear so happy. Her face lit up with a smile, radiating delight in her eyes. I wondered if my face looked the same when Ryan was nearby.

A tall blond server in a short jean skirt squeezed between tables and fixed her gaze on Ryan. "Can I get you guys anything?" she asked, not bothering to disguise the flirtatious lilt in her voice. I couldn't blame her for staring; he was hard to resist. Either he didn't notice or was used to female attention, because he barely glanced at her. His eyes landed softly on me and said, "Babe, do you want another beer?"

"I'm good, thanks."

Surprising myself, I curled into his shoulder, placed my hand on his thigh and stroked the length of his hard muscle. Everything about my body language screamed, back off, he's mine. She shot a look in my direction, like she'd only just noticed me—right there by his side. I wasn't certain if her wide-eyed expression revealed a stab of shock or disappointment. But there was no mistaking Ryan's response. His lips twisted in a wry smile, as though he knew exactly what I'd done, and he approved. Keeping his eyes trained on me, he muttered, "I'll take another beer."

"We'll have two beers, please," Roger called out. "And throw in an order of nachos."

She pointed to the guys. "Another round?"

Sam and Raul shook their heads, looking glassy eyed now. "No thanks."

Johnnie didn't take his eyes off the screen, oblivious to the server's question. I wondered how many he'd downed before I arrived because I was pretty sure I saw him miss his mouth more than once, beer dripping down his shirt.

Johnnie got up, stumbling around tables on his way to the bar. Ryan's gaze followed him. Then he was on his feet. "I'll be right back."

I kept my eyes peeled on Ryan, his brows knitting together with that worried look I knew well. But that quickly changed as they faced off in a heated conversation. Ryan's expression abruptly shifted, his jaw clenching, the muscles in his neck vibrating, his eyes shooting fierce daggers. Johnnie was doing most of the talking, and between the alcohol and his arms flailing in the air, he lost balance more than once.

I tapped Madison's leg twice with my index finger—our signal for pay attention now. A subtle chin nod toward the chaos, eyebrows raised. What the hell is going on over there?

She angled slightly toward me, studying the scene. Her jaw tightened, nostrils flared. Then came the slow head shake, her lips pressed thin—code for, there's some bad shit going down.

Finally, she slipped off Roger's lap and sat next to me again. I whispered, "Johnnie is the one who doesn't approve of me. Do you think they're fighting about me?"

Madison leaped into action before I could stop her. She sauntered close to the bar behind Ryan, presumably on her way to the restroom. But since Ryan had his back turned—and Johnnie was too drunk to recognize her—she was in.

My gaze stayed glued on Ryan, biting off my fingernails. What if he discovered Madison's covert mission? Waving my hand, I gestured for her to come back. She shook her head. Oh God, this was really bad. I nodded my head emphatically. She ignored me. I could feel my heartbeat thumping faster, my neck pulsing.

Ryan turned, spotting Madison, but she casually strolled away, disappearing into the restroom. I jumped up, walked past him, and in an oh-so-casual tone, told him I was going to the bathroom.

"Seriously? Are we in high school?" I screeched once I was inside.

"Whatever." She yanked me into a stall. "You need to hear this. There's good news and bad news."

"Oh, God." I lowered the toilet lid and sat down.

"The bad news is, Johnnie was giving Ryan a hard time for dating… and I quote, a cougar. He used the term MILF too, in a particular context, but I'd rather not repeat it. He warned Ryan that while he might be having fun now, in a few years, you'd be all dried up… like a prune." She tapped her nails against the metal door while she thought. "Oh yeah, he said Ryan was ruining his future… something about growing the fuck up if he wanted to have a family."

My head dropped into my hands, a muffled "Fuck" escaping my lips. "What's the good news?" I moaned.

"Well, Ryan basically told him to go fuck himself—that his life was no business of Johnnie's, and if Johnnie couldn't support his decisions, their friendship was done. Oh, and Ryan is a sweetie. He said you are the best thing that's ever happened to him, and he likes you because you're different from other women."

My eyes peeked at Madison. "Is that all?"

"More or less. I pretty much got the gist of the conversation. Sofia, it doesn't matter what his friends think. It only matters what Ryan thinks."

"Yes, but I'm not sure I can handle the pressure." I stood, wiped my sweaty palms on my jeans, then body-slammed her with a hug. "Thanks. If you ever consider changing careers, the CIA could use your skills. Just sayin'."

"Sadly, I've had a lot of experience in this area."

Ryan and Roger shot us a questioning stare when we returned. We shrugged in unison, our poker faces revealing nothing. They didn't ask questions, because like a woman's purse, the ladies' restroom was sacrosanct. To men, what went on in there was a mystery better left to the imagination. When I scanned the table, Johnnie was noticeably absent.

When the teams took a break, the men dissected the game; the conversation a blur of players' names, stats, and predictions about the outcome of the season. Madison's eyes glazed over, and I was sure I wore the blank look of a zombie. Ryan noticed something was off, asking me if I was okay. I made up an excuse—saying he'd worn me out—which he bought, since we'd barely slept. I didn't tell him my worries about what Johnnie had said.

Barca won in the end, scoring another goal within the last few minutes. The crowd went wild, with men yelling and fist pumping the air. Roger got doused with an entire beer when an enthusiastic college kid fell back in his chair. Understandably, Madison and Roger were the first to leave, followed by Ryan's friends.

His arm casually draped over my shoulder as he walked me to the car. It amazed me that, in such a short time, we'd come to feel so comfortable with each other—so affection-ate.

"I'll call you tomorrow." He ran a hand through his hair, grimacing. "I expect to have a busy week catching up. Are you going job hunting?"

"I almost forgot. I'm jobless. Wish I could stay in vaca-tion mode indefinitely." My body slumped, my head thud-ding squarely in the middle of his chest. I wrapped my arms around the width of his back. "Thank you for today, and last night, too."

"Oh, babe, thank you. I had the best weekend." He bent and kissed my forehead. Every part of me wanted to stay locked in his embrace. I tilted my face, probing those blue eyes, looking for a hint of what he might be feeling. But fatigue, and maybe work stress, settled over them like a cloud. His lips sealed over mine in one last kiss.

"Next weekend, I'll plan another surprise," he promised, releasing my hand.

"Ryan, please. You don't have to play tour guide here. Let's just hang out."

"Shut up." His kiss silenced me for the moment. "We will hang out, but I like doing special things for you."

I didn't have a comeback for that. Madison would tell me I should enjoy all the moments with him and make them count. But in the back of my mind, I was afraid to get accustomed to feeling so... special.

When we broke apart, I pointed my keys at my car, the lock popping in response.

He swung around and called out, "I like Madison, by the way, she's a character. And Roger's a cool guy. I'm glad you invited them."

"Me too," I agreed but didn't mention his friends and wondered if we'd ever get the chance to have that conversation. I lingered before climbing in, stealing one last peek at him as he slid into the sleek, gray BMW sports car. As soon as the engine fired up, I already missed him.

Chapter Twenty-Five

T he engine purred, a low rumbling sound that vibrated the seat. I glanced at Ryan's bicep—the way it flexed when he shifted gears—realizing how much I'd missed him this week. He kept his promise to surprise me. Maybe he planned this weekend trip to maintain our perpetual vacation bubble, just as we'd begun, but we couldn't live like this for much longer. Could we?

The week had vanished in a blur of avoided job searches and neglected responsibilities. Instead, I'd tackled the junk drawer in the kitchen, reorganized closets, and collected items for Goodwill—all the tasks I'd ignored while working. The garage project loomed like a months-long sentence. Dentist appointments, car maintenance, bills—they all waited. Even with the severance cushioning me, I'd need to get back to reality eventually.

"You look happy," Ryan said, glancing over at me.

"Your fault entirely." I squeezed his thigh, unable to suppress my grin. "I've loved the Monterey Peninsula since I was a teenager. This will be perfect."

His behavior hadn't shifted after the fight with Johnnie—if anything, he'd grown more attentive, texting throughout his workday. Still, Johnnie's words had burrowed into my brain like splinters. Eventually, we'd need to excavate that conversation. But not this weekend.

Ryan took the exit for downtown Monterey, then navigated to the pier. The moment we stepped onto the boardwalk, the aroma of steaming clam chowder thick with cream and herbs enveloped us. We sampled our way through vendors before settling into a restaurant for bowls served in hollowed sourdough rounds. If I could eat only one thing for eternity, it would be fresh-baked sourdough bread. The tangy scent alone made my mouth water before I tore off the first crusty chunk. It was my secret indulgence. On occasion, I'd been known to arrive home with only the empty paper wrapper in my grocery bag.

Ryan watched the giant sea lions throwing their two-ton bodies over one another on the wooden pier below while bellowing out throaty barks. I watched him; the way his blue eyes resembled the color of the deep, azure waters. Noticing for the millionth time how handsome he was, the sharp lines of his jaw, the way his dark eyelashes curved up almost to his eyebrows, and how the wind had tousled his thick black hair into perfect curls.

Further down the rugged coast, we strolled along the sandy path flanked by windswept cypress trees on one side, the ocean on the other. I pointed out the Victorian bed-and-breakfast where I'd spent my honeymoon, explaining it hadn't really been a honeymoon at all.

"Honestly? Your husband didn't do that. You must be joking."

"Oh yes, he did. Since his family had traveled from the east coast for the wedding, he thought it was only right to have them come to Monterey with us, considering they hadn't visited there before." I shook my head. We both stopped to stare at the delicately trimmed green and white bed-and-breakfast across the street, wedged between multi-million-dollar residential homes with a waterfront view. "They didn't stay at this same inn, but we did see them every single day."

He looked at me incredulously. "Some honeymoon."

"Unfortunately, the start of the marriage was pretty much an indication of how things would go. The priority list began with his work, then his family, and down at the bottom, I tried to squeeze in." Even as I spoke, I realized my years of experience had taught me what I wanted in a relationship. Now, I'd never agree to settle for coming in last.

"Is that why you divorced him?" His eyes probed mine, his steps halting on the path. "You don't have to talk about it if you don't want to."

"It's been a long time since I've thought about my divorce." I paused, trying to find the words to describe the slow dissolution of dreams. "It was a mutual decision in the end. To say we fell out of love would be an oversimplification. It was more like cancer, a progressive deterioration that obliterated love and turned us into enemies. I saw it coming, but there didn't seem to be anything I could do to stop it." My gaze fixed on the distant horizon, invaded by memories I would rather keep in the past. "I really did try, you know."

He moved in close, his tall frame blocking the sun's glare, and when I looked up at him, his eyes were soft. "I'm sure you did. From what I've learned about you so far, you aren't someone who gives up on anything without a fight. It's only one of the things I admire about you. And I understand why you'd have your guard up. Divorce must chip away at a person's belief in love."

I nodded. *You don't know the half of it.*

"Okay, enough of our trip down sad memory lane." He laced his fingers through mine while we walked, pausing again when he spotted something in the water. "Can you see the otters? There, just beyond the tidepools."

"Where?"

"Let's get closer." He climbed onto the craggy rocks. I followed, carefully navigating my steps.

"Oh, wow. I see them now." Sleek, black figures bobbed at the surface in the churning ocean. They glided effortlessly through the water, then anchored themselves in clumps of seaweed and floated on their backs while making a meal of freshly caught shellfish. "I could watch these animals all day. Look at those adorable faces. Don't those big brown eyes just melt your heart?"

We perched there until spray from crashing waves soaked through our jackets. He zoomed his camera lens to capture images while recounting stories from his volunteer work at a marine rescue center—the beauty of these creatures, the heartbreak of seeing them injured or sick. As he spoke, I studied his face, listened to the timbre of his voice. His brow furrowed with genuine concern, his voice gentled with compassion. The tenderness in his expression revealed something essential about him.

I had met enough men in my lifetime to identify the ones who had their hearts buried so deep an excavation team couldn't uncover it. Ryan wasn't one of them. He may have guarded it for who knows how long, but at his core, he was a golden retriever—a kindred spirit. This was the man I'd been waiting to find.

The realization unhinged me.

By the time we arrived at our hotel in the hills of Carmel, the sky had darkened, and I was a frigid shade of purple. The wind was whipping the branches of the cypress trees against the window, but inside, our suite was cozy and warm. While Ryan lit the gas fireplace, I ducked into the bathroom.

One glance in the mirror reminded me how I had not been blessed with silky straight hair, impervious to damp sea air.

I cracked the door and called out to Ryan, who was scrolling through the music stations on the TV. "I'm just going to freshen up a bit before dinner. Do we have time?"

"Sure. I haven't made our dinner reservation yet." His gaze swung from the TV and landed on the white towel wrapped loosely around my torso. His eyes gleamed with the look I knew so well, eyebrows twitching suggestively. "Do you mind if I join you?" My body responded to him without hesitation. It was as if his presence, his desire for me, was an irresistible force over which I had no control.

I tilted my chin, and his arms folded me to him. With a twist of his wrist, the towel was on the floor, his fingers tracing my spine. He dipped his head and sealed his mouth over mine, and I was lost in the sweet taste of him.

"You are insatiable," I said. The way his lips nibbled along the curve of my neck sent a wave of goosebumps down my arm.

"Apparently, with you I am."

"You won't hear me complaining."

It turns out showers can be quite fun when you have a beautiful man soaping you down. A stream of water made his caramel skin glisten over the smooth muscles. I let my palms graze over his broad chest, across the sprinkling of fine hair, while his fingers massaged the shampoo into my scalp. I couldn't remember ever having a guy wash my hair, except at the salon. He moved methodically, gently, relaxing me with his touch, then cradled my head under the shower to rinse. Water trickled down my face and mingled in our kiss. This time, I didn't bother to ask if my mascara was running. I was pretty sure it was, but I was beyond caring.

"What do you think about ordering takeout instead of going to the restaurant?" Ryan called out from the living room; a towel wrapped low around his hips.

I slid gratefully into the warmth of the hotel bathrobe, then curled next to him on the couch. "Honestly, I'd love to stay in. Pizza?"

"A bottle of wine and we're set." He tapped his phone's screen. "Pepperoni or veggie?"

"Do they have Hawaiian?"

He groaned. "Seriously? That's not even real pizza."

"You're a food snob. You know that, don't you?" I teased, running my fingers through his wet hair.

"Alright, we'll get two. Problem solved."

"Wow, that was easy. My ex and I would have argued for an hour." It wasn't much of an exaggeration.

"I don't like to argue, Sofia. There's always a better solution than fighting. I saw enough of that growing up to understand anger is no way to handle problems."

I shifted onto his lap and wrapped my arms around his neck. "I've never met a guy like you. It's refreshing. You keep giving me more reasons…"

"More reasons?" He tilted his head, studying me.

I hesitated, trying to decide how much to reveal, then kissed the tip of his nose. "More reasons to like you."

"Believe me, Sofia, you're having the same effect on me." He curled his arms around my waist, bringing me close. "I want to spend more time with you, but I'm just not sure how to manage it."

A twinge of panic clawed at my chest. "What are you saying?"

"I mean—"

The loud knock at the door startled us both.

"It must be the delivery." Ryan rushed to pull on a pair of jogging pants and a sweater while I cleared the coffee table.

"You're sure you don't want a slice of Hawaiian?" I waved the pizza in front of his nose.

"You are persistent." He laughed, and I plopped a piece of pineapple between his lips. "Not bad, without the ham." Ryan retrieved the wine bottle from the bag. I handed him a corkscrew and two glasses. "As I was saying, I want to spend a lot more time with you, but I'm going to be traveling again, first to London." A vaguely distressed look crossed his face as he slid a hand through his hair. "What are your career plans?"

The question yanked me back to reality. "I haven't figured it out. To be honest, I've been less focused since Barcelona. Why?" I tipped the glass to my lips. Admittedly, the wine didn't pair well with my Hawaiian pizza.

"I was just thinking... what if you could come with me? We could travel a bit when I can get away from work and then go back to Barcelona."

I stared at Ryan. Images of the city flashed through my mind like a slideshow of photos. In the seconds of silence piercing the air between us, I pictured us walking the streets of London, or dining at a cafe in Paris. The pictures I conjured were of my dreams. *Dreams don't come true*, I told myself. *And yet...*

"Sofia?"

"Oh, sorry. I was just thinking. It sounds surreal. I mean, I plan to travel, to do something different with my life. It may take some time to adjust to the idea, to see how it might be possible."

"If it's what you want, then I don't doubt you will make it happen. Based on things you've told me, plus what I've observed, you can be one determined lady." Ryan had already finished half his pizza, but I placed my slice back in the box. He studied me while I mulled it over, twisting the stem of the wine glass between my fingers.

Finally, I raised my eyes to meet his. "I would love to go with you."

A smile unzipped on his lips. He pulled me into a delicious kiss, tasting of pepperoni.

Fantasies swirled in my mind, dipping and weaving against backdrops of faraway places. They lingered like background music while I sat on the small sofa, Ryan pouring wine—both of us mesmerized by flickering firelight, my eyes fluttering closed.

"Sleepy?" He slid closer and draped an arm around my shoulders.

Curling my legs beneath me, I nestled into his shoulder and gazed at the flames. He smelled like home now. The feel of his soft sweater against my cheek, the comforting bulk of this man—I wanted to remain tucked in our private cocoon forever.

"A little," I said, tilting my head to look at him. The firelight reflected in his eyes like shimmering pools. I sank into the quiet and listened to the words of a song pouring softly from the speakers. "*You say I am loved... I believe...*" The back of my eyes burned with unshed tears, born from years of longing. I thought about how much I wanted to believe in love again. Ducking from his gaze, I buried my face in his chest. But there was no hiding from him.

"Hey... what?" He lifted my chin with one finger, and those beautiful blues fixed on mine, probing as if his superpower was x-ray vision. A tear escaped from the corner of my eye. How could I explain all that I was feeling, all that I longed for, was wrapped tightly with a rope of fear?

"It's just so good with you. More than I ever expected. Sometimes it takes my breath away."

"Oh, baby." He scooped me onto his lap. "Don't you know what you do to me? I'm in this with you—body, heart, and soul deep."

In the stillness, the look in his eyes stunned me. I wanted to believe. The world fell away, and nothing else mattered because he'd nestled inside my heart. In every way, he was showing me how much he cared—in the gentle look he gave me, as if saying, it's going to be okay, just trust. A powerful gust whistled through the pine trees outside the window; a branch scraped against the glass. It seemed like hours instead of seconds we held an unwavering gaze, silently confessing everything.

Slowly, irresistibly, the sound of soulful love songs drew us in, and we were drifting into uncharted waters. I let myself drown in the melody, in the mingling of our breath, in the passion swelling and crashing over me. I lost myself in his hungry, deep kisses filled with more than want or lust. My heart clenched, and I stifled a sob, rising like a plea. The words of a song ringing in my ears, *"please... don't leave me."*

As he lowered me against the pillowy mattress, his fingers skimmed a line down my belly, then between my thighs—my bare skin prickling with heat, my hips rolling at his touch. Deliberately, inch by inch, he climbed on top of me, my breath becoming more shallow with each movement until I felt the delicious weight of him.

I moaned against his lips, urging him. All at once, he was a force of strength; his arms pressing me to him, possessing me. My spine arching, hands raking down his back as our bodies fused together, moving as one. We sank into the rhythm of the music, a languid pace, and I was freefalling off a cliff; the rush sending me higher each time he pushed into me, and his words, "Oh, my baby, my girl..." landed softly in my ears.

Something unexpected shot through me when he pinned me with his gaze. I saw... something more, something new. Maybe I missed it before, or maybe I hadn't realized what his eyes were telling me. My breath caught with the realization, and I softened into his reflection as fear slipped away.

I am beyond naked. He sees all of me, down to the truth in my soul, and I know, without a shadow of doubt, I don't want to hide anymore.

As if he sensed my release, he paused, hovering above me, a gentle smile breaking across his lips. In one fluid movement, his mouth lunged at mine with a needy sound that resonated deep in my core. A tear silently slid down my temple, and I knew I was his.

Inside the fireplace, only glowing embers remained, casting a dim, golden hue across his bare chest. I lay watching him sleep, my leg slung over his, feeling the solidity of this man. My mind buzzed; a merry-go-round of images and sensations. My skin felt indelibly imprinted by his body, by the luxurious sensation of heat whenever he was near. It was hard to be so close to him and not reach out and touch him. But he looked so peaceful, his mouth slightly parted with soft snoring breaths. I willed time to stop right here, right now, while everything was perfect. I didn't want to worry about tomorrow or next month or next year.

As light as a feather, I grazed his whiskered cheek with the tip of my finger. His eyelids fluttered; his arm reflexively gripping my waist. I forced my eyes shut and let my weight sink into the mattress, relishing every nuance of this moment. My nerve endings still vibrated, only now barely returning to normal. The hairs on his legs tickled against the smoothness of my own. Our scents had mingled during the hot, sweaty sex, and something new emerged—sweet and musky and uniquely us.

Cocooned in his grasp, I felt safe and warm and fulfilled beyond my imagination. Slowly, I relaxed into this welcome comfort—into his arms—until finally, I drifted into sleep.

Chapter Twenty-Six

Morning came far too soon, in my opinion. If I had realized the windows were facing east, I would have closed the blinds last night. *Hindsight*, I thought, then pulled a blanket over my head.

Eventually, Ryan woke me with a kiss and a tray delivered by room service. Propped up on pillows, I gratefully sipped at my coffee and tore off pieces of the croissant while I stole glances at him, sidled up next to me in his black boxer briefs.

"I hate to leave this hotel." The sky beamed bright blue through the open window where Ryan stood on the balcony with his cup of coffee, while I searched for my underwear under the bed. "Found them," I called out.

He sneaked up behind me, making me yelp when he swatted my ass. "Yes, but you are going to love the view from Big Sur."

Pop's greatest hits blared from the speakers while he guided the car through the twists and hairpin turns on Highway 1. The thirty-minute drive on a road which frequently hung precariously on the edge of high cliffs would normally have sent me chewing on my fingernails. But his competent hand at the wheel set me at ease.

In fact, I felt as if nothing could phase me today. I sang along with the tunes (sometimes on key). My cheeks ached from smiling. With the window down, the wind blew my hair in every direction, but not even the prospect of a wild, frizzy mop dampened my mood.

Crossing the Garrapata Creek Bridge, a roadway suspended between cliffs high above the ocean, my heartbeat might have stuttered, but I couldn't resist taking in the spectacle below—the vast, churning blue water crashing on the rocks.

"I don't think I've been here in about twenty years. I'd forgotten how truly amazing the views are."

"Yep, it's a photographer's paradise."

"Nepenthe," I said, reading the sign on the restaurant as we pulled into the parking lot. "I've heard of this place."

"It's the most popular spot in Big Sur. I hope we can get a table." I saw the line extending out the door and wondered the same.

Ryan loped ahead to put us on the list. "They say it will just be fifteen minutes. Believe me, it's worth the wait."

Somehow, it only took five minutes. I couldn't be sure, but I thought I noticed Ryan slipping the hostess a bill, which disappeared in her palm. Miraculously, she called out his name, and we stepped to the head of the line, following her to our table on the patio.

"You weren't kidding. This is breathtaking!" I exclaimed. The tip Ryan gave the hostess must have been generous, because we had seats at a high table which practically hung off the edge of a cliff. In front of us was nothing but the clear blue sky that seemed to dip into the ocean where they joined at the horizon. Giant redwood trees filled the mountain landscape in a deep green forest. Scattered across the wooden deck, pots of brightly colored flowers overflowed with blooms. I couldn't help but get an ionic infused high, the air crisp with the scent of nature and a salty breeze.

Ryan was on his feet, focusing the lens on his camera, the click of the shutter coming in bursts. I watched the muscles in his jaw tighten as he concentrated on capturing the images. But when he tilted the camera to the sky and caught a flock of birds in flight, he whooped like an excited boy who'd just pulled the prize from a box of Crackerjacks. He looked so adorable. I had enough sense to know I was viewing him through a love lens, but damn, it felt too good to stop.

After the server interrupted his photo shoot to get our order, I asked to peek at the pictures. He scrolled through the digital images while I peered over his shoulder.

"The scenery is spectacular here, right? It's my favorite place in California to take photos."

"I can see why," I agreed. "On a worldwide scale, where are your top five places to shoot?" I leaned back in my chair and took a gulp of my beer, lifting my face skyward toward the warmth of the sun.

Ryan counted them off, raising a finger for each one. "Not in any particular order, I would have to say... the Serengeti, Machu Picchu, various spots in Thailand, Vietnam, and... Bora Bora maybe. Of course, there are endless cities in

Europe to capture beautiful scenery, but I'm thinking about nature shots now."

The server delivered our plates decorated with edible flowers. "If you need anything else, just flag me."

"Bon appétit," he said. "Where were we? Oh, yes, it's your turn. So, tell me, if you could go anywhere in the world, give me your top five picks."

I swallowed a bite of the crab sandwich, purring as the rich flavor settled on my tongue, and let my gaze scan the view spanning from the hillside to the gleaming waters. "Just five? Hmm... can I count all of Europe as one?"

He laughed, almost snorting beer up his nose. "No."

"Damn. Okay, I'll name off some places I haven't been, but my priorities are subject to change. Africa, maybe Tanzania? I've always wanted to go on a safari, and after seeing your photographs, I'm even more convinced." My fingers thrummed on the table. "Oh, Costa Rica, because of the wildlife, jungles, and beaches. The Maldives. It's on the top of my list for an island paradise, and the snorkeling there is world renowned. It would be fun staying in one of those bungalows with a glass floor so you can watch the tropical fish swimming below, don't you think?"

He nodded. "That would be cool. Where else?"

I tapped on my forehead until an idea formed. "Hmm. South America. Maybe Columbia? I'm not sure, but I've seen pictures. And..." I pulled at my pinky finger. "Cuba! I would dance my way through the streets of Havana and then stay at one of those beach resorts, drinking rum cocktails." I could sense the energy spiking through my body at the thought of traveling to exotic destinations.

Ryan's face lit up with a wry smile. No doubt because his plan was working. "Good choices. I've been to most of those places, except The Maldives and Cuba."

My brain buzzed with excitement as I returned to my sandwich, chasing a bite with a swig of cool beer. For the first time in a very long while, I allowed myself to dream without seeing the obstacles or finding reasons it wouldn't be possible.

"Of course, Europe would involve another set of at least five places, but I'll have to think about that one."

"You're on a roll. Do you remember me asking you to name the top three things you wanted out of life?"

"Wasn't that when we met on the plane to Barcelona?"

"Exactly, but the flight attendant interrupted our conversation. Did you come up with the list?"

"I can't say my priorities are set in stone. They seem to be shifting. If I'd given you an answer right then, most likely, it would have been totally different from what I'm thinking today." Somehow, I was different now. The trip to Barcelona had changed me, but Ryan had also turned my world inside out.

I took a gulp of beer while ideas percolated in my mind, trying to capture the top three on my list, then set the glass on the table. "One. I'd like to have the freedom to adjust my course—reinvent my career path. The direction is still under construction, but I don't see myself chained to a job in a corporation. Number two is easy. I want to travel—to experience living outside the comfort zone of the States. Barcelona was a wake-up call. The vacation made me remember I always wanted to see the world—to be the adventure seeker I once was."

When I reached number three, I hesitated, unsure how to frame my thoughts. I couldn't make it sound as if I planned to ride off into the proverbial sunset with him. My lips parted while I worked up the courage, my tongue darting in my mouth like a person working a loose tooth.

"Number three. I want... a relationship. I've been essentially single for a long time, so I know life isn't nearly as satisfying when you don't have someone to share it with." I studied his expression for a reaction and didn't see the usual freaked-out look of a man who felt trapped, planning an exit strategy. Instead, he seemed calm and nodded in agreement. So, I rambled on, pretending to play it cool, despite the sweat congealing under my arms, praying he wanted this as much as I did. "Either of us could have made this weekend trip alone, and the spectacular scenery would have been the same. But experiencing it together multiplies the enjoyment. Besides, eating out alone sucks." When I lifted the glass to my lips, the tremor in my hand betrayed me.

"So does having sex alone," he deadpanned.

I laughed but unfortunately, I'd been in the middle of swallowing, which left me coughing and sputtering. Ignoring the burn in my throat, I squeaked out, "You make a good point, although I can think of a few times that were so bad, I would have been way better off to go at it solo."

"Ha, so true." He tucked a strand of hair behind my ear, his hand lingering to cup my face, and gave me that look. It never failed to melt me. "But that's not the case with us."

My heart squeezed. "No. Not at all." I kissed his palm and returned his soft gaze. "Now it's your turn. What are your three things?"

He didn't hesitate on the first one. "To be successful and retire early, giving me the freedom to do as I please. I'm totally onboard with the quest for more adventure."

Number two came fast on the heels of the first. "Ditto on the goal of sharing my life with someone. I'm not convinced marriage is the answer. After all, don't over fifty percent of marriages end in divorce? And my parents certainly weren't happy, so it left me skeptical about relationships. Even so, life is sweeter when you find the right partner." He looked straight into my eyes with such honesty, it made my insides liquify. "I've had my doubts about finding happiness with a woman, but you, Sofia, are quickly changing my perspective."

My heart was doing backflips against my ribcage, but I couldn't let myself dive into expectations. Yet hope was soaring in me like a flock of birds in flight.

Just when I thought he might lean in and kiss me, the server came to our table to check if we wanted another beer. Ryan thanked her but mentioned he was driving. After she left, he took a minute before giving me his third answer.

Finally, he uttered the words I'd dreaded. They fell on me like a boulder, crushing my dreams in one swift blow.

"I want to have kids. To experience parenting a child I helped to make—to create a family life completely opposite of the one I grew up in. If I have the right partner, it might just be possible." He must have noticed my face crumpling, because he added, "I mean, someday, not now. I'm still not ready for the responsibility."

I remained silent, letting the rubble of scattered thoughts crash down around me like broken glass. My head nodded. Absently, I muttered, "Of course. Um. Yes. I totally get it."

Naturally, he would want to have the experience. I certainly had craved having a child, and even though the marriage was rough, I never once regretted it, because having my son was worth everything to me. Ryan deserved this chance. I couldn't stand in his way.

Suddenly, my appetite evaporated. I pushed the half-eaten plate to the side. I didn't look at him; my eyes would divulge too much. Instead, I kept my gaze fixed on the ocean, remarking again about the beauty of this setting. My voice sounding jagged and strained, I rambled about travel and work and things I needed to do when I got home. Anything to distract him from the topic of children. I'm sure he noticed my change in tone, but he didn't redirect the conversation back to our goals, nor did he ask me what I was thinking. I couldn't have told him, anyway.

An uncomfortable silence hung between us as we drove the winding roads, then the freeway leading to my house. Ryan kept the music going, mostly upbeat pop tunes, which prevented me from completely disintegrating. However, it didn't stop my mind from running through the calculations, risk factors, and jumping months—years ahead. Dread and fear were in control again, overriding the happiness I'd found during the best weekend ever. This time, there was no escaping those monsters.

When we were a mile from my house, I knew what I had to do. With precise timing, I waited until I could spot my home down the street before I spoke.

"Ryan, I want to thank you for this getaway. Honestly, I'll never forget it. I need you to know this." My voice sounded detached, formal by design. I bulldozed past the hope, the longing, the warmth that had filled my heart before...

"Why do I sense a but coming?" His arm stiffened as he gripped the wheel, pulling into my driveway.

"There is a but." There was no way to do this without facing him, so I shifted in my seat and steeled myself to look into his eyes. "As much as I want to be, I'm not the right woman for you." His head shot back, and I flinched at the shock in his eyes. "I can't give you what you ultimately need. I can't give you children."

He shook his head as if trying to comprehend this information. "Just hold up. First, who said I needed to have kids anytime soon? And second, I realize it would be late in life for you, but couldn't you still have a kid?"

My chin dipped to my neck. *Oh dear, he doesn't know. But why would he? We never talked about my age.* I avoided the subject at all costs and allowed him to make his own assumptions.

I swallowed hard, then took a deep breath. It was time to confess. "Babe, I'm forty-nine. My baby-making days are history. I'm sorry." I couldn't bring myself to say the word menopause. It conjured up images of shriveled ovaries, sagging skin, and a stamp on my forehead marked "expired."

The news settled over him like fairy dust, and I watched as the particles sifted through his brain, realization slowly dawning on his face. "But... this doesn't change anything, for now."

I had to remain steadfast, my survival depended on it. "But it will change everything. I'm already so invested in you." I pounded a fist on my thigh. "This is why I didn't give you my number in the first place. I could see miles ahead and predicted there would be pain down the road. Dammit." I cursed myself for letting this happen when I knew better. Tears stung the back of my eyes. "It's my fault for not asking you what you wanted sooner. Everything was so perfect. I suppose I didn't want to know."

He started to protest, to make a case, but I wasn't listening anymore. The sound of adrenaline coursing through my veins, the thump, thump, thump pounding in my ears—they blurred everything; a warning that an internal nuclear explosion was imminent. Before he could stop me, I was out of the car, tugging my bag from the back seat.

Before shutting the door, I sputtered out one last apology. "I'm sorry, I just can't do this." As the words left my mouth, my heart plummeted as if I'd fallen from a great height. And, in fact, I had.

Chapter Twenty-Seven

Ryan

"Mr. Hunter, welcome aboard. It's good to see you again. Only London this time, or is it your first stop?"

"I can't say yet. It depends on whether the buyer is interested in the deal my team has proposed."

Right now, I had no desire to run off to Dubai to handle things in person. I wondered if someone on my team could close the deal for me but quickly realized the success of the transaction was based on my relationship with both companies involved. I resigned myself to probably boarding yet another plane but hoped I could stall for a few weeks. The flight attendant handed me the menu, but in truth, I couldn't be less hungry. "Can I give you my order later?"

"Certainly, sir. Would you like a glass of champagne before we take off?"

I nodded, lifted the glass from the tray and placed it on the table, then pulled a copy of the *Wall Street Journal* from my briefcase. Forcing myself to keep my mind focused on work, I scanned the page, checking the stock value of several prospective businesses. The new tech companies I'd been following had shot up since last week. I reminded myself if I didn't stay on top of my game, I might lose a valuable opportunity. This business was too fast paced, too volatile to be distracted.

I glanced out the window, into the darkness. Fog always blanketed San Francisco, but tonight, a storm was gaining speed, raindrops now peppering the glass. The baggage truck swerved toward the plane, its headlights piercing through the heavy gray blanket like two giant, alien eyes. The weather hadn't helped my dark mood this week.

Timing was everything. What if I'd met Sofia a few years earlier? Would it have made a difference? I folded the paper and tossed it on the table. As soon as I closed my eyes, an image of her face appeared, the pain it held last Sunday. I hated seeing her in pain. Losing her was killing me too. It had been a long time since a gnawing sense of loss had hit me in the gut. Not since Jen died. I'd been drowning in quicksand ever since Sofia dropped the bombshell and walked out of my life. None of my usual strategies had worked. I'd been to the gym, hung out with my buddies, signed on for a new project that would up my game at work. Above all, I'd tried to stop thinking about her. Still, a heavy weight pressed on my chest like a constant, dull ache. I couldn't help wondering if it was the same for her. Did she miss me too?

The engine whirred, preparing for take-off. The flight attendant was rushing down the aisle, collecting glasses. An uneasy twinge of uncertainty made me want to head for the exit. *Why am I on this plane headed thousands of miles away from Sofia?* I chugged down the champagne in several gulps as she waited, then handed her the glass.

"Thank you, sir. After we're in the air, I'll bring you a glass of wine. You look like you could use another. Tough week?"

Am I so transparent? "You could say that. Something unexpected came up."

"Well, if you want, we can talk later when it's quiet. I'm a good listener. Possibly I could help, although if it's business, I'm afraid that's significantly above my pay grade. My name is Elaine." She pointed to her name tag, then winked and shot me a provocative smile.

"It's Ryan, please." Intentionally, I flattened my tone. There was no way in hell I wanted to get into a conversation with her.

She nodded, her grin unmistakably growing. She wasn't getting the hint. It had taken me a minute, but now I realized she was flirting. I was off my game, more than a little distracted. My gaze followed her as she strolled to the front of the cabin. Nice body, for sure. Tall, leggy blond. She was okay. Though even if it wasn't for Sofia, I wouldn't find her all that attractive.

But what was my type? What was I looking for? Ticking through my mental Rolodex, I realized it was usually a gut feeling which attracted me to a girl, qualities I couldn't always identify. Sure, I preferred brunettes over blonds—a nice body and a cute face caught my attention. But looks didn't matter if a woman wasn't nice in addition to being sexy. Intelligent as much as fiery. I was checking my list—brains, beauty (admittedly, I had a weakness for breasts), personality... but I knew there was more. I couldn't quite put my finger on it.

Sofia flashed in my mind, and I visualized the sweet smile on her beautiful face. She had every quality I appreciated in a woman. And yet she possessed something surprising—something I never even knew to look for. She connected with all her heart and soul, and it was fucking amazing.

Wait... I squeezed my eyelids shut when the realization hit me. The way she was with me—it wasn't on my checklist because I'd been an expert at avoiding any kind of connection. Fuck my "No freefalling" policy. I could continue to fool myself, but I'd already sailed off that cliff.

Does she love me? I felt it, though she never said the word out loud. She was so damn loving with everyone in her life—Madison, her son... me. And loyalty, that was something you didn't run across often. She'd been a good friend to me, and... Jesus, was I obsessing?

Maybe so, but it struck me that out of all the girls I'd dated, Sofia had been the first one to tick all the boxes. She was the whole package. Images of her hadn't stopped bombarding my brain for days. Looking back, I hadn't been able to get her out of my mind since the night we met. I hadn't understood it then, but I'd sensed she was the one the day we made love on the yacht.

There hadn't been any shortage of women in my life, but I'd never experienced sex like that. It was deep—way deeper than just fucking. *Totally weird, especially for the first time in bed, right?* It was so easy, so natural, to be with her. And the crazy thing was, it kept getting better. Fuck. I wished these thoughts would finally stop.

Elaine motioned me to put on my seatbelt and I buckled in while she stood in the center of the aisle, reciting the usual safety speech. I gave her the courtesy of listening, then pulled the phone from my pocket, plugged in the headset, and secured it over my head. I only wanted to retreat into some music, to drift into a space where I didn't have to think or feel. Flicking through my playlist, my thumb landed on Bach. What was it Sofia had said? She had looked so entranced, so into the piece. I had never met anyone who liked symphonies as much as I did.

An irresistible impulse made me click on the photos from last weekend. There she was. Image after image of her appeared on the seven-inch screen, and despite how things ended, I found myself smiling. She was so damn pretty. The ones I captured of her by the ocean were stellar, with the sun gleaming in her hair. And there she was with her Hawaiian pizza, biting into a slice with such enthusiasm. She'd nearly knocked the camera out of my hand to keep me from taking that pic. Without even meaning to, she made me laugh pretty much every time we were together. I could almost hear her voice teasing me; pictured the funny faces she pulled. Sometimes she snorted when she laughed really hard, then covered her mouth, embarrassed. She didn't realize I found her snorted laughter cute. At least it was cute on her.

And then, there was the way she appeared through the lens in almost all the shots, piercing me with her gaze. Her eyes went soft when she looked at me, yet they were intens e... emotional. Her feelings were always completely transparent, and I loved that about her. She never held anything back, never played games like so many women I'd met. In fact, she wasn't like any woman I'd ever been with. I wondered if her maturity was the reason she could be free to just be herself. The irony wasn't lost on me. Her age was the very thing that tore us apart.

The plane taxied down the runway, then came to an abrupt halt. I pulled the headphones off and heard the captain announce bad weather conditions were to blame for the delay. Through the small window I could see the clouds hanging thick in the air, obscuring the view even ten feet away. The rain was coming down in a torrential downpour now.

Maybe they'll cancel the flight and I'll have an excuse to stay, I thought. I shook my head, realizing I was probably scowling. I hadn't wanted to get on the damn plane in the first place. And there was Elaine again. Smiling at me, strapped in her jump seat a few feet away. I took a stab at returning her smile. God, playing this game was tiring.

My eyes drifted back to the phone's screen, and my heartbeat picked up speed. I scrolled through the pictures I'd taken of her in the hotel room, half dressed. She was so beautiful; her breasts full and her nipples taut with excitement. My body responded immediately, a visceral reaction to seeing her.

The memories came rushing back, and it was as if I was next to her—stroking the silky softness of her skin, especially that tender area on her inner thighs. Damn, that spot drove me crazy. And her hair... It must have been her shampoo, but when I buried my head there, it smelled as though she had run through a field of lavender. When I closed my eyes, I could almost feel her lips on mine—kissing me. The way she tasted on my tongue, like honey.

I clicked to close the photo app, but the memories flashed through my mind like clips of a movie. I was there—inside of her so deep—she arched her neck and screamed out my name. The melody playing in my ears built to a crescendo, reminding me of the times we came together. A breath hitched in my throat....

My eyelids shot open. Fuck no. This had to stop. I drew in several long breaths to calm down. God, what she did to me.

Why did she refuse to talk to me? If we could just have a conversation, then maybe... Maybe what? I hadn't expected it would turn out this way, that she couldn't...

I closed my eyes and focused again on the sound of the violin concerto as the airplane picked up speed, whisking me away from her. *Maybe I'll be able to think more clearly in London. Maybe distance is the answer.*

My back flattened against the seat as the wheels left the ground, and when the plane leveled off at 50,000 feet, I hit the recline switch, then grabbed the remote. Something had better distract me, because this was too long a flight to be trapped with my thoughts.

I searched for a spy thriller, maybe an adventure flick—anything to divert my mind off Sofia. As I scrolled through the channel lineup, romance films flashed across the screen. An annoying stab hit somewhere in my chest. How was it women got so caught up in romance movies, let alone the books? It was all the same. Boy meets girl, boy loses girl but gets her back in the end. The requisite happy ending. Predictable. But real life didn't work that way. Not in my experience.

A chill ran down my spine, remembering how my parents fought. It wasn't just the sting of the words, the tone in their voices. The silence sometimes spoke louder. Witnessing them made me want to steer clear of relationships altogether. Well, serious ones anyway. Ones that went far enough to pose any risk. I'd done a pretty good job of keeping things light—fuck buddies, mostly—until now. How could I trust I wouldn't end up in my parents' situation?

But when I thought of a life with Sofia, another kind of image came to mind. It was like the difference between a black-and-white photo and one drenched in bright colors. For the first time in my life, a woman had given me hope it could be different. Maybe it could be totally freaking amazing. With her, I could imagine a happy life with kids. I was beginning to wonder if fate had a cruel sense of humor.

Fuck. This feeling in my chest wasn't going away. *Have I really lost her?* I couldn't remember a time when a girl had left me. When I scanned my memory, it came to me. I was thirteen. What was her name? Susan. She dumped me after two weeks. But back then, I was pretty much a pubescent jerk, so I couldn't blame her.

Switching to the flight map, I watched as the tiny winking plane made its way across the Atlantic, and I realized there were precisely eight hours and fifteen minutes left to figure out a solution before landing. I usually had a strategy for everything. In business, I could almost always find a way to close a deal. But the situation with Sofia was complicated.

Maybe she was right, better to cut it off before one or both of us got wounded. Yeah, right. It was already too late. I couldn't just let her go. She made me feel whole—like a part of me was missing without her. What the hell was I supposed to do now?

A Bruce Willis movie was playing on the screen, but I hadn't heard a word. A fight broke out, he shot somebody... and—click. I hit the remote with my thumb. There was no use.

"Ryan, would you prefer red or white?" Elaine stood poised with both choices in her hands.

"Do you have a cab?"

"Of course."

"I'll have the bottle," I said, pointing to the red.

Her eyebrows shot up. "Um... certainly."

It might have been the tone in my voice, or the look on my face, but without a word, she passed me the bottle and a glass, then left me alone. It was a relief not to have to fake a conversation. I took a sip and decided it wasn't bad for airline wine, then gulped down half the glass.

I never told Sofia some of my friends weren't supportive of our relationship. Sam and Raul thought she was pretty awesome and only mentioned the age difference once in passing, like it wasn't a big deal. But Johnnie—he went at me hard.

"Look, Ryan," he'd begun, "you need to check your priorities. So, you have fun with her, I get it. But there are other girls who you can have fun with—young, hot girls. Grow the hell up and decide what you want out of life. Do you want to be stuck with an old lady? Fuck her for a while, get it out of your system, but believe me, it's not going to end well if you keep this up."

If Sofia hadn't been sitting there, I would have decked him. My fists clenched just thinking about it. Since then, I hadn't spoken to the asshole. Granted, he'd been drunk and didn't have a clue what she meant to me, but he didn't even try to be supportive. I was sure Sofia wasn't getting that bullshit from her friends. Then again, how would I know? Was she hearing warnings about me?

I poured another glass of wine, kicked off my shoes, and reclined the seat flat. The cabin was quiet now, the low hum of the engines droning in my ears. Some people avoided night flights, but I appreciated the way they were more peaceful. Unless there was a screaming baby on board. Yeah... Did I really want to deal with that? Why was I set on having children? My life was good. I could travel, do whatever I pleased. Life with Sofia would be sweet. Maybe it would be all I ever needed. Family life would suck anyway if the relationship wasn't strong. There were no guarantees I'd ever find the right woman to settle down with. And I'd have given up Sofia for what?

My thoughts spun and circled back to the vision slowly forming, tucked beneath my awareness. Me, Sofia, and a couple of beautiful babies. A boy and a girl. It had surfaced when she'd asked me about my goals. She hadn't realized I was actually thinking of kids with her. Now, I regretted my answer.

I stared at the ambient blue light barely illuminating the cabin. Morning was likely to be brutal, since I'd only have time to change clothes and make it to the office for a meeting. This entire week was going to bust my balls. Propping the pillow under my head, I considered trying to get some sleep before landing, but my mind wouldn't stop drifting. I closed my eyes anyway, and after a while, drowsiness slowed my racing thoughts. The wine seemed to be doing the trick.

Did everyone view me as just the guy who wanted to have fun? Johnnie certainly did. He could be shallow, but maybe that was how people perceived me. Maybe I made sure everyone only saw what I wanted them to. But Sofia's vision of me went far below the surface. She saw me for who I really was. And somehow, she liked me anyway. Wasn't that what we needed most in life? What we all craved?

My eyelids flicked open as an idea spun. It came unexpectedly like a flash, then settled haphazardly in my brain. Could this work?

Over the next thirty minutes, the idea became a fully formed plan. Possibly a ridiculous plan, but if there was one thing I knew for sure, it was that I needed her in my life. She might not agree to it, but if I didn't try, I would regret it for the rest of my life.

Chapter Twenty-Eight

It was one thing to be young and foolish; missteps could be viewed as a learning experience. It was quite another thing to be an old fool with enough learning experience under your belt to know better. Why didn't I pick up on the signs earlier? What was I thinking? How could I let my guard down?

It had been so easy to ignore the truth, to look the other way, to hold on to irrational hope. The answer was simple, really. He had been so easy to fall in love with.

My phone pinged from beside me on the bed, and I reached for it before I could stop myself. Ryan's name and recent photo filled the screen. It was the one I'd taken of him in Monterey; his gorgeous face, the angle of his jawline so perfect in profile as he watched the otters, the wind blowing his curls. Fresh tears sprung to my eyes. In the two hours since Ryan dropped me off at my house, I hadn't stopped crying. It would be a miracle if I wasn't severely dehydrated.

> *Sofia, honey, please talk to me. I'm home now. Can I call you?*

I stared at the text. What was the point? There was no magic solution to our dilemma. Hearing his voice would only increase the dull, constant throb in my chest into a sharp, stabbing pain. My thumb hit the button to turn off the ringtone, and I rolled onto my side, wishing there was a switch to stop images of Ryan flashing through my mind. Most of the time, I didn't remember what I'd had for dinner the day before or how I'd spent my birthday last year. But my brain, the sadistic thing that it was, recalled every moment with Ryan since the day we'd met, down to the most minute detail.

Even worse, my body viscerally responded to each memory with alternating waves of arousal and longing. I missed the warmth of his body next to mine, the feel of his breath on my neck as he slept curled against my back. In the aching silence of my home, I missed the sound of his voice—the endless conversations—the way he cooed loving sounds in my ear just before he kissed me, the low growl of pleasure when he pushed inside. I wondered if I'd ever stop missing him. And then, when I thought the pain couldn't get any worse, the sobs erupted again, emanating from a place so deep, it felt as though my insides would tear apart. Sobs that contained the death of dreams.

Sometime after midnight, surrounded by piles of wet tissues, I finally succumbed to exhaustion, and sleep came as a welcome respite; a temporary reprieve from pain.

A bell chimed, the noise persistent and too loud. I stared at the ocean, white spray shooting high into the air as the waves crashed on the craggy rock formations. My eyes whipped in all directions, but still, I couldn't determine where the sound was coming from. I searched for the door—to stop the insistent bell—but all around me was open space, and I was spinning...

My eyelids flew open. I heard a voice shouting my name. Panic shot through my muddled brain. I bolted out of bed, then tripped over my suitcase in the hall. "Fuck!" Limping through the living room, I finally flung the door open, my chest heaving—only to find Madison, her finger poking the ringer.

"What?" I shouted. God, my foot throbbed. "Can you lay off the bell?"

"Sofia! You had me so worried!" She pushed past me and shut the door, ignoring my foul mood.

I rubbed my eyes, probably smearing the remains of my mascara. "Why?"

"Those texts you sent me late last night. When I saw them this morning, I freaked out."

Now I vaguely remembered texting her. "I need coffee for this conversation."

I shuffled to the kitchen with Madison on my heels, my big toe now turning purple.

"You go sit down, I'll make a pot and you can explain the texts." She handed me her phone, and I sank into a chair. The words blurred without my glasses, but holding it out at arm's length, I finally saw my nonsensical, run-on sentence—no punctuation, except for a lot of exclamation points and a string of sad faced emojis.

"Oh, yeah, now I remember." My chest deflated, plunging my head to the tabletop. The cool surface felt so good on my forehead, I decided it was as good a place as any to collapse. The coffee machine gurgled, and even when the aroma hit my nose, I didn't perk up.

"So? What the hell happened?" She carried the cups to the breakfast nook, then retrieved the milk from the fridge.

"It's done. Over. Turns out, Ryan wants kids."

"He told you he wants them now? Didn't he know you were... menopausal?"

"No, he wasn't aware, so it was more like an idea of someday we could have a kid." I raised my head just enough to slurp the coffee.

"Oh, Sofia. I'm so sorry." We sat in silence for a few moments, me staring at the wall, listening to the clock ticking. I was far too worn out to talk about it. "Do you think—"

"No. I can guess what you're about to suggest. I'm in this too deep already. No way am I going to stay on this ride until he decides to look for a baby mama." The back of my eyes burned, the deluge threatening to start again. "Once again, I'm right back where I started from. How the hell?"

Madison searched in her purse, then tossed me a packet of tissues. "What does Ryan say about all this?"

I pulled my cell from the pocket of my pajamas, along with a wad of Kleenex, and slapped it on the table. "He's been calling and texting, but I can't talk to him."

She picked up my phone and scrolled through the texts. "He is persistent, I'll give him that. Sofia, this guy seriously cares about you. He's nothing like Ron. From what I see, he wants to work things out."

My shoulders sank, my chest caving in around my heart. A heart that was shattered into a million pieces, the pain unrelenting. "There's nothing to work out. I just have to live with the consequences of my recklessness." Pressing on the table, I pushed off to stand, feeling as though my body weighed five hundred pounds. My slippered feet shuffled a few inches, then I paused when a wave of dizziness hit me. Was it weird I was hoping for a heart attack to take me down?

"Are you okay? You look a little unsteady."

"I'm fine, or I will be. I just need to go back to bed. Thanks for coming over."

"Sofia," she called out. "You can't hide in bed forever."

I padded down the hallway. "Wanna bet?"

Her voice trailed after me. "I'll check in on you later. Just promise me you'll take a shower and get dressed today."

Already cocooned under the covers, I didn't respond. *I may never leave this bed,* I thought.

Several days later, when I grew tired of hearing the endless drone of the TV, I hauled myself into the shower. Even I couldn't stand the smell of me anymore. After pulling on a pair of sweats and a t-shirt, I padded into the kitchen to grab some yogurt. I'd barely been able to eat since I got home. The first stage of grief involved either starvation or binging on junk food. I was in the beginning phase, but the latter could still sneak up on me. I made a mental note to stock up on ice cream and chips—delivery only.

It was time to devise a plan, however basic. As I filled my coffee cup, then sat at the kitchen table, I considered dragging out the poster paper. But that would require a functional brain. I wasn't there yet. Routine, I decided, was the best medicine, apart from antidepressant medication, which I hadn't ruled out. I would retreat into my predictable life, forget about Barcelona—forget about the carpe diem bullshit... forget about Ryan.

Then I heard a tiny voice in my head, laughing hyster-ically. The other was shaking a finger at me, as in, didn't I warn you? Those dueling cartoon creatures were back. It was that, or I was having hallucinations. Either way, they were beginning to piss me off.

During the next two weeks, I focused only on the neces-sary tasks. I could get myself dressed in the morning, do the laundry, and clean the house. My home had never been so spotless. I started taking yoga classes, hoping the breathing would calm my nerves, and dragged my ass to the gym.

I threw out the travel magazines and read psychology journals online, hoping for some inspiration. I updated my LinkedIn profile and sent emails to a few colleagues to see if they knew of any job leads. Focusing on developing new career goals, I could put everything back as it should be. Encased in a suit of armor, I could function. I packed up all those memories into a suitcase and stuffed it in the far reaches of the closet, behind the boxes of Christmas decorations and old snow ski gear I hadn't used since the nineties.

Still, every day, I waged a battle to force the wayward thoughts back into the suitcase. Odd details came in unexpected bursts as though our time together was recorded and stored on my hard drive. Occasionally, when something triggered my brain, the memories surfaced in random patterns. It was impossible to guess when they might blindside me.

A song on the radio called up the sparkle in his eyes—how his features brightened when he looked at me. When I saw the commercial on TV advertising a romantic vacation in the Maldives, couples embracing while half submerged in the crystal-clear waters, I plummeted into despair and threw a tissue box at the screen. I didn't dare glance at the photos I took in Barcelona because memories of him were steeped in every single shot. I might as well have put blinders on my head; those things they placed on horses, so they wouldn't get distracted when they were supposed to focus on the path straight ahead. It was exhausting trying to forget him.

Ryan's texts and attempted calls pinged my phone several times a day during the first week but finally subsided by the end of the second. His photo no longer lit up my phone's screen. It was simultaneously a relief and a devastating disappointment. *Has he forgotten about me?* Then I reminded myself I had ghosted him and cringed. We'd made a promise, and I had broken it, not him.

On Thursday, day number eighteen since the tearful goodbye, I headed through the doors of Starbucks, ordered a latte, and settled in a seat by the window. Before I opened my laptop, I saw one of my neighbors sitting at a nearby table, typing furiously on her keyboard. I didn't bother to catch her attention. These days, I remained quiet and solitary. I'd only spoken to Madison a couple of times on the phone when she'd called to check in. Even my best friend was at a complete loss for words to console me, and she always had a way of spinning things around to the positive. This time, there was no positive spin. Fate had chewed me up and spit me out, battered and bruised and torn to pieces.

If I had known what was waiting for me when I innocently opened my laptop and clicked on the email tab, I would have kept the lid closed. A breath hitched in my chest. *Oh, God, it's Ryan. What should I do?*

My eyes darted around the coffee shop. I didn't see a way to manage opening the app in this public place, where lunchtime refugees from the tech company down the street sat at tables so close you could pretty much make out their meal plan for the week, find out who they'd matched with on Tinder, or take a virtual trip as they planned their next vacation. Starbucks was a voyeur's paradise. I shut my laptop and reached for my latte, cupping it between my hands, hoping the warmth would stop the trembling.

On my right, a woman with stiletto pumps sat staring at her cell phone screen, her thumbs typing at warp speed. I peeked at her shoes. They were a gorgeous maroon color, but honestly, who wore those to work?

To my left were two younger women in conversation. *Friends maybe? Or possibly coworkers,* I thought, as my ears picked up snippets of office gossip. I learned that Sandra, on the fifth floor, was four months pregnant. There was a rumor she hadn't yet figured out who the father was but had narrowed it down to the three men she most recently dated.

Angling my back to the corner, it seemed safe to risk opening my laptop. I stared at the screen, the sight of his message sending shockwaves up my spine.

To: SofiaDrake01@gmail.com
From: RyHunter@gmail.com
Sofia,

I get why you've avoided my calls, but I hope you're still reading my emails, because I need to tell you something important. I've been thinking a lot about our dilemma over the past two weeks and have come to realize, while I can't control the circumstances or influence your decision (as much as I'd like to believe I have power over all things, obviously I don't), still, I'd like to ask you to reconsider our relationship.

All I can say is I've missed you more than you can imagine. Maybe it takes losing someone to realize how empty life is without that person. At least that's how it's affecting me. I wonder, do you feel the same way? If so, please, let's talk this through.

Will you agree to meet me when I get back from London tomorrow? Are you free on Saturday? I really want to see if we can work this out. I have a proposition for you—call it a merger, where both parties find a mutually beneficial partnership. What do you say? Are you willing to give it a try? Please, please... just let me have a chance to discuss my thoughts.

Optimistically yours,

Ryan

A whimper escaped my lips as I finished his email, sounding oddly like a kitten's meow. *He hasn't forgotten me.* The stiletto lady's eyes flashed in my direction, but I no longer cared who noticed me melting.

I stared out the window at the bay waters, waging a battle to keep a tight lid on the emotions boiling inside—my armor dissolving with the heat. If he only knew how I'd struggled to forget him over the last two weeks. The way everything now reminded me of him, how I reflexively checked my phone a dozen times a day, even though I couldn't bear to answer his calls. I was certain if I heard his voice, my resolve would weaken into a pool of molten lava.

How could he possibly have a solution? I tried to imagine what he meant by a "merger," but having little knowledge about his business, I didn't have a clue about how this applied to a relationship. Despite my doubts and against my will, a rush of heat zipped up my spine like a hot flash. An intoxicating mixture of desire and love, memories and sensations ricocheted its way from my toes to the top of my head.

I read his email again, examining every word. We might still be stuck on opposite sides of this enormous barrier, but at least I could be certain of one thing—he cared for me as much as I did for him. I wasn't in this alone; he was suffering, too. Selfish? Maybe. But it brought me some comfort.

A tiny sliver of hope slipped past my defenses, and I let the words, "What if," roll silently off my tongue. I mouthed the two syllables, testing the taste. The stiletto lady shifted her gaze, catching me mid-mumble. I shrugged and dropped my eyes to the email on my screen.

How could I take this risk? If his solution failed, I could fall into a hole so deep this time I might never climb out. Still, the idea of seeing his face again was irresistible; to hear his voice... *I've missed you.* Those words rang over and over in my head, and my heart—that traitorous organ—pushed and pulsed against the guardrails, like a racehorse itching to break past the starting gate. There was no question in my mind seeing him would be painful. But how could I refuse him?

I sent Ryan a reply. He deserved that much. I told him yes, I'd meet with him—on neutral grounds—and that I missed him too, but didn't ask him more about his proposition. Emailing wasn't the way to sort things out.

After draining the last of the coffee from my cup, I closed my laptop and headed toward home. My body, more buoyant than it had been in weeks, sprung to life with a surge of energy. Despite my best judgment and attempts to stay wary, excitement spread through me like uncontained wildfire. Against all odds, it seemed I was still that golden retriever at my core. And soon, I would learn if it was safe to trust him or if I should sprint from the watering hole.

Chapter Twenty-Nine

W hat do you wear to a 'business meeting' with your ex-lover? Absurd as it sounded to me, I went dressed in professional work attire, prepared to discuss... a merger? A pencil skirt, light blue blouse topped with a cropped blazer, and finally, high-heeled pumps. This wasn't a date. It was a business meeting. Or so I tried to convince myself.

As I pushed open the brass-handled door and entered the dimly lit lounge, seeing Ryan wearing a suit only confirmed my wardrobe choice. At first sight of him, my heart hammered in my chest, and by the time I approached the table, my breaths were so shallow I couldn't be certain I was breathing at all.

"I'm glad you came. I wasn't sure you would." The warmth of his hand slid down my arm until he laced his fingers in mine. Worry lines cinched between his brows, but his eyes brightened, taking me in.

Oh, God. How did I think I could manage this? Keeping my tone neutral and guarded, I replied, "I have reservations about this, but I promised to come. So, here I am."

The decision hadn't been easy with those two cartoon characters yelling into each ear, battling to be heard. I had called a truce between the opposing sides, reasoning I should at least hear him out. And so far, I was doing a pretty good job of keeping up a professional facade. But now that we were face to face, close enough to breathe in the scent of him, my mind was spinning out of control. My body tingled, responding to a visceral magnetic force at the mere sight of him, at the touch of his hand.

"Please, have a seat."

As I lowered myself into the wing-backed chair, I glanced up at the chandeliers, at the elegance of the room... and remembered. "The scene of the crime, huh?" Despite my trepidation, a smile hitched at the corners of my lips.

"If we're going to start over, what better place than where we met?"

"Technically, we met in the private hall, but the lounge was a good call." The smooth, sultry voice of a female singer caught my attention. "Is this a track from Norah Jones?" As if a sadistic DJ had cued up the music especially for us, the lyrics, "*Come away with me*," poured through a speaker; the soulful melody threatening to rip away my facade. Was there anything more tortuous than hearing a love song when you're heartbroken?

His mouth curled into a grin. "It wasn't easy to get them to play the song."

I stared at him.

"I'm kidding. But it is perfect, right? Maybe fate is still working for us."

A cynical laugh burst out of me. "Or maybe fate is fucking with us."

"I have wondered." His gaze drifted toward the bar, the smile faltering.

I straightened my spine, desperate to get myself under control and that damn song out of my head. "How do you figure we can start over?"

A young, male server appeared with a bottle of champagne, interrupting our conversation. He poured two glasses, then tucked the bottle into a silver ice bucket. Ryan muttered, "Thank you," to the guy, but his gaze was pinned on me. I'd seen a range of feelings in those eyes. This look was different. He may have wanted to appear confident, but I could see right through him. Ryan was nervous.

Gently, I asked, "Are we celebrating something?"

"I hope so." His chest rose with a deep breath. "We can start over, knowing each other better now. All the cards are on the table, there's no guessing."

"I agree. Everything is out in the open. We both know what the other is looking for, but we're still at a stalemate." It took every ounce of strength I had to keep my voice from cracking. It was impossible to be near him and not reach out to touch him. To skim my fingers along his cheeks—his lips.

"First," he began, "let's establish the one thing that matters most. Do you want to be with me?"

Amidst the buzz of conversations, the bartender mixing drinks, and servers shuffling by, my voice emerged as a whisper. So soft, I couldn't be sure he heard me. "Yes. If it wasn't for—"

"I'm going with 'yes.' And I want to be with you. So, I suggest we find a way to make it happen."

Absently tucking strands of hair behind my ear, I leaned in, my voice sounding too desperate when the words exploded out of me. "How? Because I won't allow you to throw away your dream for me, and I can't follow you blindly into something that will eventually bring me pain."

"What if I told you having you in my life is my dream? That in the brief time we've spent apart, I've come to realize how it feels to live without you, and believe me, it was a wake-up call."

He scrubbed a hand over his hair, pain etched on his face. Seconds ticked by, waiting... while I teetered on the edge of losing it altogether; my nails digging into the leather armchair. Finally, he leaned in, clasped his hands together, his gaze fixed on the table between us.

"It took me a minute to figure it out, but being with you changed me. I divide my life into two parts—the one before you and the one since I met you. I've never felt like this before. You, Sofia, have rearranged my priorities."

Unbidden, tears sprung in my eyes. I bit the inside of my lip to stem the deluge, but I couldn't stop my hand from reaching out, fingertips stroking along his jawline. We were locked in a Shakespearean tragedy. His confirmation of love—because I knew it clearly now—made the impossible situation even worse.

"Oh, babe. Do you know how much I need you to put your arms around me? To believe everything will be okay?" His eyes drew slowly upward until he met my gaze. "But how can you make this... this monumental decision?"

"Because it's simple. I want us to be together."

I shook my head. "I can't let you do that."

He laced his fingers through mine. "Look, if it were possible, I'd welcome the chance to create a family, the two of us. But I would much rather spend my life with you and be happy than lose you for some fantasy of a family that may never happen. I'm choosing you."

My heart clenched. "Believe me, nothing would make me happier. But you might feel differently two months or two years from now. I don't want to be blindsided if you suddenly change your mind."

"I'm not going to change my mind, but I thought you would say that." His eyes shimmered with a look I recognized—like when he was planning a surprise or had an idea brewing. "So, let's make a contract. A sixty-day contract, renegotiable at the end."

"What are you talking about?" I reeled back. "You've lost me."

"Contracts aren't only for business. Marriage is a contract, but they rarely last to term. But if relationships were up for renegotiation every so often, it allows both parties to know exactly where they stand, without surprises. This way, everyone maintains control and the agreement can be adjusted to fit changing goals. You wouldn't be blindly following. Instead, you'd be setting your terms."

"How... I mean, why do we need to do... this?"

"You were upset for good reason. I can't take away what I said, and you wouldn't believe me anyway. So, I had to find a way to bring us back to the beginning—a re-do for both of us."

"I gotta say, I didn't see this one coming. But then, we did start out with a contract of sorts."

"This is totally different from the one we made before. Our agreement was vacation fun and done, no freefalling. We've moved way past that point. I want to make a commitment to you and only you. This will give you time to trust in me. Besides, I'm banking on a contract extension."

I raised a brow, still skeptical.

"Just consider it, please."

"No. What if—?"

"Sofia, come on. I know how your mind works. You could imagine a dozen 'what if' scenarios, but what if we've found something so good—so rare—nothing will fuck it up?"

I considered this for a few moments. "A sixty-day contract? Monogamous? And we check in regularly to evaluate how it's working? With an option for extension?" He nodded after each of my questions, his eyes flashing between excitement and fear. I was getting dizzy just watching him.

"Yes, to everything. I promise, I'm not looking for anyone else," he insisted. "I wouldn't be here if I wasn't positive about us being together. Are you certain you want the same? If the answer is yes, then..."

His words seeped into my brain as I sat motionless... stunned. My thoughts swirled, the needle ticking around the circle like the Wheel of Fortune. My options spun by, finally landing on the only right answer. Yes, I wanted to be with Ryan.

Oddly, his idea began to make sense. Of course, we could be grasping for some way to justify holding on—fooling ourselves. But what if this was a chance to color outside the lines and try something new? To have even a piece of the life I'd dreamed of. Was it better than nothing at all?

Long-term commitment was nothing more than a fantasy, based on my experience. Maybe relationships should be a series of short-term agreements. Could I adjust my expectations and live in the moment, as long as I'd have sixty days of moments to count on? What we had was precious—too precious to throw away. Having already tried that move, I realized I was miserable without him. Maybe... he was worth the risk, because he was risking everything—for me. He'd never let me down before. How could I resist an opportunity to be happier than I'd been in decades?

Then I recalled how Ryan, on our first day in Barcelona, had described his ideal relationship. "A best friend who you kinda wanted to have sex with every day." A partnership based on chemistry, trust, respect, and compatibility. I couldn't agree more, and we had it all. In this moment, it all came down to trust. Did I trust Ryan enough to take this leap?

I stared into my glass of bubbly for what seemed like hours while he waited. Reason faded into a blurred line, and something in me shifted. A landslide of need and want and blind hope poured through me.

Finally, I let my gaze rest on his beautiful face—a tentative smile quivering on his lips. "Where do I sign?"

I watched as relief washed across his features. His eyes lit up like it was Christmas, and all his wishes had come true.

"I'll have the papers drawn up tomorrow," he dead-panned.

"Seriously? I was kidding. There's paperwork involved?"

Beaming at me, he said, "You're adorable."

His hands weaved in my hair, drawing me to his mouth. I kissed him back, long and hard, drowning in the taste of him. His lips trailed up my cheek… a whisper in my ear.

"I love you."

Those three little words never sounded so sweet. They tumbled through me, arrowing straight toward my heart. Unchecked tears began spilling down my cheeks.

"What? You didn't know that already?"

I cupped his face in my hands. "Did you know I love you, too?"

He planted a kiss on my palm. "I was betting on it. If you didn't, you probably wouldn't be sitting here."

We must have been a spectacle in the crowded lounge, gazing into each other's eyes, leaning across the small table for stolen kisses. I didn't check to see if anyone was watching, because honestly, I couldn't have cared less. It was as if we were the only two people on the planet. Finally, Ryan raised his glass. Champagne never tasted so good.

Over the next twenty-four hours, I greedily indulged in kisses tasting of love—in his body, mine alone to enjoy. We didn't leave his apartment for the rest of the weekend. A place that somehow felt like home to me now, a safe haven where the two of us could wrap ourselves in a different sort of bubble than the one before. We ate from takeout cartons and watched movies—when we weren't clambering over each other's bodies, drenching ourselves in the scents and tastes of our union, until all traces of doubt or fear had vanished.

"Sundays are quickly becoming my favorite day. So is afternoon sex." I lay wrapped around the bulk of this man, all strength and muscle.

"Hm, I'm not sure... Saturday night sex was pretty awesome. So was Sunday morning sex."

My chin lifted off his chest in time to catch his wink. "You're going to kill me; you know that, don't you?"

"Ah, but what a way to go."

"Mm, you have a point. By the way, how was London?"

"Cold, dreary, and lacking my special girl. I came back to see you, but my team is working on a deal and I'm afraid I'll have to go back there. I wish you could come with me." He pressed me tighter against his chest, his chin resting on my forehead.

"When are you leaving?"

"Within a week. Why?"

Pushing myself up, I straddled my legs across his lap and faced him. "What if I told you I might be able to join you there soon?" I studied his expression.

"How is it possible? Don't you have to find a job?"

"Do you remember back in Carmel, when you asked me to come with you?"

He nodded, his brows knitting together.

"I started thinking, why pass up this chance? I still have four months left on my severance package, so why not travel a while? It's crazy, I know, but I've put off living my dreams for so long. Of course, the idea tanked when, um, I walked out on you. But now..."

His smile was slow to come, realization finally dawning. Seeing the joy light up his face sent me into a fit of giggles. "Oh my God, you're serious? When can you leave?"

I cringed. "I don't know yet. There are some details to work out."

Without a second's hesitation, he blurted out, "Tell me when and I'll book you a flight."

"That's sweet, but you don't have to."

He cupped my face in his hands. "I know. But I want to."

It seemed surreal. My life had spun in an unexpected direction in just a few days. A part of me wanted to put on the brakes, to slow down the changes until I caught up to this speeding train.

"Don't," he warned, shaking his head as though he could read my thoughts. "Don't overthink this. Just come with me."

"But where will I stay? What will I do while you're at work?"

"You're going to whine about an opportunity like this?"

"I'm not whining," I said in a small voice, then realized I was. "Okay, you're right."

"One step at a time, baby. You'll figure it out." Abruptly, he scooped me up and held me so tight all the air gushed out of me. "We... will figure it out, together."

Together... Just the thought of it filled me with a feeling of contentment I didn't think was possible.

I was still floating on a love-infused high when I drove to my house in the evening. It hadn't been easy to pry myself away, but reality had burst its way into our bubble. Ryan was due at work in the morning, and I had some trip planning to do.

Until I walked in the door of my home, all was right in the universe. The stars were aligned in perfect order, and the ground was solid under my feet again. Then I pulled my cell from my purse and realized I had switched it to mute since Saturday evening. Going offline was a freedom I'd rarely known, but our bubble had blocked out any need to connect with the outside world.

Except, when I saw Madison's string of texts, I was consumed with guilt at my self- indulgence.

Chapter Thirty

My hands trembled on the steering wheel, terrified of what I might find when I arrived at Madison's. I slid through a few yellow lights and interpreted the speed limit signs to be merely a suggestion. When I finally pulled up to her red brick house, two eyes peeked through the slats of the window shades, barely visible in the darkness.

"Thank God it's you, Sofia."

I threw my arms around her, my heart racing. "Are you alright? What the hell happened?"

She wriggled out of my grip, her red, puffy eyes wide with fear, then flung the door closed and locked the deadbolt. "Let's sit down. I'm afraid my legs aren't going to support me."

Guiding her to the living room, I linked my arm through hers and supported her weight as she leaned against me. She slumped down on the couch, and I claimed the space next to her. Normally, nothing rattled Madison. Seeing her like this, her body shaking with anxiety, made my stomach clench.

"Apparently, Kevin had been texting me for weeks, but I never saw the messages because I'd blocked him. I guess he got worried, or so he said, and that's why he showed up here today." She sucked in a long breath through quivering lips. "Roger was here. Not just here in my house but in my bed."

My mouth dropped open, terrifying images springing into life as I imagined the scenario. "Oh my God, Madison. Did Kevin have a key?"

She nodded. "I've been meaning to oil the hinges on my front door. It was a good thing I didn't, because the loud squeak alerted me that someone was in the house—and then I remembered the key. I heard Kevin calling my name." Her eyes lifted to meet mine. "Sofia, it all happened so fast. There was nothing I could do. I felt so helpless." Tears were streaming down her cheeks, landing softly on her sweater. I dug in my purse for a packet of tissues, frantically tore it open, and placed it in her palm.

My heart pounded in my chest. Fear, anger, and dread threatened to shatter my calm facade, but I held my voice steady. "Was he violent?"

Her eyelids fell shut, and with a nod, she confirmed the worst.

"Fuck," I hissed, heat rolling up my chest like an inferno.

"He didn't go after me, but he started throwing punches at Roger," she cried, her voice cracking. "The poor guy didn't even have time to get dressed, much less realize what or why this was happening. He could have defended himself, but Kevin caught him so off guard. I yelled at him to stop... I tried to make him stop... but he just kept swearing at me and shouting at Roger." Through hiccupping sobs, the words poured out in a steady stream.

"Oh, honey." My hand rubbed her back in circles, as if somehow this could soothe her.

"He yelled, 'You think I'm going to stand by while you fuck my girl?'" When her eyes met mine, they were filled with so much pain, my heart broke for her. "Can you imagine? He's calling me his girl and threatening Roger, while all along he's been sleeping next to his wife every night."

Now I felt helpless, watching as she used a wadded-up tissue to wipe the mascara streaks off her cheeks. But rage coursed through my veins with the force of a mother bear. I envisioned tearing Kevin apart; pinning him with a large paw, seeing him squirm with fear. Okay, maybe I was going over-board, but when someone I cared about was in trouble, there was no telling what I might do when hyped up on adrenalin. It took several deep, steadying breaths to get myself under control. Madison needed me, and ranting would only add to her stress.

"Did you call the police?" I asked, keeping my voice even.

"At first, I was too scared to move. But when he wouldn't stop, I was more afraid he might kill Roger. I grabbed my cell phone as I ran into the bathroom. Luckily, the door had a lock, because five seconds later, Kevin was pounding on it."

I swallowed hard, steeling myself for what she'd reveal next. I gripped her hand in mine, my own trembling as much as hers. "And then?"

"I have no idea if I did the right thing, but I shouted, 'You'd better leave because the police are on their way.' Sofia, I have never been so terrified in my life. Luckily, he was gone before they arrived. An ambulance took Roger to the hospital." She paused, shaking her head, tears flowing like a waterfall. "It's all my fault. Poor Roger. And I worry about what Kevin will do when the officers show up on his doorstep. I've made such a mess of things."

"Oh, no you don't." I held her by the shoulders and fixed my eyes on hers. "Madison, it's absolutely not your fault. Kevin is entirely to blame for his behavior. You are not responsible for what happened, do you hear me? I'm relieved he didn't hurt you."

When her voice emerged, it sounded vulnerable and small, like a child. "But he warned me not to see anyone else."

The words I swore in my head—words I wanted to say to Kevin—might have made Snoop Dogg blush. "He has no right to dictate to you what you can or cannot do. Madison, he has bullied and intimidated you. And today, his violence has traumatized you. That's called abuse." I held the side of her cheek in my hand. "Do you understand me? You have been in an abusive relationship, and it must stop. Now."

"Abuse? No, it couldn't be. I mean, he never hit me."

"Has he threatened you? Used his strength or words to make you fearful? Pushed you or restrained you against your will? Tried to control you and keep you isolated—like warning you not to date anyone else?"

She nodded, then sunk her head into her hands and cried—her agonized sobs cracking open my heart. I rubbed my hand over her shoulders, telling her it was going to be okay.

"Oh, sweetie, I wish you'd told me this sooner," I cooed. A part of me was stunned and embarrassed I hadn't seen the signs—I hadn't warned her.

She shrugged, dabbing her cheeks with a tissue. "I guess I never considered it that bad. Sure, he had an anger problem, but he convinced me it was my fault for doing something to make him mad." When she swung her eyes toward me, they looked like two pinpricks. "This seemed like nothing compared to what my mother endured with my father, but tonight I learned what Kevin is capable of. I don't want any part of this... this abusive shit." She spit out the words, cringing as they left her mouth.

I tucked her under my arm, her head falling onto my shoulder. "Abuse can be subtle—until it's not. It's a damn good thing you made it into the bathroom, because I don't want to imagine what could have happened to you."

"Neither do I," she whispered.

"Look, you can't stay here tonight. You're coming to my house. Tomorrow, I'm finding a therapist for you, and a women's group." She didn't argue.

In the recesses of my mind, I grasped the awful reality of her situation. This wouldn't be easy. I'd worked with survivors of domestic violence. Too many found it difficult to leave their abusers, and so, the cycle repeated. She would need to be surrounded by love and support. I also held out hope Roger would step up. If he stuck around, she'd have a chance at a healthy relationship.

As she gathered some clothes and packed up a suitcase, I noticed the bloodstains on her sheets. Picturing the scene made my stomach lurch.

"I'll help you get this cleaned up tomorrow. By the way, have you heard how Roger is doing?"

"I followed the ambulance to the hospital and waited until I could see him," she explained. "They treated him, bandaged him up. He has a broken nose but no permanent damage. He's looking pretty bad, though." She blew her nose, then said, "I apologized and tried to explain, but I don't think he's ever coming near me again. Can't say I blame him."

"Oh, Madison, I'm so sorry. But give him some time, he may come around. He's probably still in shock." Then I said with strict authority, "You must petition for a restraining order against Kevin."

"The officers mentioned something about that. I guess I'll have to go down to the police station."

"Don't worry, I'll go with you. Now, let's get you out of here."

We sat in silence during the ride to my home, and it wasn't until I'd shown her into the guest room that she asked me where I'd been all day. I paused for a moment and decided this wasn't the best time to share my good news.

"I'm so sorry I didn't see your messages earlier, but I had my phone turned off. I was with Ryan."

Her swollen eyes widened. "I thought it was over with him."

"I thought so too, but something changed. I'll tell you about it tomorrow. We're both exhausted and need some sleep. I really hope that you're calling in sick. You're in no shape to go to work. You can hang out at my house and rest. Okay? We'll make a day of it. Maybe a little retail therapy?"

She reached out a hand and folded her fingers around mine. "Thank you, Sofia."

I gave it a squeeze. "You would do the same for me. Don't hesitate to wake me up if you need anything tonight. I hope you can sleep, but if not, I have something that might calm your nerves." I nodded and added a wink before turning to leave.

"You have drugs?" Her brows shot up.

"Just some generic sleep aids."

"Gimme!" She held out her palm, and it was the first time she had smiled all evening.

I crawled into bed reeling with the range of emotions encompassed in just one day. When I sent out a silent prayer to the universe for Madison, I remembered to count my blessings, overcome with gratitude for Ryan. Just knowing I was loved by him left me feeling less alone in the world. No matter what the future held, I knew in my soul his love would always be there.

Chapter Thirty-One

"A sixty-day contract?" Madison shook her head. "And I thought I'd heard everything."

I poured my homemade sangria into chilled glasses, restraining the fruit with a spoon. A ray of sunshine poked through the fog, and while my little backyard wasn't the same as being on a terrace in Barcelona, we sat on lawn chairs looking out over the flower garden in full bloom.

"He has a point," I said. "Relationships don't often go the distance, and considering most of my attempts, sixty days isn't a bad run."

Madison snorted a laugh. "You've got that right. But aren't you multiplying the risk by running off to Europe with him?"

"Hey, you started this ball rolling with your 'carpe diem' and 'just go have fun' advice. But yes, the stakes are higher now. Now that I... love him."

"You almost didn't get it off your tongue." She took a long pull on the sangria. "This is really tasty."

"I still can't get used to saying it out loud," I said. "You know, I thought I loved Ron, but in hindsight, I think I wanted to love him—because I was determined to have a relationship. What I felt for Ron doesn't even come close to the love

I have for Ryan. It's like comparing a ham sandwich with a ten-course meal at a Michelan star restaurant."

"And if you and Ryan don't last?"

I watched a squirrel run across the grass, then leap to the top of the fence. He (or she, I didn't have a clue how to tell) ran to its mate, and they raced up the tree. I always noticed this pair hanging out together, and one day, my gardener told me it was the female who picked her partner, based on how well the male impressed her. She might stay with the guy for a while or hop around with many partners through the mating season. I wanted to believe this couple was monogamous. But clearly, it was the lady's choice.

"I'm trying to stay positive. If it doesn't last, will I fall apart? Maybe. But whichever way it goes, I've changed because of him. I have no doubt my life will be different now that I've opened myself up to new possibilities—to travel. I might even be able to manage solo travel just fine."

Madison considered this for a while, then held out her glass for a refill. "Let's slow this down a bit, though. I'm just getting used to the idea of you leaving. You're coming back in sixty days, right?"

I swiveled in my chair to face her. "To be honest, I'm not sure. I haven't planned that far ahead."

"Who are you?!" Her eyebrows arched up to her hairline.

"I know, right? But yes, I'll have to come back here at some point. Americans can't stay indefinitely abroad without a visa. And my friends are here." I leaned over and threw an arm around her shoulder. "Speaking of friends, would you care to help me pack? I have to get everything into two suitcases."

Madison laughed so hard, she had to press her thighs together. "Oh, God, I've got to remember to do my Kegel exercises. Does Ryan know how you cart everything but the kitchen sink?"

Glancing sideways, I narrowed my eyes. "Go ahead, mock me, but if we're traveling together and you need a band-aid, a sewing kit, antiseptic..."

"Okay, I get your point." She side-eyed me, giving me her signature look. "You're sure you want me to stay here?"

"I need a house-sitter, and Kevin doesn't know where I live, so it's the perfect arrangement. You'll be safe here. Later, when things are more certain and I figure out my plans, I may rent out my house."

"Sounds like a great retirement plan."

"Retire? It's a little early for that. I still need to figure out a new career move. But, Madison, having the freedom to travel for a while... it's a dream come true."

My phone vibrated on my lap, and I glanced at the screen. "Oh, my God. You're not going to believe this. It's Ron!"

Madison bounced in her chair. "Take the call!"

"Ron?" I raised the volume and turning to Madison whispered, "Shush."

"Hi, Sofia, how are you?" His voice boomed through the speaker, and I felt... nothing.

My mind ticked back to the last time I saw him—the way his eyes betrayed his true feelings. He'd never loved me. I answered flatly, "Why are you calling?"

I heard rustling sounds... of paper? "I'm... um. Well, I was just wondering how you were doing. It's been quite a while since we've talked."

I pressed the mute button for a second. "He's probably rifling through his Rolodex—old school style. How much do you want to bet I'm the tenth woman he's called?"

Hitting the microphone button again, I couldn't help the sarcasm seeping into my voice. "Funnily enough, I haven't forgotten our last conversation. Let me guess, no mother-to-be in your life yet?"

"I may have been a little hasty. I'm sorry, Sofia. We were pretty good together, don't you think?" I didn't respond. We were too busy shaking our heads. Madison mouthed dumbass. He continued, oblivious to my tone. "I was wondering if you'd like to get a drink sometime? Maybe we could pick up from where we left off. You made a fair point that night. The dating pool is pretty stagnant."

I clapped my hand over my mouth, stifling a fit of laughter, tears spilling down my face. Madison raised her palms to the sky, which summed up her response.

I resolved to be nice—to be the better person. "We were good together at the time, but I've moved on. Best of luck to you."

"Wait... you mean you have a new boyfriend?"

Madison was now miming shock, her mouth wide open, her hand over her heart. The payback, I had to admit, was incredibly satisfying.

"Yes, Ron. Oddly enough, I have an amazing boyfriend. And you won't be able to reach me at this number, as I'll be leaving to join him in London very soon."

My friend, my bestie, punched the air, whispering, "Take that, asshole."

Ron stammered, then came up empty. "Okay then. Good luck."

I ended the call and held up a glass. Then Madison raised hers. "To... karma," I said.

"May it bite him in the ass," she added.

Everything was coming together faster than I imagined possible. I was ticking the boxes on my checklist and nearing the end. It thrilled my son to know I'd be traveling back to Europe. His encouragement was surprising, considering his feelings about Ryan. I suspected Callie had something to do with his change of heart. My mother, although less thrilled about my leaving, was still supportive. While she wasn't opposed to traveling, she'd never made it outside of the States. To her, Europe might as well have been the moon.

"When are you going to return?" she asked when I called her with the news. I gave her an estimate of two months but didn't mention the sixty-day contract, because to her way of thinking, it would probably sound absurd to take that kind of risk. I might have also added a few years to Ryan's age.

There was a pause before she spoke again, as if mulling over the information. "Sofia, in case I haven't mentioned it, I want you to know how proud I am of you. If I were in your shoes, I wouldn't have the courage to go chasing around the world on some grand adventure. But then, you always could do anything you put your mind to. Just please be careful and tell Ryan I'm expecting him to take good care of my little girl."

My eyes stung at the sound of her words. Mom. She always knew what to say, doling out motherly advice during my darkest times, but this conversation surprised me. I thanked her for her unwavering love and support, even though she might have doubts about the path I was taking. Then, I reassured her I'd be fine and promised to pass the message to Ryan. I didn't mention I was a grown woman who had been taking care of herself for years, because to her, I would always be her little girl.

Chapter Thirty-Two

We lay on the living room sofa; Ryan's arms enveloping me, my head on his chest rising and falling with the rhythm of his breaths. As if the universe had rewarded us with a gift on our last night together in San Francisco, the sky exploded in hues of peach and purple as the sun drifted toward the horizon across the backdrop of a cloudless blue canvas. It wasn't often we had this crystal-clear view of the sunset from the bay windows in Ryan's apartment. We watched as the fiery sphere dipped into the sea. A blanket of fog frequently obscured the scene, but when it receded to the ocean, the sun reflected against the modern cityscape and the metal beams of the East Bay Bridge in a dazzling display of light and color. By far, it was the best show in town.

"This must be strange for you, taking a break from your career after all these years," Ryan said. We'd spent part of the afternoon discussing how much this move meant to me, but also, he'd asked more about the phases of my profession. It had been my whole life for so long. Now, he had a better understanding of the leap I was taking.

"Actually, it feels right. At first, when I lost my job, I panicked. I couldn't imagine what I'd do if I wasn't working. Now, I have the luxury of time to consider my next move.

I think all of this happened for a reason." His stubbled chin nuzzled the top of my head, and I tilted to see his face. Amber rays dappled his smooth, olive skin, illuminating a knowing smile. "Okay, what's that grin about?"

"I believe there was a reason we met at the same time your life was at a crossroads. At every turn, the fates conspired to bring us together, and now we have a clear path stretching out ahead."

I loved the way he was so sure, so steadfast in his conviction about our relationship. He was the counterbalance to my doubts, the tilt of the scale I grew more and more dependent on to remain centered. "Clear path? I hope so. It would be nice, since I'm still dizzy from the ups and downs, but who knows what curveballs are waiting to jump out and bite us?"

He frowned. "Could you try to be a little optimistic?"

"Fair point." I tightened my arm around his back and pulled him in closer, my cheeks lifting a smile against his chest. "I vow to be optimistic about the next sixty days at least. By the way, when does our contract start?"

He considered this for a moment. "Technically, when you agreed, but since we'll be starting fresh in London, why not use your arrival as a marker?"

"That sounds fair." A tingle of excitement coursed through me—I'd be on a plane to London in two weeks. It hardly seemed real. "Wait, you're leaving tomorrow, so I'll be arriving alone. How will I know how to find you?" I sat up, my head suddenly filled with questions. Although I'd resolved to go with the flow for the next sixty days, I couldn't believe it hadn't occurred to me to check those crucial details. "And where will I stay?"

Amusement fanned across his features, his eyes laughing at me. "Welcome to the party. You're a little late."

"Oh, really?"

"I've got this. Everything is arranged. When you arrive, my driver, Charlie, will pick you up at the airport since I'll be at work. I hope you'll be pleased with the suite I've reserved for us."

"For us?" I hesitated to ask. "So, we'll be sharing one room?"

"Is that a problem?" A few tiny lines formed above the bridge of his nose. Those were about the only creases he had, only appearing when his brows furrowed.

"We've only stayed together for a weekend at a time. This is a big leap forward, don't you think?"

At first, I'd maintained the dream of our budding relationship by encasing it in a vacation bubble. Then encapsulated it within a few romantic weekends. But living under the same roof would make it undeniably real—the good, the bad, and the ugly. Would my morning breath, bed head hair, and God forbid, the occasional fart, grate on his illusion of me over time? It would be difficult to keep up the appearance of youthfulness while I stripped off my makeup at night and slathered retinol cream from the chest up. Was I prepared for this transition? Or, more importantly, was he?

"Sofia, I can tell when your thoughts are spinning out of control. Your eyes flash like a neon sign. Come here." He pulled me onto his lap, my legs straddled his thighs and my arms wrapped around his neck—face to face. I obliged, giving him all my attention.

"Don't overthink this, because you'll needlessly scare yourself silly. I'm certain I want to be with you. Nothing will change that fact. If we fight, we'll make up. If we step on each other's toes, we'll communicate and smooth things over. If we have different needs, we'll negotiate and compromise. This isn't supposed to be one long vacation with sunshine and roses every day. It's life together, you and me."

"How the hell did you become so wise, so grounded?" I blurted.

"How did you become so insecure?"

"Hah!" The sound burst out of me, the many reasons flashing all at once through my mind, the memories tasting bitter on my tongue. If only my ex-husband had been half as mature as this man, I might still be married. But it wasn't the moment to offer explanations. It was an opportunity to join him in his optimism, to start fresh, to take this new chance at love and do it right this time. As my mother always said, "Don't look a gift horse in the mouth." Ryan was my gift, and I'd be damned if I was going to squander it.

I lifted a smile, love coloring my view of him as the room darkened around us. "Where have you been all my life? Wait." I stopped at the sound of my own words, at the absurdity. "Scratch that. What I meant to say was, I'm lucky to have you in my life now. Your timing was perfect, as was your choice of that flight."

He cleared his throat. "I told my mother about you." I held my breath. And waited.

When I couldn't bear the silence, I said evenly, "Oh?" I picked a piece of lint off his shoulder, trying not to picture the look on her face when he told her my age. Damn. I'd hoped we could avoid the big reveal a little longer.

He cringed, and the knot in my stomach tightened. "I'm not going to say the conversation went exactly the way I'd hoped, but in the end, she was happy I finally found someone to love. She wants to meet you, but that would involve her flying to London, so it probably won't happen soon."

"I look forward to meeting her." He eyed me suspiciously. "Okay, the thought of coming face-to-face with your mom scares the hell out of me, but I'm also really pleased you had the courage to tell her. It couldn't have been easy."

"See, these are the things I don't want you to worry about. I love you. The rest are just details, and we can figure it out as we go along."

He folded me into his arms, my chest resting on his, our heartbeats pulsing with synchronicity. "I love you, too." I declared it without doubt or reservation. I was all in, confident the feeling would only grow stronger. I only hoped the details to come wouldn't amount to more than minor obstacles, relying on faith this time that love would conquer all.

"Do you have everything?" Madison asked as I wheeled my suitcases to the door.

"Passport, wallet, phone, laptop…" I ticked off the items on my fingers. "Oh, and a book to read on the plane." She glanced down at my bulging luggage. "Don't judge me. I can never figure out what to bring, so I'm armed with a wardrobe for any occasion."

"C'mere, Sofia." She pulled me into a hug. "I am seriously going to miss you."

"Hey, you'll be just fine. I see you getting stronger every day." When I broke away, I noticed her eyes were glassy now. The back of my nose prickled, but I didn't want to let the tears loose. "I'll miss you more." Before I left her, I needed to know she'd be safe. I cleared my throat. "You have the restraining order handy, just in case?"

She nodded. "Roger is pressing charges, so even though Kevin is out on bail, most likely he'll do some jail time if he's convicted. But… I will probably have to testify." Her shoulders jerked with a shudder. Before I could ask, she added, "He doesn't know where I am, and I haven't told anyone, in case word got around. Regardless, I doubt he'd risk doing anything which would result in me calling the police again. His bail would be revoked."

"Good. That asshole deserves to be locked up. Do you have someone to go with you to court?"

"My sister will fly in from Arizona. Surprisingly, she's been very supportive. We haven't spoken in over a year, but this situation has brought us closer again. Given our fucked up family history, she's the one person who can best understand what I'm experiencing."

I breathed out a sigh of relief. "How's Roger doing with his recovery?"

"His nose has a new bump, but it hasn't damaged his looks." Just the mention of his name brought a tentative smile to her lips. "Despite the horrible attack, he wants to continue dating me. Either he's a fool, or stubborn, or he really likes me. I haven't figured out which one it is."

"If I had to venture a guess, I'd say he's hooked on you. It's hard to find that kind of dedication, so please hold onto him. Seriously, girl, you deserve a man like Roger. It may take a little time to relax into a relationship with the right guy when you're accustomed to being with the wrong one, but it will come."

"I might need some help. Can you recommend a good therapist?" She shot me a wink.

"Ha ha. I've already sent you some referrals. Give them a call and see who's the best fit. Besides, I couldn't be your psychologist since I depend on you as a friend. Don't go making me feel guilty about leaving."

"Are you kidding? I'm totally onboard and plan to live vicariously through your adventures." She paused for a moment, worry lines forming between her brows. "Are you going to be okay? This is all pretty sudden."

It was as if I'd been a missile propelling toward a target. I had to keep moving forward without looking back because if I stopped to consider my radical move, I would overthink it. I squared my shoulders, practicing my newfound confidence.

"I have a sixty-day guarantee. I'll take him, and my new life, on a test drive. Then, we'll see. Besides, Ryan has assured me he's committed to making this relationship work. His actions speak even louder than his words."

"Carpe diem," she said, grinning.

I nodded. "That's how I roll now."

"Hah!" A laugh exploded out of her.

"Thanks to you. Don't think for a minute I haven't appreciated your friendly nudges. In fact, I'm not sure how I'll manage without you, so schedule some vacation time and come visit me, please."

"Maybe, I can bring Roger?" She said it as if it was a question, but the hopeful look in her eyes told me she was already imagining a future with him.

I gave her my vote of approval. "It sounds perfect."

A text alert pinged from inside my purse while a car horn beeped in my driveway. "My driver is here. Gotta run."

I pulled her into a hug before tugging my luggage out the front door.

"Send me an email when you get settled," she called from the porch.

I nodded, waved goodbye, and while the driver was loading my bags, I climbed into the back seat. We were already sailing down the freeway when I remembered the text alert. Retrieving my phone from the inside pocket of my new travel purse, a silly, love-struck grin tugged at the corners of my mouth when I viewed Ryan's message.

You are probably on your way to the airport, according to my calculations. I just wanted to say bon voyage before I head to bed. Drink lots of champagne and get some sleep on the plane. I can't wait to welcome you home. Besos, baby.

The last few months flashed by in my mind in a visual haze as I looked at the rearview mirror, San Francisco's skyline disappearing in the distance—remembering the pivotal events leading up to this moment. They came in a sequence of memories. The ones that made my heart swell were the firsts. The first time I met Ryan at the networking event; how he took my breath away the moment I laid eyes on him. My first flight to Barcelona, destiny crashing us into each other. The first time we made love on the yacht, convinced it wouldn't be our last. Our first date back in San Francisco when we ended the night in his apartment, confirming our relationship wasn't just a vacation fling. The first time he said, "I love you," his promise giving me hope for a new future.

Now I was smiling and leaking happy tears. The driver spied me in the car's mirror, his eyes peering at me with a look that simply said, "Women..." accompanied by an eye rolling emoji. I shrugged, swiping my palms against my cheeks. I couldn't help it. Love had turned me into a raw mass of emotion, frequently spilling out of me as though the retaining wall on my internal dam had broken loose. I'd packed a stash of Kleenex in my purse for the flight, just in case. *God, I really am a hopeless romantic.* Who knew?

It was hard to believe how much my life had changed since I'd met Ryan—how different I was now. Me, Sofia 2.0. While he'd opened my heart again, I gave myself credit for being willing to take risks—for being my bravest, boldest, most badass self. Because at any point, I could have retreated from taking this leap.

A thrill whirled up my spine as I wondered what the next chapter held for us. No, not just a chapter. We were about to launch into a whole frigging novel. Even a long, transatlantic flight wouldn't dampen my excitement. Nor would I let it wipe this silly grin off my face.

As the shuttle neared the departures zone, I typed out a message to Ryan. I wanted it to be the first thing he saw when he woke.

> *Next stop, London. I plan to enjoy the flight, take full advantage of the champagne, and smother you in thank-you kisses for the biz class upgrade. The excitement has me nearly jumping out of my skin. They say home is where the heart is, and since you have my heart, I will indeed be coming home. Xoxo*

I reviewed my message and realized it sounded sappy. But instead of revising, I shrugged and hit send. With luck, I might grow accustomed to a little sap in my love life.

The End

Thank you for reading *The Vacation Bubble*. I hope you enjoyed it! I would truly appreciate it if you shared your honest review by going to my book page on your retailer's website or on Goodreads. Your opinion is invaluable both to the author, as well as other readers.

<u>COMING FEBRUARY 10, 2026</u>
THE RELATIONSHIP CONTRACT
To Barcelona with Love Trilogy, Book Two

Follow Sofia and Ryan as they navigate their sixty-day relationship contract between London and Barcelona. While Ryan plans surprise adventures to exotic destinations, neither of them could have anticipated the revelation that changes everything.

A SNEAK PEAK

Ryan

Sofia's text had made my whole morning. I couldn't stop grinning until I walked into the office and saw about a thousand emails waiting for me. Didn't matter though. Staring at my computer screen, I tried to focus, but all I could think about was Sofia on that plane, probably somewhere over the Atlantic right now.

She felt like home to me now, too. It still blew my mind how we'd found each other—pure luck or fate, whatever you want to call it. In just a few hours, she'd actually be here. What Sofia was doing was huge: uprooting her whole life, flying halfway around the world to be with me—believing in me when I said we could make it work. She was braver than she gave herself credit for, that was for sure. I had seen her adventurous spirit from the first time we'd met, even though she'd tried to convince me she wasn't about to take any chances. But then she showed up in Barcelona and I watched as she took in the sights, her face beaming with excitement. Everyone lets loose on vacation, but Sofia... she drank in every experience like she was breathing for the first time.

I swiveled my chair toward the floor-to-ceiling windows overlooking London Bridge, watching the white clouds drift by. I hadn't taken time to appreciate this city—all the history and stories packed into every corner—but I had a feeling I'd see it differently with Sofia here. We'd explore it together, like we had in Barcelona. I wanted her to be happy she'd made the jump, and I was going to do whatever it took to make these next two months count, because there was no way in hell I was letting her go after sixty days.

If you're curious and can't wait to see what happens next, scan the code below and I'll send you the first two chapters. I promise not to bombard your inbox, but I will let you know when new books are released.

Bonus Chapters

Follow me on social media. I'm always happy to hear from readers!
Instagram @marcellasteele.writer
TikTok @writerMarcellaSteele
Facebook @Marcellasteelewriter

Acknowledgements

I want to express my heartfelt gratitude to my editor and award winning author, Marni MacRay, whose unwavering support has been instrumental in my work. As a fellow author, she brings a unique understanding to the editorial process, and her genuine appreciation for my storytelling has provided the encouragement and confidence I needed to persevere in my writing journey.

Credit for the wonderful custom illustrated cover goes to Perrin at Author Buddy.